# Acknowledgements

A special thank you to Bob Erwin, who makes this author's research a less daunting task, regardless of chosen subject. If knowledge had a door, Bob would be the one opening it widely and inviting us all in, to take a spin, to indulge, to explore and savor.

A warm thank you to my New York friend Mark Freyberg, who makes judicial issues seem like a walk in the park, and whose professional expertise left no legal detail to this author's imagination.

A special thank you to Dr. Lisa Verges, for her friendship and thoughtful advice regarding the ethical boundaries of therapeutic engagement and the many challenges in treating suicidal, traumatized patients.

Last but never least, thank you to Dan Yearick for his thoughtful advice on the ethics of intervention and the essential insight into his experience working with PTSD patients. His book, *A Thousand Fireflies*, brings a unique perspective into the dynamics of trauma and the uphill path to healing.

LESLIE WOLFE

We don't welcome death; we covet the discontinuation
of life's agonizing sorrow.

LESLIE WOLFE

# 1

# The Chosen Day

He was ready to die.

Not fighting the thought anymore, not even feeling sorry for forfeiting his tomorrows.

All feeling had abandoned his weary heart, leaving nothing but hollow space behind. Nothing more than emptiness, the vacant shell of what he once was, back in the day when life was wondrous and joyful and fun, centuries ago, when he was still alive.

He leaned back farther in his seat and enjoyed the silence that engulfed the warehouse. The last of the employees had clocked out and gone home. Even Terrell, who took the most convincing to leave while he was still there looking busy in his small office, had left almost an hour ago. Most of the warehouse was shrouding itself in darkness, while one fluorescent light after another reached their automatic delays and went off, precisely sixty minutes after the last human being had tripped the respective motion sensor. It was almost like nightfall in a way; it had to do with life, but wasn't natural. There, in the realm of the immense office supplies warehouse, it was life that generated light, not the other way around.

Soon darkness would come, and bring relief with it.

His desk lamp was the only light still on, and he stared at its pale, yellowish glow for the longest time. Absentminded, he pulled two small, white pebbles out of his pocket and let his fingers play with them, rubbing and knocking them against each other, making soothing, muted sounds that filled the hollow silence. No thoughts crossed his mind; he could have stayed like that for ages, lost in the transcendence between life and death, caught between his past and his nonexisting future.

But no, he had a job to do. He forced himself to come back to reality and shrugged off the emptiness that had swallowed him whole. He let the two pebbles drop into his pocket, then tapped on the fabric to make sure they were tucked safely in there. His eyes struggled to focus on the paperwork lying in front of him on the desk's melamine surface, guaranteed to be scratch and stain resistant.

He shook his head angrily, inviting the unwanted tidbit of office product description to get out of his head, and then reviewed the list of dates printed on the sheet of paper he held with firm, cold fingers.

Only one policy left, that was all. The rest of them had passed the two-year mark that was the typical suicide exclusion waiting period. Most life insurance policies would pay the benefit even in the case of suicide, if more than two years had passed since the policy had been underwritten. His had passed that mark, except for one. He looked at the date and counted in his mind. Five more months, and that last one would reach the threshold, putting the suicide clause into effect.

*Huh...* From a risk analysis perspective, the insurance companies believed no one could hold on to the will to die for as long as he had, and that's why they were willing to pay. He reflected on that thought for a while, while his eyes wandered absently to the letters that formed his name, printed in all caps at the top of the form. The insurance companies knew how to quantify and manage risk, but they had never met nor quantified Dylan James Ballard. By the time the dust would settle on his grave, numerous actuarial busybodies would adjust that risk factor based on his precedent, and soon that clause would probably run three years instead of two. No insurance company could stand to make less than billions in profits each year.

Not his problem anymore; none of it.

All he still cared about was his wife, and he'd made sure she'd be well taken care of. The rest had stopped mattering a long time ago.

He stood with a groan and pulled the calendar off the wall, then sat back in his chair, flipping through the pages. Six months from today was November. The last of the policies would mature in five months, but he didn't want to cut it that close, so they wouldn't be suspicious.

He picked up a red pen and read through the dates, looking for one that would be worthy to become the day he stopped breathing. A Monday... what could be worse than a Monday in November, right? It would probably be a gloomy, never-see-the-sun kind of day, cold and humid and foggy and nasty, like November Mondays can be in San Francisco.

He chose the second Monday, the twelfth, and circled it firmly with the red pen. Then he squinted a little in the dim light, and read what was written right underneath the bold digits that formed the number twelve. *Veterans Day (Observed)*, it said there, in font so small and discreet, it was almost like the calendar makers had been ashamed to print those words. How appropriate a day for him to choose; how fitting. Decidedly, he revisited the date with the red pen and circled it a couple of times more.

Satisfied, he flipped the calendar pages back to May, and hung it on the wall in its rightful place. Then he turned toward his computer and opened a browser window. It was time for the next phase of the plan.

He scrolled through countless search results and spent his time reading reviews and looking at people's faces before he finally chose her. Dr. Angela

Blackwell, forty-four years old, highly credentialed, favorable reviews, published works. Not cheap at all, but he didn't care to save money this time. He needed the perfect witness, someone whose testimony would carry weight in court, someone who could swear his wife had nothing to do with his death, so the cops wouldn't suspect her of any involvement in his sudden demise. Then the insurance bastards would leave Taylor alone and have no alternative but to pay the death benefits.

He checked the time on his phone and almost smiled, noting it was probably late enough to not risk catching the good doctor still in her office. He dialed the number, and after four rings and the customary beep, he cleared his voice and spoke plainly.

"Yeah, Dr. Blackwell, hello. I need your help. I need a few sessions during the next six months or so. I will pay in cash; I believe that won't be a problem. I can't have anything like that show up on my record; I hope you'll understand. Please call me back."

He ended the call and leaned back in his seat, then allowed the silence to settle over the vast space of the warehouse, after the last echo of his voice had vanished. He closed his eyes, feeling nothing but emptiness, the familiar absence of feeling that shrouded him wherever he went.

He was ready to die, and now he knew just when that was going to happen. November twelfth.

# 2

# Anniversary

Dr. Angela Blackwell couldn't bring herself to turn on the lights, although darkness had almost completely engulfed the living room, forcing her to abandon her reading glasses on top of the book lying open on the windowsill. In the deep twilight, she could still see the ocean waves foaming as they broke against the Pacifica shore, a good 200 feet below her terrace. Yearning for their soothing sound and the salty smell of the ocean breeze, she wrapped the cardigan tighter around her supple body and pulled open the terrace door.

She stopped in the door frame and inhaled deeply, savoring the salty taste of the misty air as it touched her lips. Fog was rolling in from the sea in large clumps of restless cotton, soon to engulf the house in white silence, hiding the ocean view from her blurry eyes. She stepped outside and stood by the guardrail, keeping her gaze fixed on the horizon line, barely visible in the deepening crepuscule and the dense fog.

She closed her eyes and let herself feel the drizzle touch her face. Tiniest droplets of liquid chill she welcomed to take away the burning sensation in her forehead, to camouflage the tears that welled up in her eyes. After a while, the coldness of the mist reached her bones and sent a shiver down her spine. She shuddered and walked back inside, wiping the moisture off her face with the back of her hand.

She stopped at the fireplace and rubbed her hands in front of the dancing flames, pushing the sadness a little further from her heart. Seeing the bright colors of the lively fire, enjoying the dry warmth, after being outside, helped her chase the shadows away. When she was sure of herself again and felt confident her voice wouldn't betray her, she grabbed her phone and dialed one of the only two starred numbers stored in her favorites list.

Waiting for Shelley to pick up, she put the phone on speaker and checked the time. It was late, almost eight-thirty, and that meant well past eleven at night on the East Coast. She knew her daughter well; if she'd gone to bed, her phone would be on silent, and she wouldn't risk disturbing her sleep.

"Mom?" Her daughter's voice almost startled her.

"Yes, sweetie, it's me. I didn't wake you, did I?"

"Nope. Was in the shower, that's all. Glad you called."

Soon the new generation would speak just the way they texted and tweeted. Who needs pronouns anymore? She felt a smile tug at the corners of her mouth, and she let it bloom. The sound of her daughter's voice always warmed her heart.

"Is water dripping on the floor right now, while you're shivering and shifting your weight from one bare foot to the other?"

Shelley laughed, and the crystalline sound of her amusement filled the room. "Nah... nice try though. Good visuals. Try again."

"Bathrobe?" she offered, enjoying their little game.

"Um... close."

"Towel, then?"

"Yup. Two of them, actually."

"I can call later, you know, to give you time—"

"Nah... no need. I can talk to you while wearing a towel or two, right? You won't be offended, will you, Mom?"

She laughed in unison with her daughter, then the sound of their laughter made way for a couple of seconds of loaded silence.

"I'm sorry to be calling so late," Angela eventually said, poorly hiding a light sniffle. The cold moisture from outside must have clung to her, or something like that. Maybe fog had followed her inside the house, the unseen ghost of her lonely nights. "I hate this time zone thing. By the time I get home and I—"

"It's all right, Mom, you're not disturbing me."

Angela forced air into her lungs, while her finger hesitated above the FaceTime icon. "*Why* am I not disturbing you?" she asked, managing to sound almost cheerful. "Aren't there any interesting young men at Columbia anymore?"

"Oh, yeah, well... that, uh..."

Her daughter did that when she was uncomfortable talking about something. She poured all the pronouns and interjections she'd abstained from using in her tweet-like normal speak on a long breath of hesitation.

"Okay, I get it," she replied. "You're still researching the subject, I gather. It probably needs more study."

"Well, I actually, um, met someone. Not sure though."

Pronouns had gone missing again; she was about to share more about her someone. She waited patiently.

"He's premed," she added on the breath of a sigh. "Stars won't align, that's all."

"What's his name?" she asked gently.

"Do we have to give him a name?" Shelley pushed back. "That would make him real."

"And you don't want that," she whispered. "He must have a name, I'm assuming, but it's all right if you don't want to share for now."

A second of silence.

"It's just that doctors are better off with other doctors, Mom. I read somewhere that other professions, like business, for example, have difficulties understanding the demands of the young med student's, then later, the doctor's workload. There's no work/life balance, and they're always on call. Not to mention the hordes of hot nurses trolling those hospitals hallways, looking for prey."

Silence fell heavy after Shelley's high-pitched argument had ended. Angela thought hard for something she could say, without bringing up the one thing they didn't want to talk about.

"You don't have to marry him yet, sweetie," she eventually said. "If you like him, date him for a while, and see where it goes."

"Why?" Shelley snapped, taking her by surprise. "So I can get attached to him, then lose him too?"

"Maybe you won't," Angela replied gently. "As you might happen to know, not all doctors marry other doctors," she added quietly.

For a few moments, she didn't hear a sound from Shelley. When she spoke, her voice was loaded with tears, shaky and choked.

"I still miss him, Mom."

And there it was, tearing her heart to shreds and threatening to let out a long, wailing sob. She clenched her jaws and managed to control her emotions a little. "I miss him too, baby."

"I can't believe it's been five years," Shelley continued, no longer hiding her sadness. "Feels like yesterday."

"It does, doesn't it?" she managed to whisper. With trembling hands, she poured some wine into her glass and took a sip, hoping it would strengthen her heart.

"I wonder what he would've said about Jamie," Shelley said.

A tiny smile formed on Angela's lips. "Oh, so he has a name, after all. I'm relieved."

"I never got to talk about things with Dad. Real things, adult things, you know."

"You mean, like dating?"

"Yeah… I know I have you, but I wanted a man's perspective, that's all."

"Oh, honey, let me tell you this," Angela replied, wiping her tears. "When you turned fourteen, a friend of his from work asked him if he was ready to be the father of a dating teenager. You know what he said?"

"No, but I'm curious."

Angela could hear the smile in her daughter's voice. "He said, 'Sure, I'm ready. I bought a shotgun.'"

"What? Dad had a shotgun?"

She laughed. "No, sweetie, he was just joking."

Another moment of silence, but this time Angela didn't fear it anymore.

"How about you, Mom? Seeing anyone?"

"No... That part of my life is over."

"It doesn't have to be, you know. You're still young, and you're hot."

"What? No…"

"I'm telling you, you're so hot. I'd take you clubbing with me any day."

"So, you go clubbing? Please be careful. All sorts of creeps are out there."

"Really? Change the subject on me like that? What, you think I'm thirteen and can't figure it out?"

"You're right, I'm sorry," she admitted. Her daughter deserved more than that. She was an adult, and she'd earned the right to be treated like one. "But I'm still not interested. I'm fine the way I am, I'm okay."

"Don't you get lonely sometimes?"

"Yes, I do, but that's because I miss your Dad." She stopped short of saying how she couldn't sleep at night, tossing and turning after waking, believing he was somehow still alive, still in the house somewhere. Believing she'd had a bad dream, and he was actually downstairs, munching on one of his famous three-in-the-morning snacks. She didn't mention how she worked late these days, so she wouldn't have to come home to the nest that they'd built together, now barren. Shelley didn't need to hear any of that; all she needed was to believe her mom was all right.

She straightened her back and raised her head a little, forcing her body to act as if she were okay, in the hope that the weary mind would follow the body out of habit.

"Give Jamie a chance, Shelley. A couple of dates, and you'll find out if he's a keeper."

"Oh, he's a keeper all right," she blurted.

"You already decided on that? Only minutes after not willing to share his name?"

Shelley laughed quietly. "Test drove him a couple of times too."

"Good girl," she replied. "Now get to bed, young lady, it's almost midnight, and it's a school day tomorrow," she added, putting enough humor in her voice to make Shelley giggle one more time before hanging up the phone.

Then there was silence again.

# 3

# On A Saturday

He woke with a panicked start, while his heart thumped against his chest, rushing him back to life and filling his body with the adrenaline needed to fight, to survive. Blood coursing through his veins roared in his ears, or maybe it was the nightmare still lingering, with the resonance of explosions reverberating endlessly every time he shut his eyes.

He battled the stubborn sleep that still clung to his brain and forced himself into reality, while fighting to free himself from the tangled covers. Faintly at first, he heard a voice calling his name, and with every sound of that voice, defeated shadows made room for the light.

"Dylan, it's all right, honey, wake up. Yep, here you go."

Taylor.

Her thin, cold fingers touching his arm, the cheerful way she said his name, the smell of her, fresh as the summer morning, all cornerstones of his existence. He grabbed onto her strength to find his, and took her hand.

"There you go," she said softly. "Good morning to you."

"Uh-huh," he said coarsely, but smiled. He looked at her and took in every detail. The headband she wore whenever she went to the gym, although her blonde hair was cut short. That 2-inch strip of navy blue, elastic fabric was little more than a fashion accessory or a statement of intent, but it brought out the azure in her eyes. The snug sports bra exposed her flat abdomen, exposed all the way down to the tight-fitting yoga pants, leaving little to the imagination. All the details of her perfect body stood out when she wore her active wear, as she liked to call it, seemingly unaware of the effect her shape had on any living, breathing heterosexual male who laid eyes on her. His smile died slowly on his lips.

"Come with me," she said, leaning closer to him, her breath touching his lips. "It's still early; the gym's almost empty, I promise."

He groaned and closed his eyes, escaping the reality in which the two of them were so painfully different. She was full of life, while he was already decomposing, slowly but surely on his way out of this world. A week's worth of long hours and restless sleep weighed him down, making him hate the picture-perfect, blue sky that filled the window the moment she'd pulled open the curtains.

He turned away from the piercing light that came from that window, and curled up on his side, his back toward her. He squeezed his eyes shut, pushing her away. He felt her holding her breath for a few seconds, then her hand moved away from his shoulder, leaving him barren, hollow inside.

"Okay," she said quietly, standing to leave. "I'll give you permission for some more shuteye, Marine, but when I get back, you take me out. Deal?"

He turned toward her and opened his eyes just a little.

"Yes, ma'am," he replied, then welcomed the quick kiss she offered. Before he could help it, a few words found their way out in the open. "I'll miss you, baby," he said quietly, and the sadness of undertones in his voice got her attention.

"Then why not come with me?" she asked again, frowning a little. "Breathe a little."

"No… you go ahead, live your life. I'll just… sleep for a while."

She kissed him again and caressed his stubbly face with soft, gentle fingers. "Sleep tight," she added in a whisper, then left with a spring in her step, plugging her earbuds into her phone and jingling her car keys.

He closed his eyes and invited sleep to rush in, while the taste of her lip balm filled his mouth. The smell of it clung to him, the smell of her, and sleep wouldn't come his way. Maybe it was the morning light that filled the room and flooded his mind, even with his eyes closed.

He groaned and got out of bed, then pulled the curtains shut. A comfortable gloom engulfed the room, but he didn't feel like going back to bed. Instead, he wandered into the living room, where he pulled shut all the draperies. Unlike the bedroom, the living room curtains were a lighter fabric, and the sun's fierce rays still made their way inside, tamed, yet engulfing the room in a brownish penumbra.

He stood in the middle of the room, taking in the details. Many of their things were still unpacked; moving crates and cardboard boxes loitered in the corners in piles, some of them stacked up more than 6 feet high. They'd moved recently, and unpacking was a draining process for which he lacked motivation, because they lived in a rental house. They would definitely have to move again, at some point in the future. So why bother? Their tiny San Francisco house was a third of what they used to have before, and they couldn't afford a single square foot more. Even if they unpacked, there wasn't enough room for everything.

Maybe he'd made a mistake taking that job and coming here, dragging Taylor with him to this prohibitive place, where her things had to stay locked in boxes. Their clothes filled a rack next to the back wall, while the closets were packet tightly with boxes of all shapes and sizes. There was so much stuff… where's that stuff coming from? If she could only understand, and do away with the things they didn't really need. How many times had they moved? Too many to remember, too draining to recount. And still she wouldn't part with a single item.

They'd recently relocated from Indianapolis, for his new job at the warehouse, although *recently* might have meant a different thing to him than it did to others. They'd moved almost three years ago, and he still recalled the hope that had filled his heart a tiny bit, only to fade away quickly in the face of a ridiculous cost of living and the daily struggle to make ends meet. No wonder they didn't feel like unpacking.

He vaguely remembered reading somewhere a study about spiders, and the way they weave their webs. Scientists took this healthy, young spider and let it weave. It wove a web of beauty, all symmetrical and detailed and perfect, and then sat nearby waiting for the web to serve its purpose. Whenever a fly would get caught in the web, the spider would eat it, then quickly fix the torn net and make it perfect again, happy to work for a purpose, and finding gratification in fulfilling that purpose.

But then, the people who ran the test destroyed the web, and the spider had to build another one, from scratch. This time, it wasn't that perfect anymore; it lacked some of the symmetry, as if the spider had rushed the job somewhat, building it with fewer lines, farther apart. Then they tore it up again, and again, and again. From one iteration to the next, the web was uglier, more crooked, less perfect, its flaws speaking clearly of the spider's despair in the face of senseless adversity.

Why bother?

Slowly, Dylan walked over to the clothes rack and ran his hand against the tightly packed hangers. The gesture released some more of her scent into the air. He inhaled the air loaded with her absence and, for a second, wondered why he stood there like an idiot, missing her instead of joining her at the gym.

He weighed his options; he could still go after her, and she'd be happy to see him. She was always happy to share an activity with him, to be with him.

He almost made it all the way to the bedroom dresser where his gym shorts were, neatly folded in a drawer, but the tiredness in his bones stopped him cold.

Whom was he kidding?

He probably would go there to make an ass of himself, nothing more. Most likely he couldn't bench-press too much these days. He'd be the laughing stock of the gym goers, all too damn impeccable in their expensive gear and perfectly ripped bodies. He used to be strong, back when he could march 20 miles in full gear, M16 rifle in his hands, in the torrid desert heat, without even feeling tired. But twenty years of desk labor later, his six-pack had vanished, covered by a couple of inches of fat. Yeah, that spider's web had many facets in his case.

He walked slowly to the garage door and stood in the doorway, staring at the empty space her Jeep had left behind. Next to it, his black sedan waited invitingly, and he considered the gym once more, this time just to pay her a visit. Wait for her until she was done, then take her out like he'd promised.

He pictured himself lingering on the benches while she finished her routine, his fists white-knuckled and jaws clenched, while she stretched her lean body in front of the mirror, lifting weights and working out under the lusting eyes of who knows how many testosterone-supplementing men. What if she's not alone?

What if there's some guy, some fit, muscular guy she has more in common with than she has with him?

He closed the garage door slowly and moped back to the bedroom. He sat on the edge of the bed for a little while, then lay down and curled on his side, facing away from the door, away from the world.

"Doesn't matter," he whispered to himself, "soon it will be over."

# 4

# A New Patient

The moment the door closed, Dr. Blackwell let out a long breath of air and closed her eyes for a moment. Her last patient's twisted lamentations had left her with a migraine cloud circling above her head and threatening to take over her thoughts. Although late in the day, she still had one more appointment on her calendar, the mysterious man who seemed to know precisely what he needed.

She stepped into the bathroom adjacent to her office and turned on the lights. In the bluish, intense brightness coming from the six, high-wattage bulbs above the wide mirror, her face seemed pale, drawn. Despite the discreet makeup she wore to work every day, black circles were still visible under her eyes. Two pairs of vertical tension lines marked the edges of her mouth, an early sign of what would surely become, before long, permanent wrinkles standing in testimony of the sorrow that life had dealt her.

She massaged her brow with frozen fingers, squinting slightly, and then decided in favor of chemistry. She opened the small medicine cabinet and popped an Advil, hoping it would send the migraine cloud away. Then she touched up her makeup; freshened her lipstick; and brushed her long, curly, auburn hair; the only vivid color the mirror reflected at her. She thought of tying it back in a ponytail, to help her appearance be closer to the effective, professional look she was aiming for with each new patient, but eventually decided against it.

She checked the time and breathed deeply. She was ready and still had a few minutes to spare. Before turning off the lights in the small bathroom, she searched her eyes in that mirror, then looked immediately away, as if she'd seen a ghost. No, it wasn't the time to go there, not with a new patient scheduled to arrive in a few minutes.

She wrung her hands nervously, then corrected her posture one more time and straightened her skirt. Whenever she met a new patient, she felt a little anxious, even after twenty years of successful practice, wondering if she'd be able to help that patient the way they needed to be helped. The basis of good psychotherapy requires good chemistry between therapist and patient. Without that chemistry, her ability to help a patient effectively is hindered, as if she were climbing a mountain in winter, at night, against strong headwinds.

"Let's hope," she whispered, hearing footsteps and the sound of a closing door coming from her waiting room. She buzzed her admin, and, seconds later, the door opened and a man walked in.

"Hello," she said, smiling and looking him in the eye, while extending her hand. "I'm Dr. Blackwell."

"Hello," he replied, omitting his name, but giving her hand a good squeeze.

She gestured toward her couch and continued to smile reassuringly. The man hesitated a little, but remained standing. He seemed tired, haunted, and his eyes searched the room as if taking inventory of every single detail, piece of furniture, and décor. He was tall, about 6 foot 5, and his broad shoulders hunched forward somewhat. He'd shoved his hands into his pockets but she could tell he'd clenched them into tight fists.

Still smiling, she asked gently, "I'm afraid I didn't get your name."

He turned toward her and frowned. "No need for that."

He spoke calmly, in a matter-of-fact tone of voice that showed little insight into who he was and the reason he was there.

Nevertheless, Angela let her smile widen a bit and nodded.

"All right," she said, "but I still have to call you something. What should I call you?"

He clenched his jaws before responding, and hesitated for a while, as if considering his options. "You can call me DJ," he eventually said, just as calmly. None of the inner angst his body language betrayed came out in his voice. It was as if he'd interiorized all battles he fought deep inside, and only opened his mouth to speak when a firm decision had been made. Not before that, not even by a split second.

Angela sat in her chair and repeated her gesture, inviting DJ to take a seat. This time, he hesitated between the two sofas and chose the one where he could face her without having to turn his head.

"So, tell me, DJ, what would you like to talk about?"

Not a blink, not even the tiniest fidget. Just perfectly quiet composure. Was that earlier angst gone? This man was definitely not her typical patient.

"Before we do anything else, I'd like to understand the limits of patient confidentiality," he said.

"The limits?" she reacted. She couldn't recall in all her career anyone asking about the limits. Patient confidentiality, yes, that was a common question before patients dared to unload their deepest, darkest secrets. But limits? Never before. "Can you please be more specific?"

He groaned quietly, the first sign of emotion he'd shown by way of verbal expression. "I'm sure you understand the notion of a limit, but let me explain it to you. In which cases would you breach patient confidentiality, doctor?"

She almost bit her lip, but stopped herself in time before showing an emotional reaction to the man's condescendence.

"In situations when you could pose a danger to yourself or others. I am obligated to engage the authorities. If, during our sessions, I learn that a serious crime has been committed, I'm also required to report it."

"Where would you draw the line? How do you know if I'm really posing a danger to myself or others, or just talking?"

"Please give me some credit," she replied sternly. "I've been doing this for a while."

He chose a few moments of silence, and she let him set the pace, holding his gaze steadily but gently at the same time.

"All right, here's what I need," he finally said. "We'll do a few sessions together, every now and then during the next six months, recorded on video."

Her eyebrows shot up, but she didn't say a word.

"These sessions will be used in court to exculpate my wife from any wrongdoing after my death, sometime after those sessions have been completed."

She still didn't interrupt him, but felt her blood starting to boil. He wanted *what?*

"I've done some research; apparently, you can have someone committed for up to forty-eight hours, if you believe they're about to commit suicide. Is that right?"

"Um, yes, that is correct." She looked at the man trying to see anywhere on his face the terrible anguish that typically accompanies the thoughts of suicide, the planning of it. No matter how carefully she scrutinized that man, she saw none of that turmoil; only serene determination, fierce in its resolve. The eye of the storm, or the depths of a volcanic lake, smooth and shiny on the surface, but running miles deep in a darkened, frozen abyss.

"Then you must agree you should do no such thing, doctor. I'm not planning to kill myself imminently, so confining me for two days would be not only pointless, but also a clear indicator that you can't be trusted."

She nodded calmly a couple of times, then swallowed and replied, "I agree."

"Good," he said, again showing no trace of emotion. "Then we understand each other. Do you have any questions?"

"Yes," she said, then summoned all her willpower to remain as calm as her new patient. "If I understand correctly, you're planning to kill yourself sometime after six months' worth of randomly scattered sessions, and you'd like me to bear witness that your wife had nothing to do with your death?"

"Precisely."

"Do you know what I do for a living?"

"Yes, and that's why I chose you," DJ replied unperturbed. "You're among the best at what you do, recognized and acclaimed, a highly respected mental health professional with a dual specialty, psychiatry and psychology, whose testimony will carry weight in a statement to the police or in a trial."

She leaned back in her chair and interlaced her fingers. "You know, coming to see a psychotherapist about your plans to end your life is called a cry for help in my line of work."

"Don't kid yourself, doctor, that's not what this is about. I would've gone to a notary public, but if my case gets challenged in court by the insurance companies, they'll want a mental health professional to attest to my state of mind."

"How about a lawyer, you have one of those?" Her voice was tinged with a hint of sarcasm.

"Yeah, already got one," he replied impassibly. "He'll be in touch with you, once it's done. He'll then tell you my real identity."

She stared at him intently, but he didn't flinch or avert his eyes. The same calm resolve emanated from every pore of his body, from his clear, unchallenging gaze, from the relaxed muscles in his face, to the hands he now kept alongside his body, immobile, relaxed.

"So, you want me to sit here for six months and help you plan your death?" She shook her head, partly unhappy with herself at the climbing tone of her voice. "You want me to be a powerless witness in a man's death, and do nothing about it? Well, I don't know if I'm the right sucker for the job."

There it was, a flicker of fear in his eyes. He clasped his hands together so rushed that they made a clapping noise. Tension rose in his shoulders, hunching them higher, getting his body ready to fight.

"Are you refusing to take my case?" His voice reflected deeper layers of distress.

What was it? Surprise? Most likely. Also, a painful response to rejection, and a hint of the immense weariness that weighed him down.

"No," she replied carefully, backtracking a little, content she'd scratched the surface. "I need some time to think about it, that's all. Give me until the day after tomorrow. If you call me on Friday afternoon, I'll have an answer for you."

Her words did nothing to ease the turmoil brewing in the man's eyes. After a while, he turned his gaze away from her and stared at the floor for a few silent moments, then stood and reluctantly stepped toward the door.

"We still have time," Dr. Blackwell said, "we can still talk if you'd like."

"Why would we do that, if you don't know what you're going to decide about my case? We'd only be wasting time."

He nodded once in lieu of farewell and disappeared, closing the door quietly on his way out.

Dr. Blackwell sat in her chair for a long time, staring at the closed door and thinking about that man. It made little sense, but she felt a strong personal connection to the troubled stranger.

# 5

# An Assignment

Morning fog drizzled cold as Dylan entered the warehouse, and he made quick work of getting rid of his light jacket, covered in tiny droplets of water, and headed straight for the kitchenette. A few of his employees were already gathered around the coffee makers, mugs in hand, waiting to partake of the lifesaving fluid.

As it normally happened, his appearance in the kitchenette area silenced the small talk somewhat, while a couple of workers greeted him in various ways, reflective of how well they knew him. He acknowledged everyone and proceeded to wait for his turn at the coffee maker, despite receiving invitations to cut to the front of the line.

"TGIF, my brother," a familiar voice said behind him, then punched him lightly in the shoulder.

"TGIF, Terrell, how right you are," he muttered, but his gloomy mood colored his voice darker than he'd intended.

"You okay, man?" Terrell asked, inserting his frowning face between Dylan's mug and the coffee machine. "Which broke dick crossed your path the wrong way?"

He smiled faintly and forced himself to snap out of it enough to put Terrell's concerns at ease. That man had always been perceptive, as if he had his own bullshit radar, perfectly calibrated and always powered on.

"No one did, Big T. They've all been good, and I'm good too. Just tired. Good thing it's Friday."

"If you say so, my man," Terrell replied, after shooting him a glance that lasted a fraction longer than normal. Then he turned and left, limping visibly on his left foot, heading toward the Order Entry stations at the far left of the warehouse.

Dylan filled his mug and took a couple of gulps, feeling the burn of the hot liquid as it made its way toward his empty stomach, grateful for the jolt of energy he felt coursing through his veins almost immediately. He then trotted toward his office, where he sat behind his uncluttered desk and powered up his computer.

Following his daily routine, he checked his emails first, looking for any escalated issues or communications from corporate. There were none; his inbox was also free from clutter, with ordinary reports, questions from staff, requests for time off, and meeting invites all organized neatly in folders. Then he logged into the system and checked a few critical indicators of performance. All shipments were on time, with more than 98 percent same-day shipping achieved. Order Entry had minimal waiting times on the phones, and it was about to get better, as more employees started their shifts. It was, after all, a Friday, with work volumes not even close to a those of a typical Monday.

Then he noticed the blinking light on his phone and listened to his voicemail. Only one message from his boss, an ambitious and rather callous woman by the name of Loreen Swan, who proudly held the title of vice president, Operations. She wanted to see him, first thing.

He took his notebook and walked quickly toward the front of the building, where the brass had their offices. He climbed the stairs to the second level and arrived at Loreen's office just as the head of Human Resources was leaving. He wondered what that was about and entered the office quickly, after a short rap on the door.

"Good morning," he said, and remained standing.

"Close the door, please, and take a seat," Loreen asked, without taking her eyes off the document she was reading.

He complied and waited. A few moments later, Loreen put the document inside a folder, then locked the folder in her desk drawer.

"Dylan, I need your help. We have decided to restructure things a little and get better situated in the marketplace by increasing our margins and our competitive advantage. I believe I've mentioned this before."

He refrained from closing his eyes in despair. What happened to people that made them replace normal people-speak with such senseless, empty crap? Yet he nodded a couple of times, as if he understood and agreed with what his boss was saying.

"There's room for us to improve," Loreen continued, "especially in the Order Entry department. How many people do you have there? Thirty?"

"Thirty-four," he said, suddenly understanding where the conversation was going.

"You know, people think we're crazy for doing logistics here, in San Francisco, one of the most expensive places on this side of the world. Yet here we are," she continued, softening her voice a little, as if talking to a friend. "But that doesn't mean we can afford to be careless with money. If we can find a better alternative, we should take it."

He pressed his lips together and managed to not say a word.

"In short, Dylan, we need to work together, you and I, to find an alternative for the Order Entry team. They're costing us a fortune, when all they do is take orders by phone. Anyone could be doing that, for a fraction of the cost, from anywhere in the world, right?"

He sat silently, watching her, wondering what made people like her tick.

She was a thin, bony woman in her early fifties, with a perfectly neat hairdo and wearing a well-pressed, navy-blue shirt with narrow, white lines. Rigidly constipated was the notion that came to his mind. Her smile, all fake, didn't touch her eyes, despite the well-rehearsed body language she presented. She was showing him encouragement, but also concern. She wanted him to understand she wasn't making the decision lightly. Yeah, right.

"If we take this business unit to the Philippines, for example, we could save two-thirds of the hourly cost, and that will amount to a substantial improvement to our bottom line. What do you think, Dylan?"

He breathed a couple of times, weighing his options and trying to curb his anger. Even if he didn't care for his own future anymore, he still cared for the well-being of his people.

"I think we're making a mistake," he eventually said, and his words dropped like cold stones in the silence of the office.

Loreen's fake smile instantly vanished. She leaned back in her seat and put her hands on the armrests of her massive, leather chair. "How so?" she asked, her voice chilled and threatening.

"These people, they have years of product knowledge. Not to mention they know most of the key customers by name. They have built relationships with them. These customers trust our staff and buy more because of them."

"Are you telling me that key customers buy a million dollars a year more product because of Jim, Anne, or Julie? Really? Because that's what employing these people here, in San Francisco, is costing us. How do you justify it?"

Before rushing into the argument some more, he stopped to consider the best way to buy his people more time. Making Loreen angry wasn't going to gain him anything.

"I'm not sure what amount of upselling those personal relationships are worth, but—"

"Dylan, listen to me," she said. "You're a senior manager, one step from becoming a director, from entering the ranks of the executive leadership team. Now is the time to show me, and the rest of the leadership team, what material you're made of."

He stared at her speechless, feeling wave after wave of anger suffocating him, but she mistook his silence for approval and continued.

"Your allegiance, at your job level, should be with the company and its bottom line. I understand you're concerned about your people, and that's normal. But don't be. They'll be all right; they'll find work elsewhere, and we're probably going to offer some severance, two weeks of pay, at least."

Two weeks! What was two weeks going to do for a family of four, like Anne's? What was two weeks' pay going to do for Charlie's sick wife? Fucking bastards…

"Get this done right, Dylan, and there's going to be a ten-thousand-dollar bonus for you, maybe even that promotion we've been talking about."

He made an effort to speak normally. "Timeline?" he asked.

"You tell me," she replied. "Start selecting vendors offshore, then pick one, and have the people train their replacements. Get it done, Dylan. Fast."

He nodded, then left her office briskly and headed toward his own. Finally, behind his closed office door, he let the mask drop a little and sat at his desk, holding his head in his hands. What was he going to do?

His mind instantly filled with things he should have said, and ways he should have argued with Loreen, to make her change her mind. He beat himself up for not saying much in there, but then realized it wouldn't have made much difference. Loreen's allegiance was definitely with the company's bottom line all right, and she used him to do her dirty work for her. Gutless bitch.

Then he found himself speculating, calculating the value of a human destiny crushed. Ten-thousand-dollar bonus, for thirty-four people. That's almost three hundred dollars per person. An abject mercenary, that's what he was, nothing more, nothing less. A gun for hire, and for cheap. It made him sick, with himself, with the world they lived in.

By the time he got home, he could barely walk straight. He'd skipped lunch, too nauseated to touch the food Taylor had packed for him in the morning. Once inside the house, he closed the garage door and leaned against it, trying to get his bearings.

Taylor appeared, trotting cheerfully to greet him, the way she did every day. When she saw him, her smile died on her lips. "What happened?"

He closed his eyes and groaned, a pained sound that reverberated strangely in the small hallway. He hated bringing bad news to her, causing her lovely smile to disappear, making room for worry lines and sleepless nights.

"Dylan?" she insisted, touching his face gently. "What's wrong?"

"Layoffs…" he said, hating himself for uttering the word.

She squeezed his hand, then hugged him tightly. "Should I start packing?"

"No," he replied. "I'm not impacted, at least not yet."

"Oh," she replied, sounding almost relieved.

He walked slowly toward the living room, loosening his tie and kicking his shoes as he went. Then he let himself drop onto the couch and closed his eyes, trying to escape his reality.

He felt the couch move, when Taylor sat next to him, then she clasped his hand with both hers.

"Don't, please," she said. "Don't go there. It's not your fault."

He looked at her with pain-filled, weary eyes. "You don't understand. Give me some time, okay? I'll be all right."

"No, I won't let you," she pleaded. "Snap out of it, for my sake. Don't spend time being sad. It won't help you."

"All I'm asking for is a few bloody minutes, all right?" he replied, instantly hating himself for being angry with her.

She stood and paced the room, shoving her hands in her jeans pockets, avoiding his apologetic gaze. Then she stopped right in front of him.

"I've done nothing but support you and follow you everywhere you wanted to go, all these years. I've done nothing for myself, for my career; it was all you, always you. You could at least stop pushing me away, because it's not damn fair, you hear me?"

"All I'm asking for is a few minutes, Taylor, please be reasonable. I want to be by myself now. Do I need to leave the house for that?"

"Damn you, Dylan, don't you dare threaten me!" she yelled. "Go ahead, be an asshole. Why is it that you'd rather sit there and sulk, instead of doing something with me? Anything, just snap the hell out of it already!"

He felt his blood boil, rushing to his brain in a wave of rage like he'd rarely felt before, and never toward her.

"You drive me fucking crazy," he shouted, and she froze in place, stunned. "Don't you think that if I could, I'd do whatever the hell you want me to? Don't you know that by now?"

"Well, then, why don't you try?"

"Argh…" he groaned, then his eyes fell on the pile of cardboard boxes stacked in the corner of the room and stayed riveted to it. "I'm trying, way harder than you're trying to get rid of all this junk you're collecting. We're moving every few years, but no, you have to haul all this shit around. So, don't go telling me about how you're trying, and how you've done it all for me. You ain't done much, definitely not as much as throwing out one, single, damn, cardboard box."

He heard her heartwrenching sobs way before he saw her face; his eyes clung to those boxes for some reason, almost as if he were captivated, possessed by the sight of them. Then he turned toward her and reached out to her, overwhelmed by guilt.

"I'm sorry…" he whispered and took her hand.

She yanked herself free of him and stormed out of the room, then locked herself in the bedroom. Muffled by the distance and the closed door, he could still hear her bitter sobs, each of them tearing at his heart, shredding it to pieces.

He closed his eyes, squeezing them tightly, and let himself fall prey to a surge of interiorized agony.

"Oh, God," he whispered, while his voice trembled, filled with sorrow. "Please let this be over already."

# 6

# A Different Kind of Session

Angela inhaled the aroma of the freshly brewed hot chocolate, holding the tall mug in her palms and feeling the warmth cross into her bloodstream, thawing her heart. She kept her eyes closed for a while, letting that scent fill her mind with fond memories of a safe, cherished childhood, of Christmas Eves and foggy Sunday mornings. She blew gently into the cup to cool the steaming liquid, before she could take a sip, and let her eyes wander over the details of the familiar room.

The window sheers had yellowed a little with time, but were the same she remembered. She couldn't recall ever seeing Dr. Foster's home office with a different setup. He was aging elegantly, if that could be said about anyone, and his professional courtesy and welcoming smile had not been eroded by age, or by the thousands of patients who'd taken a seat on his couch throughout his almost fifty years of practice. Even now, he sat in his wide recliner, his feet propped on a small ottoman, his relaxed posture inviting his patients to unwind, breathe easy, and enjoy a few moments of tranquility before life's whirlwinds swept them away again.

The room was dark, yet warm, with natural, Brazilian cherry wood paneling matching the furniture and the fatigued, maroon leather of the sofa, recliner, and armchairs set. She let herself relax a bit more, leaned against the back of the sofa and folded her legs underneath her. She rubbed her cheeks against the soft, fleecy throw, and, for a while, listened to the sound of fire, crackling in the fireplace behind her. Funny how the sound of fire, in the absence of a visual sensory input, sounded just like raindrops rapping against a window or a shingled roof. How could that be possible? Fire and rain, so different, yet so similar?

Dr. Foster waited patiently and quietly, his smile genuine, touching his blue eyes and drawing familiar lines on his brow. On the wall behind him, a generous display took almost the entire space, diplomas, awards, and certifications, all attesting to his specialty in addiction psychiatry. Angela recalled, back when she was a second-year resident, asking him whether that wall of framed paper was what made a medical professional. She smiled, as she remembered his reaction.

He'd said, "It's not the paper that makes a good doctor, Angela. It's the people whose existence you touch, who lead happy and fulfilled lives because of the work you do. It's all the ones you save, all the troubled souls you don't lose." She'd been lucky to have him by her side all those years, for as long as she could remember.

"You're smiling," Dr. Foster said, pulling her back from her memories. "Care to share?"

Her smile widened and her eyes misted.

"It's about you, and what you said to me eons ago. The troubled souls you don't lose, remember that? You said, 'never stop—'"

"Fighting," Dr. Foster jumped in, finishing her phrase. "Don't look away, don't be discouraged. I've seen you do it, my dear. You have the gift," he added, a hint of pride coloring his voice.

She started to stretch her legs, but then changed her mind and folded them again, as if the tension she felt forced her to stay curled up, taking as little space as possible. She blew some more air into her mug, although the cocoa had cooled enough for her to savor it.

"You're not enjoying your hot chocolate much," he said. "Only a man can have that effect on you." His voice was gentle and warm, encouraging. Yet she stayed quiet for a while, listening to the sound of fire, and trying to see if she could tell it apart from the sound of rain. Ah, there it was… a crackle, an impulse noise that would rarely be heard in a symphony of rain drops. There had to be a way to tell fire apart from rain; no matter how similar they seemed. Their cores were at opposite ends of the spectrum. If she chose to pay attention, she'd be able to tell them apart, water from fire, truth from lies, life from death.

Satisfied with her observation, she took a sip of cocoa and relished the feelings it brought up. Family. Safety. Love.

"It's a patient," she finally said. "Well, he's not even a patient yet. I haven't decided."

"Tell me," he said, and brought his hands together and interlaced his fingers in front of him, seemingly intrigued.

She hesitated, although that had never happened before. Dr. Foster was a great resource for professional advice, and had been her mentor since she'd graduated from med school. Yet she feared that bringing someone else into that decision might skew her thinking, might make her take a different path than she wanted. But wasn't that what mentoring was supposed to do? Someone wiser, more experienced and more knowledgeable, guiding her thinking? Then why did she feel like she needed to hide her thoughts, her feelings from him? That, in itself, was a red flag, and she knew what she had to do. The rule was simple: If you don't think or feel you can talk about it with a senior physician, then you're probably making a big professional mistake.

She took a deep breath, and, before speaking, looked at the grandfather clock on the wall, an antique piece in cherry wood and gold, brought by Dr. Foster from Switzerland, more than twenty years ago. Tick-tock, the clock said somberly, and that rhythmic sound marked life passing by. Her own, her patient's.

"He wants me to watch him die," she blurted. "He won't let me help him, won't let me do anything but document his mental state for the authorities and the courts. He wants his wife to be safe and well taken care of after he kills himself."

A hint of a frown shaded Dr. Foster's brow. "Interesting... What are you going to do?"

"I've never turned away a patient, not ever," she replied, staring intently at the trembling surface of her hot chocolate, now almost room temperature. "What if he..." She choked a little, then struggled to swallow. "I can't picture myself giving him what he wants."

"So, you believe him?" Dr. Foster asked. His ruffled, almost entirely white eyebrows shot up in surprise. "Patients lie, Angela. You know that. Why do you choose to believe this man, to take his request so literally? I know for a fact he's not the first suicidal patient you've dealt with."

That was a good question. She turned her attention inward, searching for the answer, knowing it was buried somewhere deep inside her.

"I felt... chilled when he spoke to me. I had goosebumps. He was calm... incredibly calm," she added. "When a suicidal patient is that calm, it only means his mind is made up, you know that. Yet under the calm appearance, there's a storm brewing inside. I could only see a brief flash of emotion, and I had to push him hard to crack his shell open a little."

"He doesn't admit he needs help, all right, but he does," Dr. Foster said, scratching his salt-and-pepper beard. Then he pinched his chin between his thumb and his index, in the familiar posture she remembered so well from her early days as a therapist. "You've seen this before, Ang. His subconscious mind is telling him he needs help. He reached out to a therapist, out of all people, right? And a darn good one too. He probably did some research before he found you."

She flashed a crooked smile, loaded with sadness. "I challenged him about that. He has solid reasons for it, all having to do with legal procedure, the courts, and the insurance companies."

"Yeah, and those reasons are called rationalization, Ang." He leaned forward, searching her eyes.

"Cry for help, then?" she asked, still hesitant to meet his scrutinizing gaze. "Could it be that simple?"

"Definitely," he replied, "why not? But I never said it was simple. No cry for help ever is."

"He's a troubled soul, that's for sure," she finally admitted, and, as she said the words, she felt better, knowing what she needed to do. "Never stop fighting, right?"

Dr. Foster smiled widely, showing two rows of healthy-looking teeth. "Don't look away, don't be discouraged," he repeated his earlier chant. "You know the drill."

She bit her lip and averted her eyes. The same rules applied, regardless of the patients and their declared goals. It was her duty to help that man find himself, and still, the perspective of taking his life into her hands scared her, terrified her at the thought of failing. At the thought of him dying. Forcing herself to be analytical once more, she wondered about the connection she felt to the stranger she'd spent less than an hour with, and the mark he was already leaving on her life.

"What if I lose him?" she whispered.

Dr. Foster pressed his lips together for a brief moment, before replying. "That could happen. In our line of work there are no guarantees, no absolutes. But at least you'll try, and knowing you, you'll try your utmost."

# 7

# Terms

Angela paced the floor, irritated with her new patient's lack of punctuality. He could at least be considerate and arrive on time. She normally refrained from judging her patients or letting herself be upset by any of their behaviors, knowing there were many factors at play in their lives. In this man's case, she was different; everything about this patient was different, irritating somehow, as if a challenging puzzle that waited for her to solve it, but the light was turned off.

The intercom finally buzzed, and she stepped toward the door to greet him.

He entered the room without hesitation, as if attending a business meeting he was well-prepared for. He was dressed in business casual attire, with slacks and a jacket, on top of a light-blue shirt, but no tie. He seemed tired, and the same haunted expression she'd seen before was on his face.

She took a few moments to study him, while she waited for him to get settled. He was in his early forties, dark hair with a close trim, and clean shaven. He looked like many other professionals from the San Francisco business district; by all appearances, he was a well-adjusted individual, in relatively good shape. His gait hinted of time spent in the military, but not recently.

She offered him a cup of tea, which he promptly declined, then she took a seat on one of the two opposing sofas, inviting him to sit on the other one. He nodded and complied, but his posture remained tense, alert. She waited for him to speak, while he seemed to wait for her. After a while, he cleared his throat quietly.

"Um, I wanted to thank you for taking me on. I realize my request might be somewhat unusual."

She acknowledged with a quick nod.

"We'll have to put some rules in place," she said, "and I'll start by asking you to be on time for our sessions. Regardless of how late you arrive, our sessions will end promptly once the hour is up."

He frowned and looked away. "Understood. I apologize; it won't happen again."

"We will meet for weekly sessions, for the six-month period that you've stated. Twenty-four sessions," she added.

"I don't need that many," he pushed back. "This is not therapy; we don't have to meet that often. Just enough to document—"

"Don't tell me how to do my work," she replied coldly. "You requested a thoroughly documented evaluation of your state of mind, detailed enough to hold up in court. This is what it takes. If you're not comfortable with this schedule, please feel free to work with someone else. I won't be offended."

"Take it or leave it, huh, Doc?" he asked, his voice bitter and low pitched.

"Pretty much. If you follow my rules, I promise you I will hold my end of the bargain, and stand witness, wherever and whenever it will be necessary, to make sure your needs are met. However, if you start skipping sessions, or if I feel manipulated or coerced in any way, I will consider myself free of any obligations to you or your wife."

"All right, weekly sessions it is then. I'll take it."

"Then we need to discuss your payment. I won't charge you for these sessions. Instead—"

"I have no problem paying," he interrupted. "You don't need to make an exception. I can afford to pay." He sounded almost alarmed by the perspective of not paying; she wondered why.

He leaned forward, his hands clamping his thighs right above his knees, getting ready to spring to his feet, while a hint of panic dilated his irises. She raised her hands in a pacifying gesture.

"Please allow me to finish," she said gently, and he promptly settled in place, listening. "You must understand there are ethical and professional standards that govern the relationship between therapist and patient, and you're asking me to help you in a manner that puts me outside of these professional boundaries."

He stood abruptly and shoved his hands in his pant pockets. "But I thought… I agreed to do weekly sessions. Are you saying you won't work with me? You could have told me no on the phone."

"I'm not telling you no, DJ. I *will* help you. Please sit."

Disarmed and looking confused, he obeyed, but the tension remained in his forward posture, his hunched shoulders, and his firmly clenched hands.

"The way you chose to engage me is outside of what I'm allowed to do in a typical therapist-patient relationship. Therefore, I won't charge you; technically, you won't be my patient, nor my client."

He shook his head and his frown deepened.

"But won't that impact your ability to testify? How will you justify your testimony?"

"You wanted the sessions recorded on video, right? That will provide ample proof that we have talked, and incontestable evidence that will speak to your state of mind, and to your wife's innocence, in support of my testimony and written evaluation. Even if I don't charge you, my professional credibility will be the same."

His jaws clenched, his muscles bulging and rolling under his pale cheeks.

"I can't ask you to do this for free, doctor. You have to let me pay."

"And I wouldn't do it for free either. You will pay, only you won't be paying me," she said, feeling a little uncomfortable, as she explained the details of the arrangement. It sounded dirty, dishonest, as if she were a crook at a carnival, practicing without a license.

"What do you mean?"

"Every week, you will donate my fee to a charity of your choice. I hope you'll find this condition acceptable."

He remained quiet for a while, frowning and staring at the carpet, visibly troubled by something.

"Do you have a certain charity in mind?" she probed, intrigued by his persistent yet visibly anxious silence. "Which one will you choose?"

"I have to think about it," he said, avoiding her gaze and staring into emptiness.

"There must be something you care about, some—"

"No, it's not that," he replied, waving her advice away as if swatting a fly.

"Then what?"

"I'll have to find out which ones accept anonymous donations, but are willing to give receipts."

"Ah, I see," she replied. "Your anonymity is very important to you, isn't it?"

He didn't respond, not immediately. When he spoke, he had a question instead.

"Okay, what else?"

"I won't be prescribing any medication, because, technically, you won't be my patient."

"That's fine, I don't need drugs. I don't need to be cured, Doc. Don't even try."

She nodded a little sideways, as if accepting his remark but not really agreeing with it.

"We'll meet every Wednesday evening at six, here, in this office. By next week, I'll have some video equipment in place, per your request."

"Okay. I could bring the video," he offered.

"That won't be necessary," she said firmly. "Any questions?"

"No," he replied, taking her interrogation as an invitation to leave. He stood and buttoned his jacket, but remained in front of the sofa, undecided, hesitant to leave.

She smiled and remained seated, in an unspoken invitation for him to open up.

"Why did you take my case, Doc?" he finally asked. "You're obviously not comfortable with what I'm asking you to do, seeing how you won't let me pay you. Maybe I'm putting your career at risk, your license, I don't know. So, why?"

It was a loaded question that deserved a truthful answer.

"Because I believe I can help you," she said. "Even if I won't be taking you as a patient officially, that doesn't mean I won't be working with you, having your best interests in mind. Those are rules set by my own moral compass, not by the American Psychological Association."

"But you do understand you won't really be helping me, other than standing witness to what's going on, right?"

She felt a pang of uneasiness in her stomach, as if something unfurled in there, releasing fear. "Yes," she lied, refraining from adding how determined she was to try, nevertheless.

He shrugged, then took one more step toward the door.

"Women are so difficult to understand, Doc. All this charade, with the weekly sessions, your pay, and the donations, with you saying you're helping me the way you're helping your patients, when you know that you're not... Why are women so damn complicated?"

She smiled, and, for the first time since he'd arrived, averted her look. "Let's try to find that out next time, shall we? And you can call me Angela."

"All right... Doc."

He nodded and made a hand gesture, almost like a wave, then left, closing the door quietly behind him.

She remained seated, immobile, thinking what Dr. Foster would have to say about her little arrangement. Why did she feel the need to establish the therapeutic alliance with this man outside of the traditional parameters? What did she really expect would happen during those sessions? Most important, how far was she willing to go to save this man's life?

# 8

# Memories

Angela held on to the terrace guardrail and faced the ocean, still visible in the dim light of late dusk. Fog rolled in, a thick, solid bank with clearly defined edges dipped in dark, sunset hues, leaving room above it for the few early stars and the setting crescent moon to still be visible.

She breathed in the cold, salty air, and watched the fog bank advance quickly, starting to engulf the small, coastal town in silence and ghostly darkness. Soon all the burg's lights were swallowed and consumed, and only yellowish halos painted the main streets.

She felt the first needles of drizzle hit her face and bring the familiar chill, a signal it was time to go inside and start a warm fire. She pulled the French door shut behind her and, for a second, listened intently and heard nothing but silence, the thickest, most material silence she'd ever heard, yet she'd heard it every day for the past five years.

Their evening routine that she'd loved, the two of them holding hands on that terrace and watching sunsets together, waiting for the fog bank to roll in, had been, for many years, the highlight of her days. Now her sundown ritual, although unchanged, was solitary, a silent remembrance of what used to be and could never be again.

She pushed herself to start a fire, then spent a few moments in front of it, letting the cheer of the yellows, oranges, and reds in the brisk flames attempt to lift her spirits. This time it wasn't working. Resigned, she opted for a glass of wine, then sat on the big sofa folding her legs underneath her. She flipped through a few favorite movie channels. Her mind wasn't into it though; the past came crashing in, and she couldn't fight it off anymore.

She switched the TV to auxiliary input, and soon a homemade movie played, showing Michael holding Shelley's hand when she was a toddler, learning to walk. They laughed together, the two of them, and she recalled filming that scene, then leaving that camera on top of the wood rack and joining them in. Three voices, laughing together in the sharp sunlight.

Then the video switched to a later movie. Michael's hairline had started to recede, but he still looked good. He had a distinguished look, fitting for the acclaimed scientist that he'd become. It was the year that NASA had bought his thermal shielding patent, marking one of the most important achievements of his career in aerospace engineering. The video showed the three of them celebrating at an oceanfront dining restaurant, and the waiter-turned-cameraman had done a good job capturing the essence of the moment, the champagne cork popping, and the excited squeals of pure joy coming out of Shelley's mouth.

Then, another few years later, the two of them, dancing together at a friend's wedding, while she laughed, flipped her hair, and blushed like a teenager in love. By that time, Michael had been diagnosed, but his heart issues hadn't touched his handsome, loving face, nor changed his youthful ways. She recollected the moments when she had to twist his arm to get him to pay attention to his blood pressure, his salt intake, his warning symptoms. He'd always played down her concerns, only adding to her worries.

The music ended, and they stopped dancing, and soon thereafter the recording ended, leaving the screen filed with snow. The sound of static filled the room, the noise seeming surreal, almost alien, after the tones of their dance music had died. She grabbed the remote and muted the sound, while staring into the blank screen.

She knew what she wanted to do, although she feared it just as much as she yearned for it. She rationalized it by thinking that any form of grieving was better than no grieving at all, and ignoring all the other clinical terms that flurried through her mind. Obsessive thoughts and behaviors. Denial. Unresolved anger. Compulsive reliving of the traumatic event. But all those clinical terms could go spin themselves down the drain for a change. All she wanted to do was see his face once more, hear his voice again, the way he looked that last morning she'd seen him, the way his voice sounded five years ago.

Shakily, she stood and pulled open a drawer, then extracted a DVD from an unmarked case and inserted it into the player. The static on the screen quickly vanished, replaced by a blue screen with words forever burned in her memory: "Blackwell vs. Middlefield Company, Exhibit 19A—Surveillance Video."

Then she sat on the floor to be closer to the screen, staring at the grainy video, seeing every pixel of image, and straining to hear every muffled word on the bad recording, dated five years and six days ago.

She saw her husband enter the Middlefield pharmacy location nearest to his office. She knew the place well; sometimes, when they met for lunch downtown, she'd stop by to pick up makeup items or some vitamins. She vaguely remembered the pharmacy attendant, a young girl by the exotic name of Vonda, per her plastic nametag. Those were the familiar things she recalled, but that's where the familiarity ended, making room for the incomprehensible nightmare that she witnessed on that tape.

She saw Michael walk to the pharmacy counter, waiting impatiently for Vonda to wrap up business with the customer in front of him. He was fidgeting, wiping his brow with the back of his hand every minute or so, while Vonda moved slower than anyone she'd ever seen.

Finally, at the counter, he asked Vonda to measure his blood pressure. He said, "Can you please do it now? I think my blood pressure spiked. I have my meds, but I need to be sure."

Vonda shook her head and answered slowly, one indifferent word at a time. "Please take a seat and wait ten minutes. Then I'll come take your blood pressure."

"No, you don't understand," he pleaded, "if I'm in hypertensive crisis, this is an emergency. Please do it now."

"Um, I'm sorry, but I can't. There's no one else here, and the procedure says clearly I have to wait ten minutes after you've settled down before I measure it."

"Listen, I can't wait," he insisted. "I'll buy one of your damn blood pressure machines, how's that?" he offered. His voice carried hues of subdued irritation, all understandable.

"You can go ahead and buy one, sir," Vonda replied, "but there's no power plug for you to use in here."

"Then please help me, please! What's it going to take? Call your manager, and I'll explain."

"Sir, you don't need to get nasty with me. All right, I'll do it. Take a seat."

He sat on the chair and rolled up his sleeve, then waited, rapping his fingers against the table, and checking his watch every few seconds. He was still sweating, because he kept wiping his brow with his other sleeve, then tapping some more, while Vonda took her sweet time to bring the blood pressure cuff.

Then Vonda appeared in view and tried to wrap the cuff on Michael's arm, but her ridiculously long, fake nails prevented her from being able to grab the fabric and pull it through the ring. After what seemed like endless hours, but only took two minutes per the surveillance video time code, she finally inflated the cuff and took the reading.

"This can't be right," she said, "see? If you won't settle down, you can't have any drugs like this. Please settle down, sir, give it ten minutes."

"What's your reading?" he asked, while pulling his meds from his pocket and opening the small bottle.

"It doesn't matter, sir, it can't be right. You need to quiet down," she said, raising her voice, irritated with his lack of obedience.

"Tell me the damn numbers, *now*," he demanded, raising his voice for the first time.

"It says 217 over 167, but it can't be right. Like I said, you have to—"

That's when he collapsed, keeling over like something had cut his legs from underneath him, his left hand grasping and pulling at his chest, as if he tried to get it open. The EMS crew found a nitroglycerin pill in his hand, and an undissolved Captopril on his tongue. They pronounced him dead at the scene; "massive coronary" were the two words that had sealed his fate.

Angela reached forward and touched the screen with frozen fingers, right there where his body lay on the cold cement floor. Through a blur of tears, she watched the final minutes of the video, not taking her hand off those few black pixels on her screen, the last image of her husband.

He could have lived, if she'd only listened to him. That girl's indifference and the stupid procedures the company had deployed without giving employees the tiniest bit of training had killed her Michael. That girl, as slow and as deadly as molten lava, not giving a damn about anything other than her ridiculous, acrylic fingernails, had no idea that a person in hypertensive crisis is agitated and makes little sense. But she wasn't innocent, not at all. She could have called someone, or could have believed him when he'd said, "I have my meds." A year later, in court, in the history-making case of Blackwell vs. Middlefield Company, Vonda had the nerve to declare she'd thought Michael was trying to score free drugs. The fact that he was wearing an expensive business suit and looked nothing like a street junkie she didn't find relevant, per her own testimony.

Angela had turned all her anger for the senseless death of her husband into a campaign aimed at raising awareness about pharmacies' roles as first responders, even if that role was unofficial and unrecognized as such. But secretly, she wanted the company to hurt as badly as she did, and companies only hurt when they lose money.

She got the best attorneys she could find and started her crusade against corporate and individual indifference, known as egregious conduct in legal terms. Despite repeated offers, she refused to settle and continued her battle in court, where the surveillance video left little room for debate. After a brief deliberation, the jury had awarded $25 million dollars in compensatory damages and added another $25 million in punitive damages, making that case one of the largest of its kind. Against the multilocation, national pharmacy chain's $5.5 billion in annual profits, the $50 million was pocket change, less than 1 percent. The chain could afford all the egregious conduct it wanted, no matter how many lives they ended.

Angela took the money, paid her attorneys, then donated the entire amount to Michael's favorite charities. Then, a wounded warrior without a cause, she started her new existence, an endless string of lonely sunsets on the same terrace, and thick, heavy silence instead of laughter. Every now and then, she watched that surveillance video, holding her breath and hoping against all reason that this time it would have a different ending.

It never did.

# 9

# Bad News

Dylan had been up since four in the morning, going over what he had to do, how to handle the task he was forced to execute. He wanted to give people the most chances for survival, of battling the upcoming adversity that was threatening their existence, their families.

By the time he got to the office and lined up for his morning coffee, his mind was made up. Screw the company and their policies. Why would he care how the brass wanted to protect their greedy interests? He wasn't going to be around much longer anyway, and they could take their almost three hundred silver coins apiece and shove them where the sun don't shine. He was going to give his people a heads-up, one way or another, even if HR had told him to "handle the matter with the utmost discretion, to ensure a smooth transition offshore."

He filled his coffee mug, keeping his head on a swivel and looking for Terrell. He wasn't there; he must have come in early. He greeted a few of the people in the kitchenette on his way out, then walked all the way to the left of the warehouse, where the Order Entry department had its cluster of cubicles.

Terrell was at his desk, his left leg stretched out, while he massaged his thigh vigorously. He raised his head and grinned widely when he saw DJ approach.

"Had your coffee yet?" DJ asked, after a brief nod.

"Uh-huh," Terrell replied, pointing at his mug.

DJ snickered when he read the inscription on the black, half-pint mug. It read, "Marine, because badass isn't an official job title."

"If HR sees that, you'll get slapped around a little," DJ said, still smiling.

"They never venture out this far, my man. They don't care about us."

DJ's smile died, and a gut-wrenching feeling of uneasiness overtook him. Unknowingly, Terrell was right; they didn't care. "Big T, let's check out some of the paper stock levels, all right?"

Terrell stood quickly, while a frown carved two lines at the root of his nose. "Rah," he replied seriously but quietly, as he'd done many years ago in the desert, when the enemy lurked nearby.

They stepped quickly toward the farthest end of the warehouse, where print paper in bulk was stored on large pallets, an area rarely visited by anyone during the day. After a few more steps, Terrell stopped and turned toward DJ, his smile gone and his frown deeper.

"Them pallets seem all right to me and none have gone missing. So, what's crawling up your ass?"

DJ let a long, pained breath escape his lips, before he could speak. Although he'd gone over what he was going to say about a million times, he couldn't find the words anymore. When Terrell gazed at him intently, he avoided his look. "Big T, I—"

"Stop feeling my ass, man. Grow a pair and spill it already."

"They're letting you go. The entire department," DJ said, then put his coffee cup on a shelf and shoved his hands deep inside his pockets, closing his fists tightly, until his knuckles cracked and hurt.

Terrell's jaw dropped and, for a long moment, he stood there, speechless.

"What are you sayin', man? Since when are you a blue falcon, huh?" he asked, using the Marine Corps slang term for someone who'd turn on a fellow Marine to save his own skin.

"I'm not, Big T, honest to God. I probably won't be here either, by the time they get to you guys."

Terrell slapped his forehead hard, in a gesture of exasperation. "When?"

"Probably not until November," DJ replied quietly, only a hint above a whisper. "I'm doing my best to stall them, to buy you guys some time."

"But you ain't tellin' no one, so what kind of time do you think you're buying us?"

"I told *you*, didn't I?" DJ replied. "I started with you, that's all. It's supposed to be confidential, until they're ready with the paperwork and severance and all that. But I thought you could use the extra few months."

Terrell turned halfway toward the back of the warehouse, staring into thin air. "What the hell am I going to do, man?" he eventually asked.

"You can look for something else, T. I'll help you, you know I will."

"No offense, Deej, but you don't know what the heck you're talking about. If it weren't for you to give me this job, I'd still be flippin' burgers for minimum wage and eating at the food bank so my kid could go to school. I ain't got a bloody chance in hell out there. I'm a black cripple with a bad back and a limp, and not the world's greatest set of skills."

DJ stood there silently, unable to think of anything he could say to bring solace to his friend. He was right; the job market was merciless to anyone less than perfect, in everything from skillset to attitude to word choices to overall demeanor. People didn't care about people anymore and rushed into hurting others for the tiniest of suspicions, perceptions, or personal gain.

One of the halogen lights above their heads hissed, then popped loudly, and they both dropped to the ground, each extending an arm to shield the other. Then they helped each other back up, and looked each other firmly in the eye, with gazes that were devoid of all nonsense.

"See this?" Terrell asked. "This, just now, demonstrates how screwed up we really are, man. There ain't no IEDs in this warehouse, but we still drop to the ground at the slightest noise. We're damaged goods, bro, that's what we are. You think people don't see us for what we are, man? Think again."

"It's not us, T; it's the entire team they're letting go."

"All the box kickers?"

"Just the phone crew for now."

Terrell scratched his sweaty forehead and cussed under his breath.

"Maybe the others have a chance, better than us, anyway. I'll tell them, on the QT."

"No need to do my dirty work, T. I can take care of it."

"If they catch you giving us the heads up, they'll escort you out of this damn building on the spot, and then who's gonna stall them until November, huh? No, you go kiss their brass asses, or do whatever you got to do to buy us some more time, and I'll talk to the guys, one by one. No one will hear a peep, I swear."

It wasn't until later than night that DJ allowed himself to feel the suffocating rage that had been brewing deep inside. The drive home from work seemed shorter than usual, and he stopped a few times along the way, not feeling ready to get home, not feeling capable to behave normally for the sake of his wife. She didn't deserve any of that shit. She deserved to see the man she loved smiling back at her, happy to be home, happy to see her. How the hell was he going to pull that off, when he could barely breathe?

It wasn't that he wasn't happy to see her. He was, and he'd always been, ever since the day he first met her, back on that high school football field, in the rain. But she demanded him to be happy, period. To be smiling carefree, having fun in life, while his heart was breaking and his demons unyielding. If she'd only accept him the way he was, he'd curl up at her feet, as she sat on the sofa watching TV, and rest his head on her lap, waiting patiently for her soft fingers to caress his hair, while he let himself slip away into his own internal world, prey to the monsters that roamed it freely. He'd mask the pain he was feeling, and just relish her presence, her soothing voice, the warmth of her body. Later, he'd fall asleep, right there at her feet, on the floor, and she'd cover him with a blanket and turn off the lights, then spend the night near him, on that sofa, making sure he'd still feel her presence. But she didn't do any of that, and he didn't know how to ask so much of her.

Less than a mile away from home, he pulled over on the side of the road one more time, and let a rage-filled roar escape his chest, followed by a slew of profanities. Then he stopped shouting and looked at the back of his hands, intently, observing every detail, every blood vessel. Then he squeezed his hands into tight fists, watching his knuckles go white, hearing the joints crack, in a repeat of his earlier gesture, back at the warehouse. He looked around for something he could punch to feel better. The car's dashboard would probably crack and cost thousands to repair, and the car seats were too plush to mitigate his anger. With the last shred of reason he could muster, he forced himself to calm down, breathe deeply, and slowly relax his hands, regretting the tension as it left his body. His hands stopped hurting, but his entire body screamed for a release, for something that could wash away the all-consuming anger he felt.

It was almost eight when he got home, and the moment he entered the living room, he noticed Taylor was all dressed up, wearing her 4-inch heels, but didn't even turn to look at him.

"Taylor?" he asked, worried by her unusual attitude.

"How could you forget, Dylan?" she asked quietly, without turning her head to look at him. "Was it that hard to remember? You didn't even bother to pick up your phone. I don't even exist for you, do I?"

Still confused, he pulled out his phone and found nine missed calls from her, and several voice messages. He'd forgotten and left the phone on silent, after a meeting at the end of the day. His bad, no one else's.

"I'm so sorry, baby," he said, and crouched down in front of her, in time to see a tear roll down her cheek. He searched her eyes, but she turned away. "I'm here now, ready to do whatever you want me to do," he whispered.

"You still don't remember, do you?" she scoffed bitterly. "Chelsea's birthday party. The invitation was for six-thirty. I don't think there's much you can do at this time."

"Oh, crap…" he said, remembering in a split second how she'd told him time and time again how much she wanted to go, how she'd bought a new dress for that party, because her friend Chelsea's husband was some hot shot in the tech industry, and the party was going to be something they couldn't miss. She'd even reminded him that morning, right before he left the house. "I'll get dressed in two minutes. Go start the car, pull it out, and I'll catch up."

"Who are you kidding, Dylan? We're already two hours late. It will be three before we get there, all the way down to Cupertino. We'll be the laughingstock of the evening. Please, people, pass the hat and raise some money to buy these poor shmucks a watch." Her tone was bitter and trembling under the threat of tears.

"How can I make it up to you, babe?" He reached out and took her hand gently in his. Her fingers were frozen, rigid. "Just name it; I'll do anything you want."

"There's nothing you can do, Dylan, not anymore. I never get out of this damn house; we never go anywhere. You'd be happy to never see the light of day, or another human being again, but newsflash, all right? I'm alive! I'm not dead yet. Don't bury me before it's time."

She stood and walked away, and he let go of her hand, but continued watching her, hoping she'd allow him to do something to make things better.

"Where are you going?" he asked quietly.

"Where the hell do you think I'm going? To get undressed and cry myself to sleep. The usual."

"Baby, please—"

She turned around on a dime. "Don't you 'please' me, Dylan. I've begged you for years to do something, to snap out of this… darkness that you carry around yourself like a cloak. But no, you won't do anything. You won't get help, you won't listen to anything I have to say. You've turned me into a sad failure, someone who sits and waits for you all day long, only to be ignored."

Then she continued her way toward the bedroom, and soon she closed that door behind her with a loud thud.

He stood there, completely lost in the middle of his own living room, not knowing what to do or where to go. She was right, every word of her bitter diatribe was right. He'd done nothing to fix their lives, nothing to bring cheer and laughter back into their existence. The fact that he'd desperately tried all those years and somehow failed didn't seem to matter anymore. He felt unworthy, deserving of the fate he'd set for himself.

November twelfth couldn't come soon enough. Taylor deserved a happy life, and, with him in the picture, that wasn't an option.

# 10

# The First Session

DJ stood by the door, visibly uneasy, while Angela fussed with the video camera and the tripod. She was uncomfortable setting things up, not only because she wasn't tech savvy, but she'd never videotaped sessions with a patient before. To her, committed heart and soul to patient privacy, having the taped sessions leave her office was almost unconceivable.

She didn't want herself to be part of the video recording, so, for that reason, she didn't use a wide-angle view. A wide angle would have solved all problems, with the camera tucked neatly in the corner of the room, on a bookcase shelf, where neither of them would even remember it was rolling.

She'd spent the best part of her afternoon preparing for that first session with DJ, wondering which method to adopt, which tool in her arsenal she should use to engage with him better, to help him more effectively. Then she decided the first session was going to be about connecting with him, about understanding him as a human being, and not taking anything for granted. Even if she didn't know where it would lead, she had to try, fearlessly. One step at a time.

She looked at him and noticed the weariness around his eyes, the deep ridges across his brow. He seemed tired, haunted. Maybe that appearance of calm resolve was falling apart at the seams.

"Where would you like to sit?" she asked, looking through the viewfinder and adjusting the camera's height.

There were two opposing sofas in her office and a large chair, the one she sat in during most sessions. The sofas were so positioned that the patients could choose to face her chair, or face away from it, if that made them more comfortable. In either one he'd choose to sit, the camera would take a profile view of his upper body, a bit against the light, but usable.

"It doesn't matter," DJ replied. "I don't care."

"Most patients sit here," she indicated the sofa partially facing her chair.

"I'm not a patient, Doc, I thought we agreed."

"Well, you are something... what should we call you, then? A client? Psychologists have clients, while psychiatrists have patients. With me, you can have your pick."

"Whatever," he replied, making a dismissing gesture with his hand and taking a seat where she'd said most patients sat. "There, happy?"

"It will work," she replied, then adjusted the camera one last time to frame his head and upper body but little else, and took the small remote with her to her chair. "Ready?"

He didn't reply. He gazed in her general direction, but didn't make eye contact at all, not even in passing.

She clicked the remote and the red LED on the camera turned on. He fidgeted a little, then found a comfortable position and settled, with his hands clasped neatly in his lap. She saw tension lines on his face, around his mouth, and in the lines of his jaw and neck. He kept his head lowered and his shoulders hunched forward. He had strong arms, his tense muscles stretching the sleeves of his black polo shirt to a snug fit.

She smiled encouragingly for a moment, despite her usual routine that called for minimal encouragement, even if nonverbal.

"So, what would you like to talk about?"

He didn't reply; he shook his head slowly, barely moving. He wasn't going to talk; not unless she insisted.

"We have to talk about something," she added, keeping her voice gentle but engaged. He shrugged her comment off, then resumed his immobile, dissociated stance.

She waited for him to break that silence, but he seemed withdrawn into his own world, absorbed in thought. She pressed on. "Tell me a little about yourself, DJ."

He sat silently, staring at the wall, and then at the floor, at his shoes mainly. She allowed a few more moments of silence to pass, then tried again.

"You told me you were married. Any kids?" she asked, keeping her voice gentle, level, nonjudgmental.

"No."

"Tell me about your wife. What's her name?"

He waved her question away, then muttered, "No need for names."

"All right, I'll respect that, but I'd still like to hear about her."

Another long moment of silence, but she waited patiently. The microexpressions in his face told her she was close to getting a response.

"She's... fit," he eventually said, speaking dryly, yet seeming irritated by his own words. "She's a living and breathing Nike commercial."

Angela waited for him to continue, but he didn't. "That's an unusual statement about one's wife," she said. "Tell me more about what you mean."

He sighed and averted his eyes for a second, then frowned.

"She's at the gym every day," he said, his frown lingering, shading his eyes. "When she's not running or lifting weights, she's swimming. I just... can't keep up."

"Is she younger than you?"

He smiled crookedly. "Of course, you'd think that, Doc. But no, I can't even say I have that excuse. She's only five months younger than me. She's young at heart, though, she's still alive. I'm not. Corpses can't run too fast, now can they?"

She refrained from answering, but maintained eye contact and continued to listen empathically, but he didn't continue.

"You love her very much, don't you?" she asked, speaking barely above a whisper.

He didn't reply, just averted his eyes and stared into the empty air for a while, then down at the carpet.

"I believe you do," she added. "It's for her sake we're doing all this, isn't it? She must mean a lot to you."

"She does," he whispered, not taking his eyes off the carpet.

"Does she love you?"

Silence filled the room, while she waited for his reply, holding her breath. After a while he nodded once, clenching his jaws. She could see his facial muscles tensing, and it was clear he didn't yet feel like sharing anything else about his wife. She decided to go somewhere else, maybe less painful.

"Where did you grow up? Tell me about it."

"Really, Doc?" he said, frustrated and not trying to hide it. "Didn't we agree none of that therapy crap?"

"Well, then, what would you like us to talk about, that would actually prove what you're trying to prove with these recordings? Do you think a bunch of tapes with you sitting quietly on the couch would do it? I don't think so."

Angela bit her lip, angry with herself for her outburst. She knew better, and she never made such rookie mistakes, but with this man things were different, and she didn't know why. She'd never met him before he came into her office the week before; she didn't even know his name. And still, in the past few days, he'd been constantly on her mind, and the emotional connection she felt toward him, although perplexing and illogical, had only grown stronger.

"Coalinga," he whispered, surprising her.

"Ah... I can't say I'm familiar with it."

He chuckled, a quick, sad laugh, tinted with bitterness. "No one is, Doc. It's a small town built around a coaling station, in the middle of California's dust bowl. It's in Fresno County, with a population of about 12,000. It's a hole in the ground."

"Tell me about young DJ, growing up."

"There's nothing to tell, Doc. I grew up there, that's all."

"How was your time, growing up? You must have some stories to share."

He shook his head slowly, his eyes still riveted to the floor.

"I grew up in the town without a name... Coalinga is short for Coaling Station A, you know. They didn't even bother to give that place a proper name."

"What about your parents?"

"What about them?"

"Were they, um, coal workers?"

Another chuckle. "No. My father was a construction foreman, and my mother was a… she never worked. She'd slap me silly if I said she was a housewife, or a stay-at-home mom."

"What did she want to be called?"

"Homemaker," he replied. "She only accepts being called that, but she'd prefer if you'd call her Mrs. Ba—" He stopped short of revealing his last name, then groaned angrily. "Yeah, nothing special, Doc. I grew up there, all right?"

Impassible, she continued. "How was your time growing up? Could you share a thought with me? Something memorable must have happened in all your years there, right?

"Nothing really happened, Doc," he replied, a bit too quickly and too angrily. "I just went to school, came back, that kind of stuff. Nothing happened."

# 11

# An Unusual Monday

It was almost five in the afternoon when things had gone crazy all of a sudden, on a warm May school day, twenty-two years ago. It had already been a wacky, unpredictable kind of day. First, it was a Monday, and Mondays were prone to be unusually weird for some reason. Then his dad had stayed home that day, not feeling well, resigned to wobble about in his pajamas or slouch in front of the TV, dozing off at times.

He did go to school that morning though. He was ten years old, and still went there, thinking it could be fun, although most of the times it only proved to be boring as hell. His mom didn't want to take him that morning, but Nickel's mom obliged, and she drove both boys to school in her red Chevelle. She even let him ride shotgun, and Nickel didn't mind, because he was Nickel, his best friend, who'd do anything for him.

In another one of the exceptions that made that particular Monday so out of the ordinary, Mrs. Coyne picked up both boys from school at two-thirty, because she had to go to the dentist afterward. DJ didn't think to wonder or worry why his parents didn't pick up Nickel and him, if Mrs. Coyne was busy. He was happy to be driven around in the fancy sports car, and hang out some more with Nickel in his backyard. Then, about four-twenty, he ran home, hopping over a few fences and cutting through some neighbors' backyards to save a few minutes and make it home in time for dinner.

He was still panting when he opened the back door and greeted his father respectfully, as kids did those days.

"Hello, sir."

"Jumping fences again, boy?"

He didn't reply; just fidgeted a little, playing with the loose strap end of his backpack.

"Go help your mother with dinner."

"Yes, sir."

He rushed past him and dropped the backpack near the front door, then went straight into the kitchen.

"Here, set the table," his mom said, pulling plates and silverware out of the cupboards.

He was about to go back into the kitchen to get the glasses and the water pitcher, when his dad stood up, tilted his head, listening intently, then shouted from the bottom of his lungs, "Mary! Get the hell over here, right this second!"

Then, without saying another word, he pushed open the back door and shoved Dylan out of the house, so hard that he fell on his back into his mother's cherished rose garden. Not even a second after that, his father dragged his screaming mother out of the house, pulling and shoving her forcefully.

"Earthquake, woman, stop screaming, for Chrissake."

"What earthquake?" she protested, "Jim, have you lost your—"

Then it hit, the biggest, most destructive shockwave of the quake. Pale and slack-jawed, she stopped screaming and grabbed Jim's arm with both hands to regain her balance. Still sitting on his butt in the rose garden, too shocked to move, Dylan watched his home collapse in a stunned state of denial. That wasn't happening; it wasn't possible. Then his father yanked him up by his arm and rushed both of them toward the back of the yard, where loose debris couldn't reach them.

They'd survived the quake without an injury.

Not everyone in Coalinga had been that lucky on that fateful May second.

Although, lucky wasn't the term that came to young Dylan's mind when he thought of the earthquake. They'd lost everything they had.

For many days after the quake, the three of them rummaged through the rubble looking for things they could salvage, and there weren't many. The collapse of the house had ruptured water and sewer pipes, adding a different dimension of destruction to everything that was left. The gas line had ruptured also, and a small fire had started in the kitchen, sparked by the stove flame that had been warming their dinner. Fortunately, his father had kept his wits about him and had rushed to shut off the main gas line, as soon as he'd pulled his family to safety. Then the fire soon died under the gushes of water spewing from the ruptured pipes. As soon as no more smoke rose from that pile of rubble that had been their home, his father shut down the water main, then collapsed to the ground, sobbing hard with his face buried in his hands.

Back then, DJ didn't understand all the details, but his single-income family didn't carry too much insurance, and the family was broke, homeless, and still owed money on the furniture and car that were completely destroyed.

In the face of such devastating loss, no one paid attention to the young boy and his determination to scour through the rubble in search of the few things he cherished the most. The cast-iron toy truck he'd got for Christmas a few years ago from his grandmother, the last gift she ever gave him; she'd died only a few days after that last holiday they shared. His bike, rendered completely useless after the carport and half the dining room had crashed on top of it. His portable stereo cassette recorder that he used to listen to music late at night, volume set on low, after his parents had gone to bed, turned into a molten and mangled chunk of plastic. Maybe that wasn't a whole lot, but for him, those few objects were his world. His parents, burdened financially for the rest of their lives by that single catastrophic event, did the best they could, but weren't able to replace all that was lost that day.

Dylan was soon resigned to use whatever Nickel didn't need.

He stayed with the Coynes for a while, until his parents were able to secure a new residence. Still a child and ignorant of the staggering dimensions of the catastrophe that had hit his family, he remembered enjoying Nickel's clan, their laughter, their carefree happiness. When it was time to return to live with his own parents, he almost regretted it.

His new home never looked the same as the old one. Everything was cheaper, and there was less of everything, as if the spider couldn't weave its web again, stunned by the senseless destruction of its earlier work. In factual reality, his father had dealt poorly with the loss of his home, and, within the year, was battling colon cancer. Three years later, he was proudly calling himself a cancer survivor, telling his story to whomever was willing to listen, but his spider web was never again as symmetrical, as beautiful, as it had once been.

Dylan learned a tremendous lesson that fateful day. It's not worth holding on to material things, to objects, when life can yank them all away and leave you with nothing but a broken heart. His parents thought they had a plentiful home, only to see it turn to dust in a matter of a minute. That lesson, consolidated periodically for a while by the thousands of aftershocks that followed the big Coalinga earthquake, was going to leave a mark on his entire existence, although he didn't know it at the time.

He had become a minimalist.

He did cherish one thing, and held on to it dearly, and that was his wife. Sending those old memories away, he stared at the clean surface of his desk, free of the typical office clutter, and also missing the framed family photos that most employees had on their desks. Surprisingly, the company almost made it a requirement to have that framed photo on his desk, and HR had spoken to him twice, saying empty phrases like, "We want our employees to feel like home, to share the warmth and the familial feel," and so on, some more meaningless bullshit along those lines.

First, he didn't need a framed picture of his wife to remember what she looked like, to be reminded that he loved her. The icon of her was carved in his heart forever.

Second, he didn't want any of those guys gawking at her beautiful face, giving him a reason to punch their lights out.

And so, his desk remained clear of all objects, work or personal, that weren't strictly necessary, in the plainest of minimalist styles. He was fine with things the way they were; it would be less of a mess to clean up after he was gone, come November.

# 12

# Anger

To Angela's surprise, DJ showed up for his second appointment right on time. She hated to admit she'd been anxious about the session, wondering if he was going to be there, worried that he might have lied about the six months, when in fact he could decide to end things any day. She couldn't ask him for time, when he'd already said nothing was going to happen for another six months. She couldn't voice her concern; she'd risk alienating him with her distrust.

But what if there were only three months left, not six? How would she know? Or, even better, *would* she even know? She shook her head almost imperceptibly, thinking she could only work with the information she had, nothing more, nothing less. He'd promised her twenty-four sessions, and she was going to have to trust that he'd stick around for all of them, and uphold his end of the deal. She'd also have to trust herself that she'd be able to notice slight changes in his behavior, in the tumult of his emotions, when that date drew near.

It was five-and-a-half months already, not even six anymore, even if he'd been truthful about everything he'd said. Time flies.

She waited patiently for DJ to get settled in his spot and studied him. He seemed calmer, almost resigned, but did his best to avoid making any eye contact with her. Then, as if he remembered something, he frowned and stood, while his eyes searched the room impatiently.

"Where's the camera?"

"Right there," Angela replied, pointing at a bookshelf. "My other patients had issues with having video equipment in the room, even if it wasn't working. For the intent of this recording, a partial profile view should work just as well."

"Your patients don't see it over there, do they? What they don't know can't hurt them, right, Doc?"

"Something like that, yes. I cover it with that embroidered napkin, and no one knows it's there." She clicked the remote; the camera started recording and the red LED light next to its lens turned on.

They sat in silence for a while, and Angela allowed him time to gather his thoughts. The silence lingered for more than a few moments, and she couldn't wait any longer.

"What's she like?" she asked, without any other introduction. "Other than fit, I mean."

He reacted as if she'd woken him up from a dream, almost startled.

"Where were you, just now?" she asked.

He shrugged and turned his head away from her, as if averting his eyes was not distant enough. "Nowhere. Why do you ask?"

"You seemed... absent. Dissociated. What's on your mind?"

"Nothing. I spaced out. I'm tired, I guess."

"Uh-huh, okay," she replied, "Tell me about your wife."

"Why do you keep asking about her?" DJ reacted, visibly irritated with her persistence.

"You seem angry with her," she replied calmly, "and I believe the cause of that anger would be worth exploring."

He shook his head a couple of times and pressed his lips together. "I'm not angry with her," he eventually said. "You don't quite get it, Doc."

"Well, not if you don't tell me. I'm not a mind reader, you know. Why don't you tell me about her? She must be something else other than fit."

He stood and paced the floor slowly, keeping his hands buried deep inside his pant pockets. He wore slacks, shirt, and a jacket, but no tie, most likely his employer's version of business casual. His clothes were in good shape and relatively new, although not too expensive. By all appearances, his wife did a good job of taking care of him.

Yet he seemed to descend into an abyss of sadness and despair every time she brought up the subject of his wife. His face scrunched up, and deep ridges marked his brow. His mouth was tense and his lips pressed tightly together, as if trying to keep words from escaping, locked safely inside.

He walked unhurriedly to the window and stared into the distance for a long moment, while Angela only saw his back, hunched forward slightly, as if bent under a heavy weight. He leaned his forehead against the glass, and she thought she heard him let a long sigh escape.

"She... likes to collect stuff," he eventually said, and Angela had to make an effort to hear his muted words, spoken against the glass. "I guess it's my fault, after everything I've done."

"What do you think you've done?" she asked, after a couple of moments of silence.

"I've moved her from place to place, uprooted her, left her nothing but these... things, her stuff. She's got nothing; no friends, no career, no kids, nothing but me and her stuff. And I'm not..."

His words trailed off, buried in sadness and shame. He rubbed his forehead repeatedly, shielding his eyes from the milky light of day that came in through the window, as the sun's summer rays filtered through the thick, afternoon fog.

"Why did you move from place to place?" Angela asked gently. "With work?"

"Hah," he chuckled bitterly, "no, with lack thereof."

He didn't talk for a while, still staring out the window, where nothing much could be seen on a foggy day. Even the street, only two stories below, was engulfed so deeply that the cars passing by seemed surreal and distant.

"Every time I lose my job, I look for work and find it in another state. Isn't that funny how fate plays trick on us, Doc?"

"But you *choose* to look for work in another state, another place, right? It's not really fate, it's you. Your decision."

"It's whatever the hell you want to call it, Doc. When there's no money left to survive, do you think I get to choose where I want to work? I'm not such a hot commodity on the labor market; ain't got much choice in the matter. Anyone willing to throw me a bone, I come running."

"I see. And your wife? What does she do?"

She saw him shake his head again, probably frustrated with her questions. He seemed to be sensitive on the subject, all good reason to explore.

"She has to quit her job every time we move. She has to pack us up, while I'm still at work, then we move. I start work at the new place, while she unpacks us, then goes to look for work for herself. Then we repeat this drill, over and over."

"So, you know ahead of time when they let you go?" Angela asked, frowning while trying to understand what happened with her client.

"Yeah, normally I do," he replied, suddenly angry. "Believe it or not, I've never been fired for cause. But I always land on the damn layoff list. I'm never one of the keepers."

"Why do you think that is?" she asked gently.

He shrugged again, still facing away from her, staring out the window. "Ask them, if you want. How the hell should I know?"

She shifted in her seat a little. "You must have some idea, DJ."

He stood silently, still facing away and refusing to speak a single word.

"You were angry about your wife, last week," Angela insisted. "Even if not with her, per se. What are you angry about?"

"Putting her through all that," he replied. "All those moves. All those times I gave her hope, only to take it away a few years later."

"But you did what you had to do to survive, yes?"

"Yeah... so?" He was facing her now, looking at her angrily over his shoulder.

"Don't you think she understands that?"

"That's exactly the point, Doc," he replied, almost shouting. He came back to the sofa but stood in front of it, looking her in the eye from the height of his 6-foot-5 stature. She didn't flinch.

"Why don't you take a seat and explain it to me," she said calmly. "I'm not sure I understand."

"What's so damn difficult to understand? She's done nothing but help me and wait for me, all her life. She lived the life I asked her to and never complained. And now I can't even keep up with her at the gym; I resent her for going, for not wanting to bury herself alive the way I do. How's that? Clear enough for you, Doc?"

He resumed pacing her office, taking long, slow steps muffled by the thick carpet. Every now and then he checked the time on the digital clock that hung on the wall, behind the sofa.

"Every time she wants something, I manage to screw it up and I don't deliver," he continued bitterly. "She doesn't want much, but when she does, she can always count on me to fuck it up."

Angela shifted in her seat again, to keep her eyes on him and his posture. His body language gave away significantly more than his words.

"If I understand correctly, your wife, whom you love deeply and who also loves you, is helping you with your career, putting herself second, and giving you all the support you need, right?"

He nodded once, while his jaws clenched.

"Yet you're planning to leave her, in the worst possible way a faithful, loving wife can be abandoned, right? Her entire world will fall apart the moment those cops ring that doorbell and let her know what you've done."

She sounded harsh and judgmental, two solid breaches of therapy technique, but she didn't hesitate, looking to crack that shell of calm resolve. What she normally had months, even years, to achieve with other patients, she had to manage in only a few short weeks, with a patient who didn't want to be treated, didn't want to feel better. Not many of the textbook techniques applied, not in this man's case.

His hands closed into fists inside his pockets, but he continued to pace the floor unperturbed. He'd obviously thought of that many times, and she didn't rattle him a single bit.

He stopped in front of her desk and looked intently at Michael's framed photo, but didn't touch it. After a second or two, he turned toward her and looked at her with a hint of a smile.

"He's a lucky guy, this man. You're both lucky."

She felt her blood boil and, before she could restrain herself, she let him have it, raw, unfiltered.

"Do you have any idea what devastation such loss can bring?" she said, raising her voice and walking briskly toward her desk. Within a split second, she was standing inches away from him, inserted between him and Michael's photo, as if to shield his image from DJ's eyes. "How it leaves you empty inside, gasping for air, just wishing you could die, so the pain would stop? You say you love her, but you're about to make her go through hell," she added, lowering her gaze. "The one hell no one ever comes back from."

She moved away from him, seeking refuge near the window and staring outside, mirroring his earlier stance. She breathed deeply, trying to get her emotions under control.

"Doc, I'm so sorry," he said quietly. "I had no idea. What happened?"

She swallowed hard, before replying, and didn't turn to face him. "I'm afraid we ran out of time for today."

"No, we haven't," he replied, "but I understand if you want me gone."

She forced one more deep breath of air into her lungs, then released it slowly, focusing on the sound the air made while leaving her body.

"Tell me how the two of you met," she asked, then walked back to her chair and sat down.

"We went to high school together. Same year, but she didn't even know I was alive until junior high."

Unwillingly, she found herself smiling. "Tell me more."

"Uh… nothing fancy. We met one day in the schoolyard, that's all. It was raining, there isn't much to tell."

# 13

# The Fall

It rained all through that football game, soaking Dylan's jersey and making it cling unsightly to his shoulder pads. There, in the middle of the driest patch of California desert, on the night of his second football game, it had to rain.

But that didn't stop him. He ran through that rain savoring it, tackled like a pro, and scored like he'd played in the major leagues. He was a little surprised with himself, because he didn't think he wanted to be on that field that much; it was all Nickel's doing, not his.

Secretly afraid he was going to die a virgin and willing to do anything to improve his chances with the girls, Nickel had dragged the both of them onto that stadium, hoping that the white tights and broad-shouldered jerseys would compensate for their skinny arms and scarce facial hair. After only a few months of training, Coach had allowed them both to get off the bench and play at the beginning of the new season.

Far from being the only seventeen year old who believed there's no tomorrow, DJ had worked out heroically all summer long, finding some value in Nickel's dating strategy, especially after having attended the last game of the previous season and having noticed the attention the players got from the girls. The quarterback had his choice of dates, he had a new girlfriend every week, and still managed to do just fine. And that quarterback was a couple of inches shorter than him, and as pimpled as yesterday's leftover pizza. But in the nocturnal lights that flooded the field toward the end of any game, only his broad shoulders were visible from a distance and nothing else mattered. The girls were lining up.

Six months later, he was in decent shape and started to like what he saw in the mirror. His scrawny arms and legs had covered nicely with muscles, and his posture had straightened, erasing all evidence of the hunchback he'd developed while growing up too fast. Rain or no rain, he was getting good at the sport and was starting to enjoy every minute of it. When that second game was finally over and their team had won, he and Nickel welcomed the cheers coming from the thin, soaked crowd, in no hurry to leave the field, despite the unrelenting downpour.

Then Nickel disappeared, reeled away by a red-haired cutie who'd materialized on the grass and grabbed his arm in lieu of an introduction. Left alone in the rain with his dignity in shreds, seeing that no one else was there, he started running toward the locker room, among the last people to leave the soaked field.

Then it happened. After an hour of running back and forth during the game and managing to remain upright the entire time, he slipped and fell hard into a puddle of rainwater. He'd lunged to jump over that puddle, but he must have stepped on something slippery, because his feet ran from underneath him in an instant, slamming him to the ground. The fall knocked the air out of his lungs and made him dizzy, leaving him confused, seeing stars. His right buttock smarted badly, and, by the pain and warmth that spread quickly, he realized he'd cut himself. Groaning and cussing, still unable to get up, he took his hand to his butt to assess the damage and brought it back covered in blood. His tight pants had ripped, and he felt the rip spreading as the stretched fabric gave under the tension. Next to his thigh, the torn head of a sprinkler stood in testimony of what had happened.

He was still cursing the bent piece of metal when she appeared next to him and he froze, unable to say another word. The only thing he could think of was his naked cheek bleeding and smarting but, thankfully, staying hidden from her view.

"Sitting comfortably, aren't you?" The girl giggled, as she leaned forward to look at him. The nocturnals were shutting down, and only a few lights remained. The fewer the better, considering the state of his rear end.

Of course, he knew who she was. He'd known who she was for some time now, probably since she'd grown into a stunning creature, svelte and curvy at the same time. Her blonde hair was short, and she wore it in a cute, sporty cut. Rain had pasted it against her face, but she didn't seem to care. She moved and talked naturally in that downpour, a beautiful, wild animal, a wonder of this earth.

She extended her hand to help him up, but he stared at that hand, petrified. How was he going to get up, with his bruised butt hanging out? No... he was going to sit there in that puddle until the earth split open and swallowed him whole. Yep, great plan. If only it would work.

"No?" she asked, laughing. "You're that tired, huh?"

He nodded, unable to take his eyes off her beautiful face.

"Then I'll keep you some company," she said, and sat next to him, in that same puddle, relaxed, as if she'd sat on a dry, plush carpet. "Hope you don't mind. I'm Taylor, by the way."

"Uh-huh," he replied, and took her hand. Electricity coursed through his fingers when he touched her skin, and briefly he wondered if she'd felt the same jolt.

"Uh-huh what?" she laughed. "Uh-huh is your name?"

He felt his face catch fire. "Uh-uh, it's Dylan," he managed.

"Ah, he speaks," she said, still giggling. "For a while there, I was concerned."

He smiled awkwardly, unable to think of anything intelligent to say. It was as if words had decided to leave the general area of his brain, leaving him tongue-locked and behaving like an idiot.

"Great game tonight," she said. "On behalf of Coalinga High, we thank you for your contribution to the first winning game of this season."

He nodded, still unable to say much. What could he say? That he couldn't believe his eyes she was there, holding his hand in the rain, sitting so close to him he could feel the heat of her body burn his skin through the sodden jersey? For a brief moment, he wanted to blurt all that out, to get it off his chest, but decided that silence was golden, or at least less damaging than a spew of nonsensical words.

She looked at him briefly, then turned her gaze sideways. She had the deepest blue-green eyes he'd ever seen, and he was already getting lost, sinking, out of breath, yet flying so high he wasn't even touching the ground anymore.

She ran her fingers through the short blades of grass, then shook away some water off her hand, sprinkling it toward him.

"Are you here to stay?" she asked, all of a sudden serious.

"Where? Coalinga?" he asked back, confused. "I was born here, so, I guess, yeah."

"No, dummy, here, on this field, in this lovely weather," she giggled again.

"Oh," he replied, then turned away from her. "Yeah, I guess I am," he replied, and she instantly burst into laughter, sending the echo of her voice across the empty stadium.

The rain had thinned and was about to stop. A few stars were already visible above the western horizon line, and the ghost of the moon was struggling to poke through the clouds.

"I can see why you want to stay here forever," she quipped. "So cozy, right? But I'm getting cold. Would you let me freeze to death?" she asked, putting exaggerated worry in her voice.

"No one freezes here, it's never cold enough," he replied matter-of-factly, but then felt like an idiot again when she burst into renewed laughter.

"Come on, Dylan, let's go," she said, hopping promptly to her feet and extending her hand.

"I… can't," he eventually said, avoiding her gaze.

She suddenly turned serious. "Why? Are you hurt? I saw you fall."

"It's nothing."

"Then?"

"You go ahead, all right?" he said, already sad at the thought of her leaving. "We'll catch up tomorrow."

She stood upright in front of him, propping her hands firmly on her hips. "Nope, not budging from here until you tell me what's wrong."

The earth wasn't showing any signs of opening up to swallow him whole any time soon, and Taylor seemed just as stubborn as the earth was. He gave up, feeling his cheeks burn and his ears tingle. "It's my pants," he whispered, mortified. "When I fell, I ripped my pants. I'm not moving."

"Is that it?" she asked, still serious.

"That's all there is," he replied, unable to look her in the eye.

"All right, then," she said, unzipping her wind jacket and handing it to him. "Tie this around your waist and you'll be fine."

He obeyed, then stood, biting his tongue when his wound smarted some more, sending shoots of pain deep inside his muscles.

He tried to walk normally, but when he put his weight on his right foot, the pain was too much and he limped visibly. Without warning, Taylor pulled the jacket away and looked at his back side.

"Oh, crap, you're bleeding," she said. "Let's take you to the hospital."

"It's not that bad. Just a cut. When I get home, I'll put some Band-Aids on it and I'll be fine."

"It'll leave a mark," she insisted, sounding less convinced.

"It's my ass, not my face. No big deal, you know."

They both laughed and chatted as they walked toward the gymnasium, but then she followed him inside the men's locker room.

"What are you doing?" he said, stopping her at the door.

"What? You mind? No one's here; they've all gone."

"Yeah, but I need to shower and change."

"I'll help you patch up your gluteus. It's my duty as a cheerleader to preserve the values of our home team."

"Oh, no, you're not," he reacted, "uh-uh." No way he was going to let her see him, or, even worse, touch him. He looked away, hiding his face from the intense fluorescent lights that revealed the crimson in his cheeks.

"They have a first aid kit in here for sure. If not, I'll grab the one from the girls' locker. Come on, don't be silly. If you do as I say, I promise I'll let you buy me coffee one of these days."

Twenty-five years later, he still recalled the feeling of her thin, cold fingers dancing on his skin, barely touching, yet moving with dexterity and confidence while applying butterfly bandages, one after another, quickly, painlessly, while he didn't dare to breathe. The cut wasn't too deep, but it was three inches long and worthy of a visit to the ER, in her opinion. She was glad to help, and she felt he'd been an idiot for sitting that long in the soaked grass with that bleeding injury. He took the scolding quietly, savoring every word she had to say to him, no matter how harsh, while deep inside he knew she was the one.

He smiled at the distant memory, a timid smile clouded by sadness and regret. He wondered what had happened to them... Had they grown old already? Maybe not yet; he still felt the same electric jolt whenever she touched him. Nevertheless, they'd let life's hardships smother and erode that wonderful feeling they both used to share, little by little, more with every passing year. Even so, he was thankful for that rainy day, and for the broken sprinkler that had left such a beautiful mark on his destiny.

A quick rap on his office window pulled him back to reality, and the fond memories dissipated, scattered by the intrusion of his daily routine.

A middle-aged woman wearing a reflective vest opened the door a crack and popped her head in. "Boss, can I ask you a question?"

He waved her inside, and she quickly entered, then closed the door gently behind her. She fidgeted in place, clasping and unclasping her hands, hesitant.

"What's up, Nancy?"

"Um, I hope you won't take this the wrong way, boss, but I need to know if I'll be able to make my mortgage payment this month. I have three kids; I need to know."

He bit his lip and swallowed his rising anger, triggered by the way Nancy's anguish resonated with his own. He resented all that misery, dealt generously by reckless, ignorant people who didn't know when to keep their greed in check, who didn't care how many lives they destroyed for those almost 300 pieces of silver.

"Yes, Nancy, this month you'll be fine, and next month too. Beyond that, I don't know. But don't wait for the shoe to drop, okay? Start looking."

She nodded, unable to speak as tears started flowing from her eyes and her chin trembled. Then she left without another word, leaving Dylan alone to battle the demons of his own despair, of his suffocating powerlessness.

# 14

# Fears

Angela touched up her lipstick and ran a hairbrush through the curly mane of shoulder-length, auburn hair, her typical routine before each patient session. She was preoccupied, going through the motions absentmindedly, mulling over the same question she couldn't easily answer.

How does one treat someone who doesn't want to be treated?

She didn't even stop to think about whether she should. With other patients, she made sure they wanted to improve their lives, and they showed the commitment necessary to discover and adopt the changes needed to make their goals happen.

DJ was different; she thought of him as a dying patient and of her office as an emergency room. No time to ask permissions, set goals, and evaluate or secure commitment for change, and even less time to build a strong therapeutic alliance with him. She'd seen in his eyes the fierce determination to follow through with his plan to end his life, and the calmness of his demeanor whenever they discussed it reinforced her sense of urgency. There was no doubt about it; he was ready to die.

She'd hoped he would open up and start talking more about his personal history by now, but it seemed that whenever she led him toward a painful area, he pulled away and refused to talk about it. Yet he'd chosen to see a therapist, and that couldn't have been by accident. Somewhere buried deeply inside his mind, under thick layers of anguish and pain, a part of him still wanted to live. His subconscious mind had led him to choose a therapist to be his witness and had provided him with a plausible enough explanation to make him accept he needed to be in her office every week. That wasn't an accident; that was nature taking over. Instinct.

In every living thing lies a strong will to survive, even if it's not a conscious intent. Seeds buried under inches of frozen soil will germinate and the little plants will push toward the sun, always in the right direction, always toward life, never getting lost in the darkness. And yet, not all seeds manage to survive and thrive to become strong, enduring trees. Some are buried too deep, others are too damaged or too weak to push through, but the survival instinct is always present, hard-coded in every living strand of DNA. She counted on that.

Maybe there was a chance. There had to be.

She turned off the light and left the small bathroom, closing the door behind her. She glanced at the wall clock and noticed DJ was already late by two minutes, and she found herself worrying again. Was there really enough time? Or would she read in tomorrow's news about yet another Bay Area suicide? How would he do it? Jump in front of an incoming Caltrain, like at least a dozen other people had done that year? Or would he—

The intercom buzzed and she rushed to press the button, hardly registering the wave of relief she felt. Seconds later, when DJ came in, he found her standing near the door, composed, professional, instilling confidence, engagement, and a sense of safety. By the book, even if only in appearance.

"Hey, Doc," he said, making eye contact for less than a second, then walking past her to take his usual seat.

"Hello, DJ," she replied, with a bit of a smile.

He looked his usual self, calm, resigned, yet burdened by something. He sat hunched forward, his back not touching the sofa, and he stared into thin air like he always did.

She started the video recording and gave him a minute, but he still wouldn't speak.

"What would you like to talk about today?" she finally asked, painfully aware of each passing minute.

He shook his head slowly and remained silent, grim.

"We have to talk about something," she insisted. "That's the way it works. It's up to you what we talk about, how's that?"

He shook his head again, a little more vigorously. "I'm afraid I don't have anything to tell you, Doc."

"Does that happen often?"

He frowned and glanced at her. "What?"

"You, being afraid."

"Don't twist my words around," he said, his voice tinged with sadness.

"What are you most afraid of, DJ?"

"I didn't say I was afraid," he replied with a frustrated sigh. "You're not keeping up here, Doc. It was a figure of speech."

"Sometimes, the words we use are windows into our subconscious minds. We can choose to open this one and peek inside."

"I thought we agreed, no shrinking, but whatever. I guess you can't help yourself." He shrugged and looked her straight in the eye, his brow still furrowed, and his mouth flanked by two deep, vertical ridges. "I'm not afraid."

"Of anything, ever? Wow, that's rare."

"No... I mean right now, I'm not afraid. I thought that's what you meant."

"Ah, I see. Okay, then, what are you the most afraid of, in general?"

He riveted his eyes to the floor again and spent a few moments thinking. Flickers of internal turmoil danced in microexpressions on his face, barely visible.

"There was this diner, many years ago, in Cleveland," he said, then cleared his throat quietly. When he spoke, his voice was still choked. "I used to go there on my lunch breaks, during winter. I used to smoke back then, and it was too cold to smoke outside, so I went in there for coffee."

"No lunch? Just coffee?"

"Heh... I used to make ten bucks an hour, so yeah, no lunch, just coffee, a tasteless but warm swill at a cheap, downtown diner. It was okay though. I took the same booth every day, and this waiter brought me my coffee. The same guy, every day, the same coffee. A buck-ten, with refills."

He stopped talking and his shoulders hunched forward a bit more, and he lowered his head, as if exhaustion pulled it down, making it too heavy to bear.

She waited for him to continue, but he'd stopped, lost in his memories. She gave him a few more minutes, and eventually he continued.

"He was old, that waiter. His hands were shaking, stiff with arthritis, and he could barely walk. When he brought the coffee, he always spilled it, almost half of it landing on the floor or on the saucer. I remember being afraid he'd slip and fall, break his neck or something."

She nodded once, encouraging him to continue. He still averted his eyes, but every now and then he glanced at her, as if to gauge whether she was still listening.

"I asked him one time, why work anymore? He was almost eighty years old," he continued, visibly affected by the story. "He said he had to; his wife was sick. I remember asking, in my youthful ignorance, if Medicare wouldn't cover his benefits, if he really needed to work to have health insurance. You know what he said?"

"No, what did he say?" she replied.

"He needed the money for his wife's medications. Medicare didn't cover all that, or something, and he dragged his tired old bones into that crappy diner every day, just to buy her the meds she needed. Working for tips on buck-ten orders like mine."

"That's love," she said, moved by the story.

"Yeah, Doc, and that's me," he added, shifting from sadness to anger in less than a second.

"What do you mean?"

"I'm that waiter, Doc, can't you see?" He stood and started to pace the office, as she'd learned he did whenever he was frustrated, an expression of fight-or-flight response to stress. He felt the urge to distance himself of what bothered him, and that made him restless, like a caged animal who wanted to break free.

"No, I can't, not without assuming, and I'd rather not do that. Let's discuss it."

"In a few years, that's who I'll be if I let it happen. That waiter, barely walking straight, desperate to get money for his wife's meds, that will be me. Not letting go. And her? She wouldn't get the healthcare she needs, because I won't be making more than a few bucks an hour, not even enough to feed and clothe us. That's me, that waiter."

"Why do you believe that? You seem to be a successful professional, gainfully employed, who has the talent to survive, to adapt, right? Didn't you say that every time they let you go, you bounce right back, even if you have to move from place to place?"

"You don't get it, Doc. You've probably led a plush life and never struggled to make ends meet; that's my bet when looking at you, at all this," he said, gesturing vaguely toward her office walls. "I'm guessing no one's ever yanked your job from you and shoved you to the curb. No... you don't get it."

"Okay, so explain it to me then."

"You asked what was my biggest fear. It's failure. Failing her... failing us. I've already let her down, more than once."

He clasped his hands together forcefully, until his knuckles turned white, and held on like that, standing still in front of the window, looking outside. She could see his profile, the tension in his jaw, the frown that ruffled his eyebrows.

"I'm letting her down every day," he eventually continued, "every time she wants me to be alive, and I'm dead inside. She deserves a happy home, some peace and stability in her life, not... what I'm able to offer."

"But she loves *you*, doesn't she?"

"Unfortunately for her, she does," he replied, while the tension in his body still remained. "Every few years, I'm the one they pick for their damn layoffs, and I'm the one to drag her away again, to another place where she has nothing. I'm the one who has to pack up and leave, looking for yet another master to serve, while she... only wants a home. It's not too much to ask, is it, Doc?"

"Have you asked her? How she feels about it?"

He shook his head angrily and shot her a burning glare. "Jeez, Doc, do you think I need to ask her? She won't say anything, she understands, but I can't do this. Not anymore."

He unclasped his hands, still standing in front of the window and staring outside, and reached inside his right pocket. After a few moments, he pulled out two small pebbles and started rubbing them together, making soft, clicking sounds, barely audible despite the silence in the office.

From a few feet away, Dr. Blackwell squinted to discern more of what he was doing. They seemed to be regular pebbles, nothing special about them, but they had to be important for DJ. The hand gesture he was making while rubbing them seemed well-rehearsed and rhythmic, something he'd done many times before.

"How much more of this do you think I can take, before I run out of options?" he added, after a few minutes of silence. "Before I have to start selling our stuff to put food in our mouths? Before I'm that waiter?"

She didn't answer, and he wasn't expecting a reply. She let a few silent moments pass by.

Then he turned toward her and walked toward the door. The two pebbles were still in his hand, but he had his palm wrapped around them tightly. He stopped a few feet from the door and turned toward her. He held her gaze steadily, unperturbed.

STORIES UNTOLD

"We die slowly, Doc, we all do. I'm already dying. You probably can't see it, but I can. I only want to speed up the process, that's all. Put myself out of my misery, be done with it already. Set her free, save her from me, before it's too late. Before I take her down with me."

# 15

# Pebbles

It must have been two years or so after the big earthquake; Dylan didn't remember exactly. It was summer, a dry, hot summer that had already turned the fields a crisp brown and made the leaves fall from the trees as if it were already fall.

He wandered around the yard, dragging a stick and scratching the dirt with it, occasionally kicking a stone. It was hardly a yard; just a patch of dust around an off-yellow, modular home, the only dwelling his parents were able to afford after the quake. It gave them a roof over their heads and a place to come home to every day, but little else. The heat was suffocating inside, and, despite his father's promises, a window air conditioner was still not showing up.

Normally he didn't care about the heat that much. Unlike his mother, who was stuck in the house cooking and cleaning, he roamed free, hanging out with Nickel, doing his homework at his place, and exploring what little adventure Coalinga had to offer.

But his best friend had recently disappeared without a word. He'd been sad for a few days, talking less, and resigned to sit under the oak tree in the Coynes' lush backyard, then he vanished. Dylan knocked on their door one day, and Nickel didn't rush down the stairs with a holler, like he usually did. Instead, Mr. Coyne opened the door, grim and unshaven, and told him that his friend wouldn't be available for a while. Maybe he should try again next week?

School was out, so he couldn't see Nickel in class either. For the lonely twelve-year-old boy, not knowing what had happened and why his friend had disappeared, every scorching day dragged on forever, strings of slow-moving minutes filled with worry instead of childhood's blissful joy. More than a week had passed since he'd last seen Nickel, and Mr. Coyne still didn't let him inside the house that had once been his home, even if a temporary refuge after a catastrophe. He felt banished, abandoned.

When Dylan's father came home from work that day, the boy didn't look up from the ground, where he was trying to dig a pointless hole with a stick, a dry branch fallen from a nearby dying tree, right by the creek bank. His mother came out of the house, wiping her sweaty brow with her apron, and greeted her husband with a quick peck on the mouth. Then they both turned toward him.

"Aren't you forgetting something, son?" his father asked.

He stood reluctantly and dragged his feet until he got in front of him, but stayed at a safe distance. "Good evening, sir," he whispered, not taking his eyes off the ground.

His father leaned forward until their eyes were at the same level. "What's on your mind, Dylan?"

He shifted his weight from one foot to the other, unwilling to talk, but the weight on his heart was too heavy. "Why doesn't Nickel play with me anymore? What have I done?" Tears flooded his eyes, despite his desperate effort to control them, then came rolling down, leaving streaks on his dusty cheeks.

His parents looked at each other briefly, then his mother sat on the wooden steps and took his hand.

"Peter's mother is sick," she said, referring to Nickel by his given name. "She… might not be around for too long."

"She's going to die?" he asked, his voice trembling with renewed sorrow, as he recalled Mrs. Coyne's warm chocolate chip cookies; her hands tucking him in at night after the quake in the rustling of fresh, cool sheets; and her red Chevelle as she drove the boys to school.

His mother pressed her lips together and nodded slowly. "Yes, Dylan, she is," she whispered gently, caressing his hair. "I'm so sorry, baby."

He yanked his hand from his mother's grip and ran behind the house, where he could let his tears flow freely, shielded from anyone's view. Late that night, he snuck out of bed and ran over to the Coynes, sneaking in the moonlight like a prowler, unseen, silent. He climbed the big tree in front of the house and crawled on the branch that came closest to Nickel's bedroom window. Then, holding his breath, he threw little branches he tore from the tree until Nickel's pale face showed up in the window frame.

Nickel smiled when he saw him and opened the window, beckoning him to come in. Dylan shook his head and invited Nickel to come outside instead. The boy straddled the windowsill in his pajamas and leapt ahead, grabbing the same tree branch Dylan was holding on to. Under the added weight, the branch bent and swung dangerously, and the boys giggled quietly as they made their way back to the ground. If it were daytime in a happier era, their descent from the tree would have been accompanied by bold imitations of Tarzan's jungle cries.

Without a word, they bolted toward the creek, hiding from the occasional car's headlights and the late passersby. When they got to their favorite spot on the Los Gatos Creek banks, they dropped to the ground, splayed and breathless, and stared at the waning moon.

"I'm sorry," Dylan eventually said, "about your mom."

Nickel sat and hugged his knees, but didn't say a word for a while. The crickets grew louder and louder, encouraged by the stillness of nature.

"She doesn't know who I am anymore," Nickel whispered. "My dad said it's the pain meds."

Dylan sat and turned toward Nickel, as the boy grabbed a fistful of pebbles and threw them into the creek. The crickets fell quiet for a while.

"I wish it was over," he whimpered. "What's the point, huh?" Another angry fistful of pebbles flew out. "She's never coming back. She's not Mom anymore; Dad said she's just a heap of pain waiting to be set free."

Dylan touched Nickel's shoulder, but he turned away and sniffled, then wiped his nose on his pajama sleeve.

"I'm going to miss her," Nickel said, after a while, still sniffling. "I miss her already."

Dylan jumped to his feet and grabbed Nickel's hand, tugging hard. "Come on, let's go."

"Where?"

"You'll see."

He led the way to an inlet on the creek bank and knelt in the dirt, squinting in the pale moonlight. He dug with his fingers and picked up pebbles, one after another, then discarded them, unsatisfied. Finally, he found one that he liked, rubbed the dirt off it, then held it out for his friend to see.

"Got one," he announced proudly, then resumed the search, under Nickel's perplexed eyes. As soon as he found another pebble, he stood and showed both of them to Nickel, in the palm of his hand.

"These are special, you know, they sparkle in the sunlight, like diamonds. You'll see tomorrow." Then he offered one to Nickel. "This one's yours."

Nickel took the pebble and studied it closely. "What's it for?"

"It's for luck."

"And it works?"

"Sure, it does."

"Mine's bigger than yours," he said.

"You're older than me," Dylan replied.

"Huh... only by one month and three days."

"Yeah, but still, older. And bigger too."

He watched Nickel as he scraped away some dirt off the pebble with his fingernail, then looked at it from all angles, rubbing it between his fingers, his face lit up by the moonlight and his sadness gone, at least for a moment.

"Brothers," he whispered, then glanced quickly in Dylan's direction.

"Brothers," Dylan replied quietly, barely covering the sound of the crickets.

"Dylan?"

The voice of his boss dispersed those fond memories and yanked him back to the reality of the conference room, filled with people staring at him, waiting for him to answer.

Hesitant, he looked at a colleague, then at another, still reeling.

"Are you all right?" Loreen Swan asked, her fake concern unmasked by the glint of irritation in her eyes.

"Yes," he replied, then cleared his throat. He opened his portfolio and pulled out his team's activity report, then started to give his weekly update.

# 16

# Lois

DJ was late again, and Angela had gone from anxious to irritated, then back to anxious again. She made a conscious effort to refrain from worrying; he'd been late before. Typically, when patients arrive late for therapy they're trying to communicate a message, even if they're unaware of it. Maybe they're not comfortable with the direction their therapy is taking, maybe they'd rather stop coming altogether. Maybe the feelings and thoughts they grow aware of during therapy are too upsetting for them to handle, and they struggle to keep the appointments; things "happen" to them that deter them from arriving on time.

Or maybe he'd given up and taken his own life.

She checked the time again; he was already seventeen minutes late. That was unprecedented. She poured herself a tall glass of cold, sparkling water and drank it all, trying to quench more than her thirst. Then she went to the window and looked outside, hoping she'd see DJ approach the building.

There was no one on the sidewalk, or in front of the mid-rise professional building. There was a car parked at the curb, a black sedan, and the driver was seated behind the wheel. She couldn't tell who it was; from her higher vantage point, she only saw the car's hood, roof, and windshield, nothing more, parts of it being shielded by the lush crown of an old cypress tree. She didn't believe that was DJ inside that car, but, absent other distractions, she kept her eyes on the mysterious vehicle and its driver.

The man kept both his hands on the wheel, completely still. She could see his knuckles through the windshield from her second-story window, tightly gripping that steering wheel, almost like holding on to it for balance. He didn't move; for many minutes, he didn't budge an inch. Then his hands disappeared from view and, within seconds, the man got out of the car, looked up straight at her window, and nodded in her direction.

It *was* DJ after all.

He pressed the remote in his hand and his car locked with a chime, then he walked toward the entrance. Perplexed, Angela took a step back from the window and inhaled deeply, getting ready for whatever was left of her session with him. Twenty-three minutes. Should she break one of the golden rules and extend their time past seven?

He came through the door with his hands in the air, defensively and apologetically at the same time.

"I know I screwed up, Doc. I know I'm late."

"Why are you late?" she asked, while closing the office door and inviting him to take his seat. "Did something happen?"

He pressed his lips together and threw her a frustrated glare, but then looked away immediately.

"I don't know what you're doing to me, but it's messing me up," he said in a low-pitched voice.

"What do you mean?"

"I thought we agreed you're going to evaluate me and nothing else. Last week though, you took it too far."

She wondered if he'd started to feel the effect of their talks, stirring up old memories, forgotten feelings, maybe even uncovering whatever trauma he had buried in his past, not only hiding it from her, but, most important, from himself.

"When we discussed your fears, and the waiter who used to serve you coffee?" she asked. "That's what you're referring to?"

He nodded a few times, still staring at the carpet.

"You can always choose a different topic of conversation, DJ. You're the one who's in charge here."

"Well, then, how about we don't talk today?" he asked, looking her in the eye with an intensity she didn't expect. "How about we sit here in silence, and wait for the time to be up? I need a damn break."

He closed his eyes and leaned against the sofa, allowing himself to relax a little, but most of the tension in his jaw and his neck remained.

"All right," she replied gently. "Let's take a few minutes and just breathe." She watched his chest move with every breath he took. He kept his eyes closed, but he wasn't relaxing, not as much as she would've wanted. The same clenched jaws, the same deep lines that flanked his tense mouth stood in evidence that his relaxation was superficial at best.

She checked the time and bit her lip. They had less than fifteen minutes left. She couldn't afford to waste any time. Weeks were flying by, and his deadline loomed like a bad, unavoidable omen.

"And breathe," she said, "let the air fill your lungs and bring you the peace you're looking for."

He opened his eyes briefly.

"There's no peace for me, Doc. Not yet."

"Would you like to talk about that?"

"No." His reply was quick and firm, undisputable.

"Why don't I do some talking today, then?" she offered, and, in the absence of any response from DJ, she continued. "Are you familiar with Maslow's hierarchy of needs?"

"Vaguely," he replied, but opened his eyes and straightened his back, leaning forward.

"It's a theory that illustrates the psychology of human motivations. It's drawn as a pyramid, with the base being the most fundamental level, the physiological needs. That's where we put food, water, shelter, and so on, everything we need for our bodies to survive. Then comes safety; personal security, health, some say even insurance satisfies this level of need. Financial security and job security are at this second level."

"I think I remember, yeah," he said, then frowned a little but continued to listen.

"Then the third level is for social belonging, where family and friends come into play. One level higher is esteem, a person's need to be respected, appreciated. Finally, the tip of the pyramid is self-actualization. The need to discover all that you can be, and fulfill that need, following your true passion."

"Uh-huh, I get it."

"Where do you see yourself, on this scale?"

DJ promptly crossed his arms at his chest, and his frown deepened. Then a crooked, bitter smile tugged at his lips. "Really, Doc, you have to ask?"

"Yes, I do. I don't like to assume."

"I'm at rock bottom. Right there with food and shelter and whatever else you said in there."

"How come? Seems to me you have these basic needs covered; you've moved past level two, maybe even three. You have a family, a few friends, I'm sure."

The same crooked smile appeared briefly on his face, loaded with bitterness.

"What do you think happens with the damn pyramid if it's built on sand? If the base can collapse overnight?"

"You think the base is collapsing?"

"Jeez, you still don't get it, do you?" he muttered under his breath, visibly frustrated. "Do you have any idea how short the distance is between living a decent life and being homeless? Do you know how little it can take?"

"Ah... I see," she replied. "You feel vulnerable, insecure in your ability to provide that decent life you were talking about."

"I don't *feel* anything, Doc. I *know* it. I *am* vulnerable. I've seen it. With others, but with us too. We came close a couple of times, too close. What happens if I can't find another job fast enough? With age, it will only be getting worse. No miracles expected there, huh?"

"But you survived, every time. You learned from it, and you moved on. You might not realize it, but you're a strong person."

"Ha," he snapped. "I've seen stronger men than me, better men than me, rejected by everyone, thrown out to the curb. I know it will happen, and I can't do that to her. It will kill her."

"You seem quite confident this doom scenario will happen, no matter what."

"Every time I'm out of a job, I fear the day I have to tell my wife we need to start selling our stuff to downsize, to put food on the table. I don't have much… but she has all these things she cares about. It would break her heart to part ways with all her cherished objects, and for what? Because she married a loser? A man who's falling apart, who can't provide for his family? At least we don't have kids; I managed that much, to not ruin yet another innocent life."

With every word he spoke, he turned darker, as if clouds of anguish rose from the depths of his mind and cast thick shadows over his entire being. His anger rose, close to the surface, threatening to erupt. Was he ready for that yet? Probably not.

"I understand how difficult this can be, to live with such burden," she said warmly. "Help me understand your wife a little better. Tell me about the two of you, when you used to date. You said you met her in high school, right?"

The shift in conversation worked, and she watched the signs of that deep darkness dissipate somewhat, as he recalled days when he'd been happy and hopeful.

"Yeah… She was amazing," he said, and she thought she saw a sparkle in his eyes. "It didn't matter we were in such a godforsaken place like Coalinga; she made it interesting, exotic even. Not much we could do, other than go for long walks, or sometimes sneak inside the theater to watch a movie. She held my hand… she always held my hand."

"Where did you two go for your walks? In the park?"

"In *the* park, yeah, the only one they have in Coalinga, or by the creek. We used to take the dog with us, and she loved the creek better, because I let her off the leash and she could run."

"Was that your wife's dog?"

"No, she isn't much into dogs." He turned away, hiding his eyes, then added in a whisper. "Lois was mine."

"Tell me about your her," she asked, intrigued by the change in his demeanor.

"There's nothing really to tell," he replied, deep undertones of sadness coloring his voice. "She's gone now; she died many years ago."

# 17

# The Deal

Dylan closed the door to his office and sat behind his desk, then opened a Styrofoam box filled with Caesar salad. Taylor had fixed lunch for him, and that meant the salad probably needed more Caesar dressing, but he didn't complain; she'd grated some Parmesan on top of it, even added a couple of anchovies. He unwrapped a plastic fork and started to eat, while watching from a distance, through the glass panel next to his office door, as the warehouse workers pushed their pick carts back and forth, collecting orders from the shelves and packing them inside cardboard boxes.

Soon the workers and their carts seemed to fade from view, leaving only the rhythmic sound of the cart wheels to be heard, as they traveled over the seams in the floor, echoing almost as if hammers drove nails into wood, somewhere in the distance.

He saw himself as a teenager, kneeling on the half-built deck, with Nickel by his side, driving nails into the wooden planks, securing them in place on the joists. It was a windy October day, and Dr. Soto watched the progress of their work with a slight frown, from behind a closed French door. A few feet away, next to the wall, Lois lay on her side, with her eyes half-closed and her pointy ears moving slightly with every bit of noise. The constant sound of hammering probably kept her awake, but she didn't seem to mind.

He'd lost count of how many nails he'd driven into those planks and joists, but he didn't mind. Every now and then, he looked over his shoulder toward Lois and felt content with the deal he'd struck with the potbellied and rather austere Dr. Soto. He'd never worked so hard in his entire life, but he wouldn't have had it any other way.

It all started about two weeks earlier, when he came back from school one day and found Lois lying listless near the house, in a pool of her own vomit. She barely lifted her head to greet him and fell back on her side, breathing with difficulty. He'd knelt next to her, grabbed her head with both her hands and tried to lift her, but she was too heavy. He called her name, but she didn't open her eyes. He let her go and ran screaming to the house, hoping his mother had arrived home from her temp job at the hospital.

"Mom! Mom!"

His mother appeared in the doorway, wiping her hands on her stained apron.

"Why the hell are you screaming like a scolded banshee? Didn't we talk about this?"

"It's Lois, Mom, she's not moving."

She scrambled with him and crouched next to Lois. She lifted the dog's eyelids, looked at her mouth, felt her weak and thready heartbeats and her shallow breathing. Then she dashed inside the house and called his father at work, telling him to rush home. She'd never done that before, not ever since he could remember.

There were very few good things about Coalinga being so small a town. Dylan couldn't think of many, but the short time it took his father to get home that day was one of them. His father took one look at Lois, then loaded her into the back seat of his car and drove like a maniac all the way to Dr. Soto, the town's veterinarian.

They stormed inside the vet's office and, in one long breath and a rush of panicked words, Dylan explained what was going on. Dr. Soto gazed at him over the thick rim of his glasses, then dispatched his assistant, a balding, young man by the name of Jake, to help carry Lois inside.

Her body seemed lifeless on the white, tiled table, but she was still breathing. Dylan kept his hand on her neck the entire time, scratching her gently behind her ears, telling her everything was going to be okay.

After he examined her, Dr. Soto looked briefly at Dylan, then gave his father a long look.

"She's been poisoned," he announced, "her liver and kidneys are shutting down. If we would've seen it earlier, maybe we could've done something. I'm afraid that—"

"No!" Dylan shouted. "No, you can't let her die."

Dr. Soto pressed his lips together. "I'm sorry, son; there's not much I can do. Even if I keep her here under intensive care for a few days, there's no telling how things will turn out, and it would cost you thousands of dollars," he added, looking at Dylan's father at the end of the phrase.

Mr. Ballard averted his eyes and shoved his hands inside his pockets. "I can't... we can't afford it, Dylan, and even if we did, she'd be in a lot of pain—"

Dylan grabbed Dr. Soto's arm with both his hands, unable to hide his tears any longer. "Please, I'll do anything. Anything you want, for as long as you want me to. I'll work the kennels at night, do your cleaning, wash your car, anything you want. Just don't let her die, please. She's only three years old. Please."

Dr. Soto looked at him thoughtfully. "How old are you, son?"

"Fifteen," he replied, feeling a shred of hope swell his chest.

"Almost fifteen," his father corrected him, but nodded almost imperceptibly, probably for Dr. Soto's benefit.

Dr. Soto took off his glasses and started wiping the lenses with the front part of his lab coat. For a long minute, he didn't say anything; he meticulously wiped each lens, probably thinking what to do.

"You'll work the kennels every day, starting now, until she's back on her feet. Then you'll build me a new deck. And you won't skip a single day of school."

"Yes, yes, I'll do it, thank you!" he said, and hugged the perplexed veterinarian.

"But there are no guarantees, son," Dr. Soto added. "I meant what I said; she might not make it."

He shook his head, between tears. "She'll live. She's strong, and she's a fighter. Let's not waste any more time."

Dylan's father went home alone that day, as Dylan took his new job seriously and started working at the kennel every afternoon, wearing Jake's old lab coat, and helping Dr. Soto with whatever he needed done. He cleaned the cages, fed the animals, swept the floors, and typed invoices for the doctor's customers. Then, at night, he curled up next to Lois in her kennel, and dozed off with her. In the mornings, he rushed to school, where he laughed in the face of anyone who told him he stunk of dog piss.

Lois survived, only barely, but managed to pull through. A couple of weeks later, she was still weak, not yet willing to run or fetch a ball, and endured patiently the loud hammering in Dr. Soto's backyard. Dylan had folded a blanket for her next to the house, where the sun's oblique rays warmed the deck in the afternoon, to have her keep him company, while he held his end of the bargain.

Nickel was not part of the deal, but he contributed nevertheless, because that was Nickel, a heart of gold with a sharp tongue and a keen sense of humor.

"What's in it for me?" Nickel asked. "I could go to the movies, pick up a girl, have some real fun. Instead, I hand you nails and beams and stuff. Boring!" he added in a sing-song voice.

"You get to hang out with us," Dylan replied. "It's not like you're really working. You're only handing me stuff, like you said. I actually deserve better, now that I'm a qualified carpenter."

"Who told you that? Most of all, why did you believe them?"

"See this?" Dylan said, standing and gesturing widely at the finished part of the new deck. "I built this!"

Then he saw the grin on his friend's face, and added, "Okay, *we* built this. We're so cool! Wait 'til we tell the other kids. We could make some serious money next summer."

The French door slid open and Dr. Soto's head popped outside. He looked at Lois first, then at the two boys.

"I hear a lot of chatter and not a lot of work, and I'm getting worried. I have guests coming on Saturday. Am I going to be embarrassed with this deck?"

"No, sir," Dylan replied, all serious.

"Will it be done by Friday night?"

"Yes, sir," he replied.

"All right, back to work!" he commanded firmly, and then closed the door, not fast enough, not before Dylan saw him smile.

# 18

# Timeline

The coffee tasted bad that morning, although it was probably the same coffee they normally brewed in the office, made with the same machine as always, in the exact same way. Yet the bitterness in Dylan's mouth didn't go away, and coffee didn't wash it off either; it made it worse.

Judging by the way people reacted in the small kitchenette, Terrell had finished talking to everyone. They were quiet, avoided his looks, and the typical chatter had simmered to barely audible whispers. They knew, and they'd all withdrawn inside themselves, joined by the common threat, yet divided by their individual agonies, painted in different shades of the same misery.

He spilled the stale coffee and poured himself a fresh cup, then added a bit of milk, hoping the bitterness would wash away. Then he checked the time, mumbled a curse under his breath, and rushed upstairs to meet with his boss. She was expecting him to discuss the timeline of the upcoming reduction in force, as the brass liked to call it when they throw people out in the street.

Loreen's office door was open, yet he stopped and knocked on the door frame. She lifted her eyes from the computer screen, and one of those fake smiles instantly appeared on her lips as if she'd touched a button to display it.

"Ah, good morning, Dylan. Take a seat."

He closed the door behind him and sat, open portfolio in his lap, ready to take notes.

"So, where are we with finding a vendor?"

He cleared his throat before speaking and made an effort to maintain a professional, calm demeanor, while presenting the competing vendor offers. It wasn't easy; anger swelled his chest, suffocating him, choking him, making him want to shout endless slews of epithets. Instead, he took out three vendor profiles and handed them to Loreen.

"These are the shortlisted vendors. Two are from the Philippines and one is from India. The Philippines are better priced and more flexible. The Indian company is more expensive, and I wasn't thrilled with their terms. They reserve the right to use those employees as they see fit and reassign them among their clients, which means we could be training people all day long."

Loreen studied the three offers quickly, making notes on each sheet of paper with a green felt-tip pen.

"Yeah, I agree. Let's stick with these two," she replied, and handed him back the two Philippines vendor profiles with her scribbled notes. "Confirm pricing on both these contracts, make sure there aren't any hidden fees, setup fees, or whatever else they'd want to charge us."

"Understood," he replied, and closed his portfolio, getting ready to leave.

"What's your timeline? When can we pull the plug?"

"Um, by the way things are moving, I'd say not before November fifteenth, maybe even December first."

Her fake smile vanished, leaving ridges and lines of irritation on her brow and around her eyes.

"It's the middle of July, Dylan. Why is it taking so long? Are you stalling?"

*Damn right, I am, you heartless bitch,* he thought, but instead of speaking his mind, he leaned forward and shook his head a couple of times, looking her in the eye with confidence.

"No, ma'am, I'm not stalling. Vendor selection takes time; we can't rush into a relationship without doing our diligence. We might wake up one morning and find our vendor has vanished and no one's answering our phones. That's why it took so long to finalize the shortlist. As soon as we pick the final vendor, legal has to review the contract, and that's typically two weeks, then the vendor's legal department might take some time on back-and-forth with our legal; you know how these things go."

"I'll speak with legal, make sure they clear their agenda and turn this around in two hours, not two weeks," Loreen said, with such fierceness it made Dylan shudder, as if he'd seen a viper coiled in a corner. "If we can't let these people go before December, we won't show any of the financial benefit on this year's profit-and-loss statement. We want to close the year with a bang, don't we, Dylan?"

"Yes, ma'am," he managed to say.

"Okay, what else needs to happen?"

"Um, after we've finalized the agreement with the vendor, they are requesting at least two months to hire the staff and put them through their initial training, orientation, and so on. We're also involved in the interviewing process; we want to make sure their English is up to par, and that they have the necessary business acumen to handle order entry for office products without screwing it up."

"Which one of these vendors have the shortest hiring time?"

"None do. They've all asked for the same time frame, two to three months. We'll keep it at two, if possible even shorter, but it ultimately depends on the candidates they find."

"I see. Then, what else?"

"Once the offshore reps are hired, we start training them, and that will take us at least a month."

Loreen scribbled something on her notepad, then frowned some more. "That puts us to three-and-a-half months, maybe four. November first, maybe the fifteenth, that's what you're saying?"

"Yes, that's correct."

"What needs to happen to make this happen October first instead? Maybe we can have one good trimester on the financials before end of year."

"I'll try my best to make that date," he replied firmly.

"Let me know the minute anyone stalls. This has the highest priority possible, you understand? The moment someone, anyone, doesn't reply to your emails, or doesn't review materials the same day, you call me. I don't care if it's Legal, or Finance, or whomever. This has to happen. What else?"

"Communication timeline, with the employees," he said. "But first, is it possible we shift some of these roles internally, instead of laying people off? Aren't any other departments hiring at this time?"

Loreen leaned forward, as if to get her message across better, more clearly. "San Francisco is an expensive place to run a business, and the company wants to reduce its footprint. No one's hiring anyone; actually, most departments are letting people go."

"What if we moved operations elsewhere?" Dylan asked. "Nevada is giving great tax incentives to move business there, and the cost of living is nothing compared to here. Many of these people would relocate, if you gave them the chance."

Loreen groaned and took a sip of green tea from a white mug bearing the company logo. "It's not worth it, Dylan, think about it. They'd want the same pay, and we want to pay cheaper, right? If we relocate them and cut their pay, they'd be disgruntled. It's not worth the complications."

"But they're trained, knowledgeable, experienced. They bring a lot of value to the company."

She leaned back in her seat, and her eyes shot him an irritated glare that she controlled immediately. But when she spoke, her voice had a finality in it he knew he couldn't ignore.

"The work isn't rocket science, Dylan, it's warehouse logistics. How hard can it be? The new employees will pick it up in a week or two, and they'll be enthusiastic, eager to impress, not disgruntled. Don't you like that?"

Dylan clenched his fists under the table and managed to force out of himself a nod and a hint of a smile.

He didn't remember how the meeting ended; for some reason, the rest of the conversation and the walk back to his office were a blur. His mind had gone into overdrive, trying to figure out a way to push back the timeline that Loreen would do anything to move forward.

# 19

# By the Fireplace

Angela walked slowly, staring at the office walls, as if she'd never seen them before. Sometimes she touched an item, a framed photo, or, closer to Dr. Foster's desk, an award or certificate, then she moved on, step after slow step. She felt the plush carpet under her bare feet and relished its softness, the familiar feel of the Persian rug, the fringes, then the coolness of the hardwood at the edge of the rug.

"You seem restless today," Dr. Foster said, a hint of worry causing a slight ruffle in his bushy, white eyebrows. He sat in his usual spot, comfortable with his feet up on the leather ottoman, but watching her move through the room with undisguised interest.

"Is this new?" Angela asked, touching a framed certificate of achievement in gold lettering on aged parchment, recognizing Dr. Foster for his contributions in the field of addiction psychiatry.

"Yes, it is," he replied proudly, with a wide smile. "Although, after a certain age, when all these organizations rush to recognize your life's work, it's never a good sign."

"Ah, don't be silly. You taught me that recognition is valuable, and you should savor it. You've worked hard for it, so you might as well enjoy."

He nodded a couple of times. "Couldn't have said it better myself," he laughed, and Angela joined him in laughter.

She continued her slow walk around the room, then stopped in front of the fireplace and listened to the sound of the crackling fire. It still sounded like rain; that wasn't a passing thought, a furtive impression she'd had when she'd visited last.

"Why don't you sit?" he invited her again.

"I sit all day long, and I do feel a bit restless; you're right about that."

"What's on your mind?"

She didn't say anything for a while, thinking, letting her mind wander freely. She pushed her thoughts away from the man who called himself DJ, but her thoughts, stubborn as hell, came back rushing, anxious, obsessive, grim.

She watched the flames dance into the fireplace and didn't feel the joy she usually did when she looked at the fire. She felt anguish, turmoil, and heard the screams of each dying wood fiber, as it was consumed and turned to ash.

"Do you have some wine?" she asked, "I'd love some, if you have it handy."

Dr. Foster smiled widely. "I have a great Cabernet Sauvignon. A patient brought it to me last week. It was a parting gift."

He stood and went to the bar, built into the massive cherry bookcase, and opened the doors. He took out a bottle and held it in front of his eyes, squinting a little. "Diamond Mountain," he read off the label. "Napa Valley. It must be good."

"Ah, I've heard about it," Angela replied, "but I've never tried it."

"Let's see," he said, and uncorked the bottle. He poured wine in two glasses and handed one to her. They clinked glasses and tasted the liquid.

"Uh-huh," Dr. Foster said, "yes, this is an excellent wine."

"Thanks, I needed this," Angela declared, and turned her gaze to the dancing flames.

Dr. Foster went back to his recliner and sat, watching her silently for a while.

"Are you going to tell me what's wrong, my dear?" he asked.

She took another sip of wine, then turned toward him. "It's my patient. I… he drives me crazy. I've been seeing him for almost two months now, two out of the six, remember? And I don't even know his name."

"Ah, the suicidal man who needed your help. I was meaning to ask how that was going."

"Not well," she snapped. "I've tried everything I could think of, bent every professional guideline, and I still can't get him to open up. I can see he's reliving things, but he won't share, he won't discuss them with me. He could disappear one day, jump off Golden Gate or whatever else he decides to do, and that would be the last I'd hear of him."

"That can't be easy for you, knowing that it could happen. How does that make you feel?"

She bit her lip before answering. Too many words were crowding her mind, desperate to come out. Too many feelings, contradictory, confusing.

"Powerless and angry too. Frustrated. He doesn't even want to try, doesn't let me show him there could be another way. His mind is made up, and I can't seem to reach him. All the arguments he's making are so plausible, so rooted in reality, it makes me wonder sometimes."

"You've had little time," Dr. Foster replied, "and this patient doesn't acknowledge he needs help. That notion is still buried deep inside his subconscious mind. It's normal to experience—"

"He's stubborn, and if the time runs out before I can bring him out, he'll die. And it's going to be my fault."

"Ah… did you hear yourself just now?"

She sipped the remaining wine and put the empty glass firmly on the desk, next to the bottle, in an unspoken request for a refill.

Dr. Foster obliged, and poured the red liquid slowly.

"I can't think of anything else but him," she confessed. "Nothing else matters, none of my other patients, nothing. I can't let him die, and that's all I can think of. What else to try, how else to talk to him."

"Tell me about him, what's he like?"

"He's tall, six-four or six-five, and well built. He appears calm, but that calm doesn't run very deep. He's strong-willed, and not at all psychologically minded. He doesn't want to talk about anything, doesn't want to think differently, although, intellectually, he definitely has the ability. He's intelligent and perceptive. He has inadequacy issues, he's terrified of failure, his self-confidence is—"

"Are you falling in love with this man?"

His question stunned her. The thought hadn't even crossed her mind.

"No. He's married and loves his wife deeply," she replied, staring at the flames.

"You know that's not really an answer," he pushed back gently. "I was asking about what you feel, not what he feels. Quite different things, you must agree."

She looked at him sheepishly.

"No, I'm not falling in love with him. I'm obsessed with him, consumed with the desperate need to know that he's going to be all right. I even thought about hiring a private investigator, to find out who he is."

"Whoa… that's some serious overstepping of boundaries," he reacted, this time with a full-fledged frown on his brow.

"I know. If he senses anything, he could spook and disappear forever. I can't do that, I know it."

Slack-jawed, Dr. Foster shook his head slowly in disbelief. "That's not what I meant, Ang."

"I'm not sure what to do anymore. He wants to die; he's determined, and I can't let him do that, do you understand?" She lowered her voice to a whisper. "He can't die."

"What do you think is wrong with him? You have enough experience to be able to formulate an opinion after six sessions."

"Seven."

"Okay, seven," he acknowledged with a shrug. "Is he depressed? Was there a recent traumatic life event that has triggered his decision to end his life? Is he terminally ill?"

She let a long, pained breath of air escape her chest. "He seems healthy, and he's never mentioned anything about an illness. He's loaded with anger, so depression could be a factor. I'm guessing some old, untreated posttraumatic stress, maybe brought up by a recent trigger event."

"Is he military?"

"He hasn't mentioned it, and I didn't ask. He looks ex-military though, at least to me. He's hypervigilant, even hostile at times. If I ask questions, he shies away from the areas we should be discussing the most, the areas where his feelings are closest to the surface."

"That's normal for nonpsychologically minded individuals, especially those who believe, at least on a conscious level, that they don't need therapy, that they don't need to work on their issues." Dr. Foster said. "Why does it bother you so much?"

"Because there's no damn time!" she snapped. "I don't have years and years of weekly sessions to help this patient uncover who he really is and how to live a better life. I have seventeen more sessions left to figure out how to keep him from ending his life. I'm counting every damn minute, and I'm not getting ahead." She downed the rest of her wine, then abandoned the empty glass on the mantle. "For some reason, the thought of this man dying deeply upsets me."

"Is this about Michael?" he asked, his voice barely louder than a whisper.

Tears flooded her eyes and started rolling down her cheeks, as if they'd been collecting in there, in a hidden pool of liquid pain, waiting for the opportunity to escape.

"Maybe it is," she said, looking at the flames that seemed unreal through the veil of her tears. "Michael died because no one cared."

She didn't look at him; she couldn't bear to let him see her sorrow. But she felt his presence there, by her side, and the thought of that gave her courage.

"I know I can save this man, I can feel it. I don't know how, don't know what I'm missing."

"You'll find it, Ang. But promise me, you'll take care of yourself too. Otherwise, you won't succeed."

She sniffled, still avoiding his look.

"Thanks, Dad, I will."

He stood and walked toward her, then hugged her tightly and kissed her forehead.

"Can I crash here tonight?" she asked, inhaling the familiar scent of his aftershave.

"Tonight, and any night, Ang. Let's get you upstairs, in your old room. That bed is always made, waiting for you."

She shook her head with a smile and lay down on the sofa, by the fire that sounded like the rain.

# 20

# An Evening

Dylan let the shower run and turned to face the white, tiled wall. He leaned against the cold surface with his open palms and closed his eyes, letting the flow of warm water attempt to wash away his torment.

He saw himself delivering the separation packages to his people, letting them go, one after another. To Terrell, a single parent and a wounded war veteran, who'd probably never recover and whose child would probably end up in foster care in less than a year, when he'd lose his home and the state would be quick to take his son away from him, instead of throwing him a lifeline. To Anne, whose aging mother had started to show signs of Alzheimer's. To Jim, who had the most chances to make it okay, and had recently got engaged. He opened his eyes and stared at his hands, under the steady flow of water, expecting to see blood on them. He didn't care that he wasn't the one who gave the order; he was the one who was going to have to pull the trigger.

Or was he?

Was he being a coward for wanting to not be the one who delivered the inevitable layoffs? How hypocritical could he be, preparing everything for the offshore transition, yet avoiding being the one who looked his people in the eye when they got fired from their jobs?

He slammed his hand against the wall, and then slammed it again, harder. He didn't feel any pain, nor any relief. But after a few seconds, he remembered he was stalling the layoffs as much as possible, delaying the inevitable as long as he could. That was his fight, and it was a just one, even if fought cowardly through lies and deceit. And still, no matter how he chose to look at it, he was being paid to terminate thirty-four people, to derail the destinies of thirty-four families. He had blood on his hands, and no amount of running water would cleanse that.

What if he refused to have anything to do with it and left his job? Then the ones who'd struggle the most would be him and Taylor, while whomever took over in his place would probably be ready to fire everyone by mid-August. He'd hurt his people more by taking himself out of the equation. He was trapped, a powerless tool in the hand of a ruthless master.

He leaned his head against the tiles and let the water run on his back. The sound of the shower melded into a different sound, and images started to form against the darkness of his closed eyelids.

An endless road covered in dust, somewhere in the Torgan Valley of Afghanistan, on the way to Sorkh Deh. The compact convoy of Humvees, raising dust in the air, a dust so thick he could taste it, blocking his view of the vehicle in front of him, even if they weren't too far behind. The sound of the Humvee's engine, the chatter of his crew. Navajo's endless supply of dirty jokes, and the roars of laughter every time he told another one. Terrell's nonstop humming of the Jennifer Lopez hit, "I'm Gonna Be Alright." Jack Austin's stories of riding stallions bareback in his native Texas and hunting wild boar with an Atchisson assault shotgun, loaded with 12-gauge ammo he made himself using ball bearings, nails, and gunpowder he bought by the barrel. Crazy bastard... Behind the wheel of the Humvee, the grimy face of—

The shower curtain pulled open and he froze, knowing it was Taylor, knowing she was about to touch him, while his mind was still captive there, in the middle of the Afghan desert. He willed himself back to the present and shook away the lingering ghosts of the past.

"I did good work, didn't I?" she said, her voice low and loaded. She ran her fingers on the old scar still showing on his right buttock, and his blood caught fire. He turned toward her and grinned widely, when he saw she was naked, ready for him.

He turned off the faucet with a quick move and stepped out of the shower, water dripping on the floor. Without a word, he lifted Taylor up in the air and she wrapped her legs around his waist. With long, hurried strides, he took her into the bedroom and lay her on the sheets, then stopped to look at her, to fill his heart with images of her yearning body.

He touched her soft, silky skin with burning fingers, taking his time, savoring the little sounds she made, and didn't stop until she writhed and moaned, calling his name, wanting him inside her. He made love to her slowly, savoring every second, every touch. He held back until she was ready and begged for her release, then he took both of them to the heights of shared pleasure, sinking into the depths of her eyes, breathing in her cries of ecstasy.

Spent, he cuddled her against his body and caressed her hair, not daring to close his eyes, not wanting to miss her, not even for a second.

"Welcome back," she quipped, running circles with her fingers on his chest. "I missed you."

The darkness returned, sudden and unwelcome. It had been a while since they'd been together like that.

"Hey, come back to me," she said, touching the newly formed ridges on his brow. "Don't go there, stay with me."

He attempted a smile, but didn't manage to wipe the frown off his face. Instead, he reached for her lips and kissed her, then tightened the grip of his arms around her body.

"Okay, that's better," she whispered, "but not good enough. What's on your mind?"

He groaned and closed his eyes, in a futile attempt to evade the reality that came crashing in. "Nothing."

"Let me help you get another job, okay? What do you say? I'll sift through online postings and find stuff you can apply for. Let's fix this problem before it hits, for a change."

"And move again?" he asked, feeling all energy drain from his body. "It's not easy, with all the stuff we have."

"Then, let's stay here," she offered. "Change jobs, but stay here. San Francisco is big enough for you to find another job."

He groaned. "Life's too expensive here. We're paying a fortune in rent for a tiny place, so cluttered we can't move. Every month, half my income plus more than half of yours go to the landlord. That's not a way to live."

She lifted herself and leaned on her elbow to see his face. "So, you don't want to move, but don't want to stay either. You have to choose one, you know."

Another wave of darkness engulfed him, when he remembered he wasn't going to move again. Not ever.

"Why don't you give me a few months. Things will sort themselves out, you'll see."

"How many months? If things are shabby at the job, maybe it should be sooner rather than later, don't you think?"

"Yeah… we'll decide on Thanksgiving, how's that?"

She studied his face for a moment, and he had to fight himself to hold her gaze. He wasn't going to be there for Thanksgiving. It would be her decision, where to move, what to do, where to go. All hers. Alone. Without him.

"All right, deal," she replied. "But you have to feed me now. You know, sex makes me hungry."

He managed to smile and followed her into the kitchen. Minutes later, they'd finished munching on some snacks and had taken their usual seats in the living room, in front of the TV. She sat on the sofa, remote in her hand, flipping through the channels. He sat at her feet, leaning against the sofa next to her legs, anticipating her soft hands tousling his hair or rubbing his nape.

"Look, it's *The Patriot*, with Mel Gibson. Want to try it? It started ten minutes ago."

"Sure," he replied, feeling himself slip away the moment she'd turn on the TV.

For a while, he forced himself to pay attention to the action flick, and it wasn't a bad one. Lots of shooting though and cannons, against a backdrop of epic film music. Gunshot after gunshot, his memories invaded, and soon he was feeling the taste of the Afghan desert dust on his lips, and he struggled to answer one obsessive question: Who was driving the Humvee that day? Who was he sitting next to? He remembered the grimy face, covered in sweat and dirt. He remembered his white teeth, when the man had laughed at one of Navajo's jokes. He remembered knowing who that man was, but not anymore. His identity was hidden behind a wall of darkness. He had to remember; he absolutely needed to tell that man something, before it was too late.

He let himself sink deeper into remembering, into reliving, and almost felt he could reach out and touch the man's arm, to get him to turn his way, so he could see who he was. His chest swelled, and something choked him, as if a scream struggled to escape, and it felt as if he could—

"Why didn't Martin kill the colonel first," Taylor asked, "then lead those guys into battle? That's what I would've done."

"Huh?" He turned his head toward her, utterly confused. "I'm not sure what you mean."

She pursed her lips and frowned at him, shooting him a glare he never wanted to see again.

"You're not here anymore; you're not watching this with me," she stated in a disappointed voice, searching his eyes. "Where the hell are you, again?"

# 21

# A Smile

"Is that a new chair?" Dylan asked, as soon as he took his usual seat on the couch.

"You're observant," Angela replied. "Yes, it's new."

"What was wrong with the old one?"

She gave his question a bit of thought; his interest in anything outside his grim realm was new, and while typically she didn't encourage personal questions from patients, she decided to follow his lead. After all, it was the first time he'd opened the conversation or manifested any interest in his surroundings. That aside, she couldn't tell him the truth. She'd replaced the old recliner with the new one because she wanted to be able to keep her eyes on him with ease when he paced the office. The new chair was mounted on a swivel.

"It was time for a new chair," she said with a tiny smile. "The old one was getting uncomfortable and had developed a squeak that was disruptive to my patients."

"I didn't hear any squeaks," he said.

"I'm happy to hear that," she stated serenely.

He was quiet for a while, and beneath his apparent calm, hints of his internal turmoil were showing. A flicker of a frown, the tension in his jaws, his hunched-forward position he always took while seated on her couch.

"Must be nice," he said, "to get new things every now and then. To get rid of the old stuff."

"Yes, it is. It's refreshing."

A hint of that crooked smile tugged at the corner of his mouth. "It's a privilege."

"How so?"

He shook his head and sighed, but didn't say a word.

"Is your wife working?" she asked, going after a hunch. There was something about DJ's wife that deeply troubled him, despite his unrelenting love for her.

"Yes, she is," he replied morosely.

"Tell me about her career. What does she do?"

"Her career?" he snapped, switching from that apparent calm to the heights of barely controllable anger in a matter of milliseconds. "You mean, whatever's left of her career, after I've destroyed everything that could've been destroyed?"

"Why do you feel you've destroyed her career? Help me understand."

He shook his head, frustrated.

"I told you before, Doc, but you're not paying attention. Every time we had to move, she left her job because of me. Then we moved, and she had to find another job in a place where I've decided to take us. You think those places were like San Francisco, with thousands of jobs open? No, we lived in rural Indiana, where the best she could get was clerking at the local tax office, for nine fifty an hour. When I got laid off in Indiana, they'd just promoted her to supervisor."

"So, then, why did you move from Indiana?"

"Because I couldn't get any other job there. She... always believed in me, invested in me, so self-sacrificing. Then I got the job here, and the difference in my pay was worth almost her entire paycheck. She was happy to leave, thinking we could get ahead this time. But the cost of living here is awful."

She nodded. "It is. Did she find a god job here?"

He scoffed again, angrily. "No... Her résumé has employment gaps in it, and those bastards don't care that she did whatever she had to do for me. She was a store sales rep in Cleveland, and worked at the Waffle House in Milwaukee. Then the tax office in Indiana. What do you think her chances are to find a good job, with that résumé, with more holes in it that a piece of ripened Swiss cheese? That's why she'll never have to work again after November. She's done enough for me. Now it's my turn."

"I understand how overwhelming it can feel to deal with so much change. Most people don't move half as much as you have, and they still feel overwhelmed. Maybe it would be helpful if we tried to explore some alternatives, don't you think?"

"Alternatives to what?" he asked, his voice cold and tense.

She bit her lip, angry with herself for tipping her hand so carelessly. "Maybe we can discuss some better ways to adapt to the challenges you both are facing in your professional lives."

"I thought we agreed, Doc. Don't explore anything with me, I'm not interested. Is that clear?"

"I understand this is your preference; I only struggle a little to understand why you'd go to that extreme for a challenge most people face on a daily basis? Life is tough for many, and yet they choose to hold on and fight."

The same crooked smile tugged at the corner of his mouth. "Yeah, and some fight they're putting on. We're all popping pills, drinking, or drugging our heads off, trying to ease the pain, to find the courage to face another day. You call this living, Doc? 'Cause I don't. I can't live every day of my life knowing that I'm powerless, and that at any time I can end up on the street, dragging her down with me. I can't expect every day to bring us that single, devastating event in our lives that could spiral us both into hell. What if I get sick and can't work anymore?

What if we get into an accident? No, I'm done trying, end of story. I'm an educated, rational man who's out of any other viable alternatives. Not depressed, not on any drugs, just realistically seeing that the odds are stacked so high against me that I want to at least *choose* the way I lose this game, with some dignity left."

She listened attentively, trying to find faults in his logic, but couldn't, and that was a troublesome thought. She waited for him to continue, but he'd interiorized his anguish and seemed to continue his argument in his mind, unwilling to share.

"Tell me about your parents," she eventually said, seeing that several minutes in a row brought nothing but grim silence.

"There's nothing to tell. They're not relevant to any of this." He shook his head, then gazed at her quickly. "They did their best, and that's it. For whatever I've screwed up in my life, they're not to blame."

"Are they still alive?"

He nodded, but didn't say another word.

"How about Lois? Want to tell me more about her?"

He smiled for a split moment, a genuine smile that touched his eyes.

"Was she named after Superman's girl?" she continued, hoping she could keep him in the positive emotion for a while longer.

"Yeah," he replied, looking her briefly in the eye with a renewed smile. He seemed different when he smiled like that. His features relaxed, the tension in his jaw vanished, and his eyes softened, warm with kindness.

She crossed her legs and leaned back a little farther in her seat, ready to hear more. "Tell me."

"The movie had just come out, and I think I saw it fifteen times with Ni— ... never mind."

"Do you have a picture of her?"

His eyebrows shot up and he fidgeted a little, then he reached for his wallet in the back pocket of his pants. He took out a weathered, black-and-white picture of a dog and put it gently on the coffee table, right in front of her. Then he sat back on the couch, a hint of that genuine smile still lingering on his lips.

She took the small, fragile photo carefully, and studied it closely. She didn't know much about dogs, but she could tell Lois was a beautiful one. She looked like those K9s that the police used. Must have been great for a young boy growing up with such a strong, beautiful companion.

DJ watched her anxiously, as she looked at the photo. After a short while, he stood and started pacing the room. She put the photo back on the coffee table, concerned he must have grown uncomfortable with her touching it. By all appearances, that photo was a valuable memento of his childhood.

"How old were you when you got her?" Dr. Blackwell asked.

He stood by the window again, looking outside at the foggy evening. He kept his back turned to her when he replied. "I was twelve."

"How did she come into your life?"

"It was after my... after someone died. My parents brought her home one day. She was little," he added, and she could hear the smile in his voice, a strangled smile, as if beyond it, a wave of tears threatened to push the floodgates open. "Those big ears, bigger than her head, trying to stand up. She grew into those ears, eventually."

"How was she, growing up?" she asked cheerfully, glad she found a topic he was willing to talk about, a tiny crack in his shell.

For a while he didn't speak, staring into the rolling fog. Slowly, the smile returned, barely visible from her vantage point, where she could only see his profile.

"She made those faces, you know, tilting her head left, then right, while staring at us. Her big ears flopped to the sides, then tried to stand up again. We'd say something stupid, like, 'Lois, who's the meanest dog around?' and she'd tilt her head, over and over again. Nickel and I, we rolled on the ground, laughing."

"Nickel?"

The smile vanished, and his head dropped forward until his forehead leaned against the window. His right hand reached inside his pocket and Angela thought she heard the faint sound of the two pebbles rubbed together.

"He… we grew up together, that's all."

"I see. Were her ears always floppy? In the picture, they seem quite firm," she steered carefully toward the source of that elusive smile.

"No. She grew into them. She was about six months old when they stopped looking as if she'd stolen them from a bigger, meaner dog." He laughed quietly, and shot her an amused look. "One day we looked at her and she was a big dog, all serious, guarding the home, taking care of Nickel and me, barking at every drunk and every mailman visit. She still made us laugh, though. She always tilted her head like that. We used to go by the waterhole, the one by Los Gatos Creek that is, at night, and jump in there naked, hollering, with Lois by our side. She loved a good swim. Then she came out of there, stinking of bog and mud and wet dog, and my mother always grilled us the following day."

"Keep going," she encouraged him, smiling.

"Then I met Taylor," he said in a quick breath. "She wasn't crazy about our threesome dates, as she used to call them."

"Who's Taylor? Your wife?" she asked, ready to jot down the name in her notebook.

"Uh-huh," he said, still looking out the window. "She wasn't thrilled with Lois. Her fur clung to Taylor's clothes, and she always worried that her hands smelled of dog. I didn't have the heart to tell her, but she smelled of dog altogether, not only her hands. I loved her smell."

Angela listened intently, not daring to interrupt or ask any questions, still amazed she'd learned the closely guarded name of his wife and so many details of DJ's childhood, only because she'd found the right way into his heart. People are complex beings, and to understand the myriad facets of someone's mind, their intricate and compounded emotions, was like exploring a labyrinth with nothing more than a flashlight, only seeing a tiny stretch of the convoluted road ahead. Yet sometimes, in complete darkness, that flashlight could find the right turn, the unique path that led to uncovering someone's inmost being, who they really are deep inside. Her only chance to reach him, even if against his conscious will.

She looked at DJ briefly and saw he was still standing near the window, staring intently outside, at the early, foggy dusk. She then reached inside her pocket and pulled out her phone, discreetly, then made sure it was on silent. After checking one more time if DJ could see what she was doing, she took a picture of the old photograph of Lois, then put the phone back inside her pocket.

"She thought it unromantic of me to kiss her while holding a bag of dog crap in my hand," he added, chuckling softly. "One time she got so mad… We were making out in the park, but I had to stop and bring Lois to order. She was chasing squirrels. It took me a while to get her to stop, and by that time, the moment was gone. Taylor was mad, frustrated, feeling neglected, and I was out of breath, after chasing Lois through half the park. Any hint of sexual arousal was gone at that point," he clarified, still smiling, but this time fondly, the way people smile when they look at old pictures of their happy days.

He stopped talking for a while, but Angela let the silence take its course.

"God's tennis balls…" he sighed. "She loved God's tennis balls."

"What are those?"

"Squirrels."

"Ah…" she acknowledged with a quick, quiet chuckle. "What happened to her?"

The smile vanished, and she regretted she asked.

"She lived many years," he replied dryly, "but we're out of time."

With little delay or protocol, he picked up the faded photograph and left, only a few minutes after seven, making her wonder what wrong turn she'd taken in the labyrinth of his memories.

A few minutes later, still unsettled, she started pacing the floor, just as he'd done earlier, wondering what was at the core of DJ's grief. He'd explained the decision to end his life in a rational, factual manner, yet she felt there was something else buried inside him, something that made him crave the moment he'd stop breathing.

In most cases, suicide isn't about wanting to die, as much as it is about wanting to stop living to end the pain that accompanies the realities of living. Suicidal people don't fantasize about seeing themselves as a bluish corpse lying on the coroner's table with a bullet hole in their head and half their brain matter missing. No, they envision the moment when they'll be able to rest, in peace, without feeling any guilt, or fear, or sorrow. Without feeling shards of pain tearing them inside, ripping them apart, and leaving them breathless, depleted, vulnerable in the face of life's incessant attack.

She leaned her head against the cold glass and watched the rolling fog for a while, and the hues of oranges and purples at the edges of the fog bank in the distance, toward sundown. Below her window, at street level, the mist was gray, engulfing everything slowly, inch by inch. Street lamps, the massive cypress trees, the cars parked at the curb.

She recognized DJ's car, right where it had been since earlier, and she saw him sitting behind the wheel, holding on to it with both hands, frozen in time. She couldn't see his face from her vantage point, but she knew it was him. She considered going downstairs to talk to him, but quickly rejected the idea. Whatever monsters he was battling, right there behind the wheel of his parked car, he needed to battle alone.

# 22

# Meatballs

Dylan could barely breathe. He kept his hands clenched on the steering wheel, trying to steady himself. Waves of suffocating anger pressed against his chest, tearing at him from the inside out, fresh and palpable, as if it had just happened. Mrs. Vilhein's visit.

Lois had barely got back on her feet after being poisoned, and Nickel had insisted, the night before, that she was ready for a dip in their favorite splashing place. They took Lois swimming, and she ran like a maniac, as soon as they let her off leash, then plunged into the muddy water, all four legs hitting the water at the same time. The next day, their entire home stunk of wet dog, and his mother gave him an ultimatum before going to work: no more swimming in the waterhole, or no more Lois inside the house.

He was still deliberating what to do, when he heard Lois growling and then someone knocked on the door. After recognizing the wrinkled, flabby face of their next-door neighbor through the tacky sheers hanging at the front window, he opened the door and let her in.

"Good morning, Mrs. Vilhein," he said, then watched Lois sniff her feet with a quiet, restrained growl. Then Lois walked away from her and curled up on the floor in a corner. "Mom's not home. She'll be back at three."

"Oh, it doesn't matter, sonny. I brought you these, for your doggy," she replied, handing him a small plate with several meatballs on it. They smelled good, and Lois flicked her tongue over her nose, but, like a well-behaved dog, she didn't come begging.

"Thank you—" he started saying, then froze. He remembered, as if experiencing a sickening déjà-vu moment, that he'd lived through that exact scene before, and the mystery of Lois's recent poisoning, unsolved until that day, was hence figured out.

Mrs. Vilhein had brought meatballs for Lois before. Only once. The morning of the day Lois had fallen sick.

His mind raced, desperately thinking what to do, trying to refrain himself from beating the crap out of the wicked, old woman. Then he had an idea, maybe not the brightest he'd ever had, but an idea that helped him squelch the screams of rage inside his mind.

"You're very kind, Mrs. Vilhein, please sit," he said, with the most courteous smile the angry fifteen year old could muster. "My mother would give me a beating if I didn't at least offer you a cup of coffee."

The old hag, flattered by the attention, quickly sat at the dining room table, and let out a solid stream of words, neighborhood gossip, her opinions about everything under the sun, and her absolute commitment to petition the city to have the garbage pickup days changed for their neighborhood, because the noise made by the trucks disrupted Wednesday morning church service.

Dylan brewed her coffee, made to her order, and wondered why. Why would a dog like Lois motivate someone like that old harpy to poison her? What kind of person poisons a dog anyway? Why aren't there laws against it, laws that have teeth in them, laws that could make people think twice before harming an animal? What had Lois ever done wrong to that woman?

When the coffee was ready, he poured it for her in a clean cup on a matching saucer, offered her milk and sugar, put napkins on the table, and even popped open a box of fresh cookies. His mother would have been proud.

Then he sat across from Ms. Vilhein, the plate with meatballs right in front of him, and looked her in the eye for a few seconds. The witch didn't even blink. She sipped her coffee and smacked her lips, satisfied.

Dylan took a meatball with his fingers and held it in the air for a while, as if planning to give it to Lois. The dog, smart enough, manifested no interest whatsoever, probably recognizing the smell of the food that had nearly killed her. Mrs. Vilhein smiled encouragingly.

Without hesitation, Dylan put the meatball in his mouth, chewed it quickly, and swallowed it, washed away with a gulp of water. Mrs. Vilhein stood quickly, flustered, all color drained from her cheeks.

"Sit," Dylan commanded, and took another meatball. "They're quite good and tasty. Too bad they're deadly."

Mrs. Vilhein's hands were shaking visibly, her eyelids battered, and her chin trembled. A sickly shade of purple colored her chest, rising toward her face. "Why... what are you saying?" she managed to articulate.

He grinned at her, a crooked grin filled with disdain.

"You see, Mrs. Vilhein, my dog was poisoned and nearly died," he said, taking another bite of meatball.

"So sorry to hear that, so sorry," she mumbled, her voice now trembling in unison with the rest of her body.

"I bet you are," Dylan reacted, the sarcasm in his voice searing, despite talking with his mouth full. "And I swore to myself that whoever poisoned my dog would pay for it, no matter what it takes." He chewed the rest of the second meatball and gulped down some more water. "Yup, no matter *what* it takes," he repeated, his features firm under the shocked gaze coming from her rounded eyes.

"What are you talking about?" she said, feigning ignorance, then stood again, ready to leave.

"Sit. The. Fuck. Down," he said coldly, and she obliged, letting herself drop back onto the chair, probably weak at the knees.

"What are you going to do?" she asked, barely a whisper.

"Throw you in jail for attempted murder," he replied calmly, as if talking about last week's game scores. "There aren't any good laws against poisoning a dog, but there are quite a few against poisoning a kid. This plate, right here, has your fingerprints on it."

Her eyes flickered with unspeakable fear, and she reached out to grab the plate, but Dylan, faster, blocked her hand and took the plate away.

"Uh-uh, don't even try. Get used to the idea, my dear Mrs. Vilhein, you're going to jail for the rest of your evil life. You should enjoy the experience; there aren't any dogs in there."

She started sobbing hard, wailing, imploring. "Please... please don't do this. I'm so sorry... please, I'm begging you."

Dylan took a bite out of the third meatball and watched her squirm, feeling nothing but vindication for Lois, experiencing that strong elation most people feel when justice is finally served, albeit after a long time.

"Don't eat anymore, please," she pleaded between sobs.

"Afraid of a murder charge, Mrs. Vilhein?" he chuckled, and took another bite, a smaller one. He'd just felt a pang of excruciating pain in his stomach, almost making him keel over. Poor Lois, what she must have endured.

"What's in them, old bat?" he asked coldly, feeling beads of sweat breaking at the roots of his hair.

Her jaw fell, but then she replied, keeping her eyes riveted to the floor. "Rat poison."

"Yeah, that's what we thought," he said casually, then took yet another bite. "Vilhein, what kind of name is that? Never heard it before."

She stared at him in shock for a long moment. "Um, Hungarian. My late husband, he was—"

"Did he teach you to poison dogs?"

"No, he—"

"Why? Why did you do it? What did Lois ever do to you?"

She shook her head slowly, keeping her eyes lowered. "I'm so sorry, please forgive me, I'm begging you. I have a son."

"What did she ever do to you?" he repeated the question, grabbing his abdomen, feeling the poison ripping at his stomach lining.

"She barked. Sometimes she barked. But I'm so sorry."

He stood and looked at her with unspeakable disdain. "Get the hell out of here."

She rushed to her feet and toward the door. She had her trembling hand on the door handle when she turned and asked, "What will you do?"

"I guess you'll find out sooner or later, won't you?" he replied, then gestured her away.

She vanished, and, as soon as the door closed behind her, he rushed to the kitchen and fixed himself warm water with salt and drank it down in huge gulps, just like he'd seen Dr. Soto administer to poisoned dogs as a first-aid measure. Seconds later, he was retching violently, holding on to the toilet bowl for balance and fending off Lois's long tongue. Then he let himself drop to the floor and writhed in pain for a while, with a whimpering Lois by his side, but the pain slowly subsided, after a second round of warm brine.

By the time his mother came home, he was lying in bed, claiming food poisoning; he hadn't lost his sense of humor. His mother fixed him a chamomile tea and didn't worry too much about it.

The following day he saw a moving truck loading Mrs. Vilhein's possessions, and at the end of that day, she was gone from their lives forever.

Good riddance.

He slowly unclutched his hands from the steering wheel and breathed deeply, letting his head lean back against the headrest. After a few moments, he turned the key in the ignition and shifted into gear. Before pulling away from the curb, he looked up and thought he saw Dr. Blackwell watching from behind the second-story window.

Maybe she understood a few things, but he wasn't sure if that was a good or a bad thing.

# 23

# Candlelight Dinner

The following Friday, Dylan made a point to get home early. For a change, he was among the workers who stormed out of the building at precisely five o'clock, and he jogged to the car to beat the traffic going out to the freeway. Twenty minutes later, he was home.

"You're early," Taylor greeted him at the door, smiling excitedly. "Any plans I should know about?"

He leaned and kissed her lips, lingering, tasting their softness. She responded, wrapping her arms around his neck and moaning softly into his kiss.

"Let me make it up to you, baby," he said, "it's been a rough patch. Want to go out somewhere?"

"Ooh, let the weekend begin," she cajoled, with a quick, delighted laugh. She looked him in the eye playfully while she considered his invite, then shook her head. "Uh-uh. I want you to grill us a steak, a big one. We'll share it, then you'll take me for a drive on the coast, to watch the sunset."

She wanted so little. At least that much he could do to make her happy.

"Deal," he said. "Ribeye or T-bone?"

"Ribeye, Marine."

"Yes, ma'am."

He changed quickly into a pair of cargo shorts and an old, stained T-shirt and started the grill. He added a couple of charcoals to it, for a hint of smoke flavor. Ten minutes later, beer in hand, he pulled out the biggest ribeye he could find in the freezer and put it on the heated grill, then grinned with satisfaction when it sizzled just right. He kept an eye on the grill's thermometer, but mostly he watched Taylor set the table. Two placemats. Two plates, two sets of forks and steak knives. Two glasses, although she'd also grabbed a beer and was drinking it from the bottle.

Then she warmed up a bowl of roasted potatoes and set it on the table, while he flipped the steak onto the other side. He inhaled the mouthwatering smell and then looked at Taylor again. The final touch to their dinner setup, a tapered, scented candle, she was putting in a candleholder.

He checked the time, then took the steak off the grill and went inside. A few feet away from the table he stopped, his eyes glued to the fake marble candleholder.

"Wow," he reacted, recognizing the object, "you still have that?" The candleholder was quite old and chipped in a couple of places. The white color of its marble-like finish had stained with yellow here and there, and the base of it was cracked, but still holding. Yet that single object carried so many memories, the essence of who they were, and who they had been.

She lit the green candle, then admired the setting with a smile. "Yeah, you know me, I never throw anything out, right?"

He sat at the table, staring into the candlelight, mesmerized, while she cut the steak and served the potatoes. That tiny flame, burning brightly at the end of the fragile candlestick, reminded him of her strength, her resilience, her wonderful love for him.

They were about twenty years old when that candleholder came into their lives. He didn't remember exactly what month it was, or if he'd already turned twenty or not, but it didn't really matter. They'd recently moved in together in a small rental apartment, sick and tired of Taylor's mother, Sara, butting in all the time, unrelentingly critical of her daughter's taste in men. Her daughter could have done much better in her uncensored opinion; she could have been with a wealthy man instead. Not that there were any wealthy men readily available for Taylor to choose from in Coalinga, but Sara didn't care. She still believed Taylor wasted herself on Dylan, threw her life away. Consequently, she hated Dylan, and didn't pass on a single opportunity to express her honest thoughts.

Frustrated with her mother, Taylor had encouraged Dylan to get a place of their own and move in together, and he'd been deliriously happy for a while. He didn't make much money in the oil fields, because he wasn't qualified for any work other than basic labor, but he didn't hesitate. He signed a lease, then struggled badly to put up the cash needed to secure the place and cover the deposit, first month's rent, and all the utility deposits he didn't know he was going to have to pay.

A month and a half into their new residence, they still struggled to make ends meet, and they'd fallen behind on a few bills. He worked twelve-hour days, but the pay was low, and they didn't start with anything.

He'd come home late that evening, tired to the bone, feeling his way in the dark to the apartment door, and mumbling cusses under his breath because even the porchlight had gone out. He pulled out his key and didn't get it into the lock on the first attempt, but, before trying again, Taylor had opened the door for him and grabbed his hand, leading him inside.

Everything was completely dark, except for one bright candlelight, sending shadows and glows into the entire room. It was a big pillar candle, green, with a faint scent of pine, he recalled, smiling, a little confused. As he reached for the light switch, Taylor had grabbed his other hand quickly and took a finger to her lips.

"Shh... don't say a word," she whispered. "Don't do anything."

Then she led him to a blanket she'd laid on the carpet and slowly took her clothes off, under his burning gaze. The candlelight made her skin glow, as if she were a supernatural being, a goddess descended on earth only for him.

Then she approached him and started to undress him, taking her time. Feeling an urgency like he'd never felt before, he tugged at his shirt, eager to unbutton it, then gave it up and tried to pull it off over his head. She grabbed his hands, again forcing him to take it slow, and he obeyed, hypnotized by the way her blue eyes reflected the candle's vivid flame, fascinated by her smile.

When she finally finished undressing him, she looked at him from head to toe, biting her lower lip, still smiling. Then she lay down on the blanket and crossed her arms under her head, ready for him.

He remembered the way they made love that night, forgetting everything, lost in each other for hours, whispering each other's name. That candle had burned faithfully the whole time, bringing warmth and a soft glow to the room where they found togetherness like never before.

Hours later, he didn't recall how many, he made an effort to pull himself out of her embrace. It was getting late; he'd lost track of time, and soon he'd have to wake again for another work day in the oil fields. He started getting up, regretfully untangling himself from her embrace, but she was quicker than he was, and sat up next to him, holding his hand.

"Um, there's something I need to tell you," she whispered, and her smile was gone, replaced with a half wince, a grimace of guilt and sorrow.

He remembered how he'd panicked that instant, thinking she might've been pregnant. They were in no condition to start a family, not when they couldn't afford to pay their bills for just the two of them. He held his breath, but managed to respond encouragingly.

"What's wrong?"

"There's no power. The bastards cut it off today; they said we didn't pay."

He recalled how he bit his lip, until he felt the taste on blood in his mouth, to control the tears that threatened his eyes. The candle, their lovemaking in the dark, the wonder of Taylor.

"I didn't want you to come home to a dark, despondent home, that's all," she whispered. "I hope it wasn't too bad."

He wrapped his arms around her and held her tight for endless time, rocking her gently, wondering what he'd done to deserve her. Twenty-two years later, she was still there by his side, still lighting candles in the same candleholder, and still he'd failed her all the way. Never gave her stability, a real home, a family. Never gave her children.

"Be here," she urged him, touching his arm, "be here with me. This steak is too good for you to let it get cold."

He laughed, a quick, quiet chuckle. "I was remembering that night," he said, gesturing toward the candleholder. "Where did it come from? I never knew."

"A garage sale down the street. Got it for five cents," she replied, then took a sip of beer.

"And the candle?"

"That I borrowed from a neighbor," she replied, blushing a little. "I had to tell them we had no power."

He chewed slowly, barely feeling the taste of his steak. The smell of cardboard filled his nostrils, threatening his appetite.

"So, you've had it all this time?" he asked, unaware he was frowning.

"Yeah," she replied, a little standoffish. "Don't tell me you're sorry I didn't throw it out."

"No, I'm not," he said, but his eyes turned toward the piles of cardboard boxes stacked up in the corners of the room. "I was wondering how we got from this," he pointed at the candleholder, "to that," he added, gesturing toward the pile of unopened boxes.

She leaned back, and a flicker of disappointment glinted in her eye.

"It's not so bad," she replied after finishing her food. "We have a good life."

"No, we don't," he reacted, and pushed his chair away from the table. "We're living paycheck to paycheck, barely getting by. We can't get ahead, and not for lack of trying."

She sighed and closed her eyes for a brief moment.

"We have a home, a roof over our heads. Many people don't even have that."

"Ha! Don't I know that," he replied, allowing the darkness back in. "For how long, huh? For how much longer will we have that home? One goddamned wrong step and we're done. You call this a good life?" he'd raised his voice in anger, and seeing the hurt in her eyes only made him angrier. He was a damn bastard, nothing short of that.

She watched him with sadness and a bit of frustration in her eyes, probably waiting for him to be over, to finish spilling his ire. Paradoxically, her supportive, patient attitude made him even angrier; letting her down fueled his exasperation, as if the gasoline of renewed failure were poured on top of his blazing self-resentment. He wanted her to yell at him, call him the names he deserved, pummel him down to the ground where he belonged. Instead, she looked at him with sadness in her eyes.

He stood and walked toward the pile of cardboard boxes and gave them a good, thorough look. Some of them he recognized; he'd moved them a few times, loaded and unloaded them on and off moving trucks in various zip codes. Others were new, and he wondered what on earth could she be keeping in there, so precious, so valuable she wouldn't let go, move after excruciating move? He'd tried to open a box before, but she'd turned angry all of a sudden, screaming and yelling at him, and he'd given up knowing, seeing how much it upset her.

"You make it so damn hard for us to move," he eventually said, anguish tinting his voice, "to stay nimble, to survive."

"So, what, now it's my fault?" she reacted with a wry laugh and an undertone of animosity, like she always did when he threatened her precious boxed possessions. "It wouldn't hurt if you managed to keep a job for a while longer, you know. Wouldn't hurt if you left your damn past behind. We're here…

we're alive, for goodness' sake. Tell me, is there a single good thing in your life?"

He stood, grimly leaning against the wall next to the pile of cardboard boxes, unable to answer.

"Can you think of one? One good thing you have in this life?"

He frowned, unable to speak, feeling his clenched jaws resisting his will.

Under his disheartened gaze, she burst into tears and rushed out of the room.

"You," he whispered, long after the bedroom door had slammed shut.

# 24

# A Decision

Dylan let himself slide to the floor, right next to those damned cardboard boxes, and leaned his temple against the wall. He stared at the candlelight, hating how the candle grew smaller, threatening with the onset of darkness. He listened intently, but couldn't hear a sound coming from the bedroom. He wanted to rush in there and beg Taylor for forgiveness, but he sat on the floor, paralyzed, knowing she'd forgive him only to be disappointed again, and then again.

Guided by candlelit memories, he realized he was the only one who had changed through the years; she hadn't. She'd stayed the same devoted, loving woman, the same wonderful girl he'd fallen in love with. The same woman he'd married almost twenty years ago.

He closed his eyes and invited the cherished memories to invade; he didn't have to wait too long. Soon enough, carried away by the past, he could smell the oil in the dry desert heat, mixed with the stench of sweat and the funky odor of heavy-duty hydraulic lubricants.

He and Nickel had been working in the oil fields for four years, and Nickel had just celebrated his twenty-second birthday, a celebration with little fuss, because he was still single and poured his entire paycheck into the family home. His father's pension wasn't enough to keep the property going, and Nickel didn't turn a blind eye, even if he'd moved out of his family home.

Coalinga offered few options of gainful employment; the town's official profile listed agriculture, oil, and incarceration as the main industries, and, of course, there was always the hospital. Out of all choices presented, both boys agreed the oil fields held the most promise in terms of higher pay. After giving the fields four years of their lives, they had little to show for it, other than sunburned skin, calloused hands, and low paychecks.

They worked hard and bore the roughneck nickname proudly, although during weekend beer talks, both agreed they would've wanted to do something else with their lives. Becoming a driller seemed a worthy goal, only it didn't touch their hearts nor occupy their minds. Yet, unable to find viable alternatives, both young men carried on, day after long, scorching day in a mind-numbing routine of hard labor.

DJ and Nickel always hung together over lunch, finding a place in the shade somewhere and sharing their meals. Taylor packed twice the food, knowing that Nickel was a slow riser, always running late for work in the mornings, almost never packing his own lunch. That mid-September day was no exception; Nickel had jumped out of bed, only when DJ had honked for the third time, and he'd barely had time to put on his coverall and grab his boots on his way out.

A cool breeze blew that day, a breath of fresh air they both welcomed, as they sat behind the tool shed, wiping their hands against the worn, stained fabric of their pants, and the sweat off their brows with their sleeves. They chewed and talked at the same time, and soon enough Nickel noticed something was different about Dylan.

"That grin on your face, DJ, that ain't coming off, is it?"

Dylan's grin widened, but he didn't say a word.

Nickel punched him in the shoulder jokingly. "Spill it, brother."

"Nah... it's nothing," Dylan replied, but still smiled, staring at the distant fields, where pumpjacks seesawed up and down, incessantly, busy insects against a backdrop of brown, scorched earth.

Another punch, a little bit stronger. "Spill. Now."

"It's Taylor. She, um, proposed to me last night."

"Whoa... what?" Nickel jumped to his feet. "You're one lucky son of a... chicken! Getting a girl so tired of waiting, she had to propose to you. Jeez... How the hell did you get so lucky, huh?"

Dylan's smile vanished, and his stare moved from the horizon line down to the ground under his boots.

"We have no future," he mumbled, squeezing the sandwich wrapper into a ball and throwing it into the trash can. "I can't say yes."

"Pfft..." Nickel reacted. "Double chicken. Let me spell it out for you. First, you didn't propose to your girl for so long, she had to grow a pair in your stead and ask you herself. Then, you're about to say no? You're never going to forgive yourself for breaking that girl's heart. Tell me, did she propose with a ring and all?"

Dylan still stared at his boots, but that earlier, persisting grin had returned in some measure. "No, it wasn't like that. I'll... do it, the ring piece, if it comes to that."

"If, you double-chicken sandwich? If? Are you kidding me? Girls like Taylor, they don't happen twice in a lifetime. For some guys, they don't happen, period. Look at me. Don't throw your life away."

Dylan stood and looked around him, as if seeing the oil fields for the first time. "Do you like this? Working here, in these fields?"

"What, you crazy, or something? Of course, I don't," Nickel replied, frowning.

"I can't do this for the rest of my life, I just can't. This isn't the life she deserves, stuck here, in the middle of nowhere, in the town with no name."

"What are you saying?"

"I'm going to enlist," he blurted, after a short hesitation, knowing how his friend would react. "Then I'll have money for college, and a chance to be somebody, to get us out of here."

"Yeah?" Nickel snapped, stomping the ground a couple of times angrily. Then he grabbed his hard hat and threw it out as far as he could. "Then what the fuck will I do, huh? What happened to brothers for life? What happened to this?"

He shoved his hand in his pocket, then took out a white river pebble, showing it to Dylan. His scrunched face trembled in anger, and his eyes drilled holes in Dylan's.

"You still have it," Dylan said quietly, then reached inside his jeans pocket and pulled out his own pebble. "So do I."

Nickel grabbed DJ's elbow tightly, and Dylan grabbed Nickel's forearm, in a strong, brotherly handshake that extended to their entire beings.

"Brothers forever," DJ said.

"Brothers forever," Nickel repeated, then patted DJ on the back, twice, as he cleared his throat.

"Then come with me, Nickel. Let's join the Marines together. Let's see the world."

"What about Taylor?"

"I think she'll wait for me... No, I *know* she will. There's no other way, there's no future here."

Nickel scratched his head for a long, silent minute, then started unzipping his coverall. "Ah, to hell with this shit. Let's put these babies to some real work," he added, flexing his biceps.

"What, now? Really?" DJ danced around Nickel, stomping his feet in the dust, as if he were one of those old-day shamans celebrating rainfall after drought.

The return-to-work horn sounded in the distance. The young men looked at each other, then Nickel grabbed his yellow hard hat from where it had landed earlier and walked toward the field office. "No time like the present time, Deej. Are we doing this or not?"

"Hell, yeah!" Dylan replied, catching up with him.

On their way out, they stopped by the office to drop off their hard hats and talk to their boss. The balding, potbellied man gave them a disgusted look.

"Where do you schmucks think you're going mid-shift?"

"We're enlisting today," Dylan replied. "We're joining the Marine Corps."

The man's expression changed, as he stood and shook their hands. "Oorah, boys. Make me proud."

Taylor wasn't too happy to hear they'd enlisted, without even asking her. With misted eyes she said she understood, and only had one condition.

They got married the weekend before the two young men had to report to Marine Corps boot camp. All through the wedding, Dylan's chest swelled every time he looked at Taylor's beautiful face, happiness exuding through every pore of his body. He had to make an effort to stay serious during the service, and not grin ear to ear, or dance in circles around his dazzling bride.

Taylor's mother didn't show, and didn't support her daughter's decision to marry "the broke roughneck on his way to becoming a meaningless grunt." In a rarely seen act of protective defiance, Dylan's mother somehow managed to raise the money and bought Taylor a beautiful dress, catalog-ordered from Los Angeles. As for Nickel, he beamed as best man, doing his duty with the utmost solemnity, and doing justice to his father's old tuxedo.

Even Lois had a role in the event, although she had to wait outside until the church service was over. Later, after they'd all gathered in Nickel's backyard for the wedding party, Lois followed DJ everywhere, and she had a central spot in most of the family pictures. Toward the end of the shooting session with countless family photos, Dylan arranged with the photographer to take a few shots of Lois. The best one, a black-and-white portrait of Lois sitting, looking straight into the camera, he had ordered a print in a 2 by 3-inch size, small enough to fit his wallet.

That photo had never left his wallet since. On the opposite pocket, he carried another cherished keepsake, a photo of him and Taylor at their wedding, both mementos of the happiest day of his life, both milestone markers of the moment his life had started to change.

# 25

# Bread Crumbs

Angela had cleared her Wednesday afternoons, allowing herself the time she needed to prepare for DJ's sessions. As such, she had the entire afternoon to think of the best way to reach him. It was the end of July, November was approaching fast, yet the only real progress she'd made was by accident, when she'd stumbled upon Lois, the good-looking dog whose story was the first thing DJ had wanted to share.

Although getting her patient talkative would've normally been considered a major win, she wasn't so sure with DJ. His apparently calm resolve seemed unshaken, and the real, emotional-rather-than-rational reason behind his decision seemed just as elusive as it had been the first time she'd met him.

There was another breadcrumb trail she could hope to explore, and that was his military service background. He hadn't said a word about it yet, and she was hesitant to push in that direction, being how he only recently opened up enough to share details about himself, the things he cared about, his childhood.

After thoroughly considering pros and cons, she decided to give him some more time, in the hope he'd bring it up himself; a week or two, not more. Three months had passed, out of the six he'd initially mentioned, and whenever she thought of time running out, she felt waves of panic and anxiety. What if she couldn't stop him? What if he was going to die?

Her father had repeatedly reminded her that no physician can aim to save every single one of their patients; sometimes the unavoidable happens, despite all the efforts, all the fervent determination to alter the unfavorable outcome. Yet that wasn't good enough, and she didn't care whether DJ's death would be statistically or professionally acceptable.

She just wanted him to live. She *needed* him to live.

She felt as if she'd known him for a long time, although she didn't know that much *about* him. He felt familiar somehow, and that familiarity she had difficulties placing or explaining. He looked nothing like Michael, so that couldn't have been it. She was sure they'd never met before, but she felt as if saving his life was the most important thing she could do, not only for him, but for herself at the same time.

The intercom buzzed, and she glanced quickly at the digital wall clock. Six p.m. sharp, and DJ was on time. She opened the door and greeted him as usual, showing no hint of her own turmoil, then took her seat and crossed her legs, ready to listen and identify any useful bit of information he might divulge. Hints and glimpses into his adaptive defenses, ego strength issues, potential repressed memories of significant trauma. Anything that could help.

She waited for him to speak, but other than a quick nod, in place of hello, he said nothing. He'd taken his usual spot and seemed unnervingly calm. She took a quick, sharp breath, and went for the core issue, the precise point where he'd blocked her the last time.

"So, tell me, how did Lois die?"

This time he didn't flinch. "Old age, I guess."

"You guess?" she asked gently.

He averted his eyes, focusing on the wall in front of him. His shoulders hunched forward a bit more, and he clasped his hands in his lap. "I wasn't there... I was overseas, deployed."

She saw tension take over his body, transforming him under her observant gaze. His knuckles turned white, and she thought she heard his joints crack. His jaw tensed, and muscles danced in tight knots on his face, his neck, his arms. Then he turned farther away from her, hiding his face almost completely, and squeezed his eyes shut. His lips, pressed tightly together, didn't let a single sound escape. Yet he was reliving something, a memory so terrible that his entire body reeled from reliving it in silent screams of pain, right under her eyes.

She waited patiently for a few moments, but then asked gently, "Have you thought of getting another dog?"

He reacted as if he'd awaken from a deep sleep, raided by nightmares, and crossed his arms before speaking.

"Taylor, she, um, she's not that much into dogs. It would make it hard for her, for us. We're at work most of the day." He chuckled bitterly. "Have you tried renting a place in San Francisco with a dog? You can forget about it."

"I see," she replied. "Let's talk about Taylor, then."

"Let's not."

"I think we should. She's at the center of your universe, from what I can tell. She's the reason we're doing all this." It was interesting she had to plead the same argument every time she wanted him to talk about his wife.

He nodded, still partially turned away from her. "What do you want to know?"

"You told me she likes to exercise, to stay fit. She works, she has a job. What else does she do? What does she like?"

He bit his lip before speaking, hesitant, still unwilling to open up.

"She likes her stuff," he eventually said. "She collects things."

"What kind of things?"

He shrugged and scoffed, visibly displeased. "All kinds of things. She says she wants to be ready for any circumstance that life could throw at us."

"That's laudable, isn't it?"

"I guess her intentions are good, but we've been hauling a pile of her shit around with us. It makes it difficult, but not for her. She'd never throw anything out."

Dr. Blackwell frowned a little. "Not anything?"

"She'll throw household trash and all that, but she'll keep anything else, like old clothes, magazines, things we don't use anymore."

"Ah, I see," she replied.

"I never understood why she does that. We need to move quickly, to stay lean, nimble, not weighed down by all the old phones we've ever had, or whatever the hell's in those boxes. I guess she's a packrat."

"Maybe she's nesting," Angela offered. Seeing his confused stare, she explained. "Women have the instinct to nest, to arrange their homes and make them comfortable and plentiful. You've moved around a lot, so she wasn't able to do that. Maybe she's preparing herself for that moment, compensating somehow."

"It'll come soon enough. After November, she'll do whatever she wants, wherever she wants to do it. She won't have to worry anymore."

"Have you thought that maybe she's trying to weigh you down?"

"What do you mean?"

"You said you moved a lot. Sometimes, our subconscious minds make us do things we don't understand. Maybe deep down inside she wants to set roots somewhere, have a more stable livelihood. What do you do with something that's adrift? You anchor it down, weight it in place."

He looked at her with raised eyebrows and ran his hand through his buzz-cut hair a couple of times. "Really, Doc? How about my theory, care to hear that?"

"Sure, I do. Tell me."

"What if I failed so miserably to provide the financial safety of our family that she feels compelled to collect this junk, out of fear she'll need things and she won't be able to afford them? What if I made her walk the edge for so long that she can't envision a normal life anymore, when she'd be able to buy whatever she needs?"

"It's possible," she agreed gently, "but I feel you're quick to assign that blame to yourself. Did you do these things on purpose?"

"No," he mumbled, barely audible, staring at the floor.

"You did the best you could, didn't you?" she asked, matching the low pitch of his voice, but loading the question with empathy, with kindness.

"The best I could wasn't good enough, Doc. Let's leave it at that."

Silence took over the office for a while.

"Does Taylor want children?" she eventually asked.

He glared at her for a split second, then resumed staring at the carpet. "Another failure on my part, right?"

"I didn't say that," she replied.

"No, *I* did." He stood and started pacing the floor, as he normally did when she touched a nerve, his preferred form of acute stress response. Most likely he preferred to be anywhere else but there, in her office. "What would you have done, in my place? Bring another innocent being into this world, to a family that can't make ends meet, fathered by a man who can't provide steadily for his family? Do you realize we live in an unsafe environment that I've created? What would you have done?"

"It's not about me, DJ, it's about you. Are you happy with your decision to not have children?"

He went to the window again, hiding his face, intently looking outside at the gentle light of summer dusk.

"It's a necessity, nothing else. I can't be sure my family will survive; why make it worse?" He cleared his throat quietly. "I'm actually sure it won't, not as a family. Taylor will survive, and she'll have the life she deserves."

"Is that what she wants?"

He let a wry laugh escape his tense lips. "Probably not, but it's what she needs."

"Tell me, do you believe things happen for a reason?" she asked, hoping to steer him clear of the dark cloud that hovered around him.

"You're funny, Doc," he reacted. "You of all people should know better. No, we're just insects caught in a dance of random, uncorrelated events that play tricks on people and their lives."

"That must feel quite lonely, thinking like that."

"Lonely or not, I'm done lying to myself."

"How's that?"

He didn't speak for a while. He dug the two pebbles out from his pocket, and held them in a tight fist at his chest for a while. Then he started rubbing the two stones against each other, making that subdued clicking sound she'd become familiar with.

"Back in Indiana, there was an ant colony dangerously close to the house. Busy, hard-working little guys, those ants. I decided to deal away with them; I didn't want to foot the cost of an exterminator, in case the ants got to the house eventually. So, one day, I poured hot water mixed with orange oil on top of the ant hill, and they were gone. To them, what happened can be described as a natural disaster, an extinction-level event. Most of the ants died; only a few remained and those scattered, never came back. What took me minutes to achieve on a Sunday evening caused the deaths of thousands, a civilization destroyed within seconds. So, now, you tell me, Doc, do things happen for a reason?"

The dark cloud had grown denser, engulfing him altogether.

"Who cares about the fate of a single ant in that colony, when no one cares about the thousands that have perished?" he asked, still looking outside and talking calmly, almost like in a trance.

"It's not the same thing—"

"It's precisely the same thing. Stop trying to save me, Doc. I'm beyond that; I'm already dead. I'm only going through that instant of time between the extinction-level event and the actual onset of death. It's already happened; it's irreversible."

He turned and walked out of her office with another quick nod in lieu of goodbye, still holding the two pebbles in his hand. It was precisely three minutes to seven; their time was up.

She let a long sigh out of her chest, as soon as the door closed behind him. Then she stood and went to the window, looking for him.

He walked briskly toward his car and drove away immediately. This time, he didn't spend time in his car, thinking, reliving who knows what nightmare. Just as his resolve, his calm had deepened.

She was running out of time.

She stood there, at the window, frozen, watching the early evening fog roll in, wads of turbulent cotton bringing salty, gray mist from the sea. Unstoppable, unescapable. She covered her mouth with her hand, as if to repress a wail, then rubbed her forehead for a while, thinking hard, desperate for a solution.

She had an idea, but would it work? Or did she risk pushing an already fragile, unstable man over the edge? It wasn't even a fully fleshed plan yet; it was only a heading, like knowing she needed to drive south to leave the city. Yet she didn't have anything else other than time, running out faster than she could afford. That day, more clearly than in any other day before it, she realized she was going to lose DJ.

She took out her phone and browsed through her list of contacts, then chose one. First, she sent Lois's photo by text message, then dialed the number.

A man picked up in a hoarse voice filled with a big smile.

"Dr. Blackwell, what a nice surprise," the man said.

"Hello, Barney, how are you?"

"Doing good, can't complain," he replied. "It's great to hear from you. I was talking about you the other day. I never got to thank you, for everything you've done for me."

"You're welcome, Barney, glad I could help."

"I see you sent me a picture," he said, "that's a beautiful dog."

"What kind of dog is that, Barney? Do you know?"

"Of course, I do. I work with dogs, remember? Cats too. It's a German Shepherd, and a beautiful one. See those ears, how perky they are? And the demeanor, the strength he projects?"

"She."

"My bad," Barney said quickly. "Sometimes you can't tell. Fine dog, pure-breed German Shepherd."

"I don't know much about dogs, Barney. What kind of dog is that? Is it good for a boy growing up?"

"I can't think of any better choice. Protective but gentle, a great play buddy and a fine companion. Great energy. That dog would die before anyone harms that kid. Needs a firm hand though. He, um, *she* needs to know who's boss."

"Good to know, Barney, thank you very much."

She hung up after inviting Barney to come by some time, to catch up and have a cup of coffee together. Then she went back to her new chair and sat, folding her legs under her body, and swiveled around so she could watch the fog through the window, the flushed hues of late dusk as they lost color and changed to grays. She was in no hurry to get home, where nothing but silence awaited.

# 26

# A Cup of Soup

Angela savored a spoonful of soup, then admired the golden color of the dense liquid. Exquisite. She looked at her father, seated across from her at the table, and noticed the satisfied smile on his lips.

"Wow, this is fantastic. How come you cooked? You never do."

"I felt like I was coming down with a cold, and I panicked; I made myself a lot of chicken soup. Now I need you to help me work through it," he chuckled.

"Gladly. Aren't you having any?"

"Already did," he replied, rubbing his stomach in circular moves, accompanied by a satiated sigh.

"For dinner?"

"And lunch too."

"I don't blame you. Did you put sour cream in it? I also smell some garlic."

"Yes, the works. I sprinkled some feta cheese crumbles in there, and some fresh parsley."

"Great, thousands of calories in a bowl of dinner soup. Thanks, Dad." Angela laughed, then took another spoonful and savored it with eyes half-closed. "I needed this."

"Anything wrong?" Dr. Foster frowned a little, and his ruffled eyebrows arched with concern.

"No," she replied, "it's this fog. Dense and cold, gets to my bones. I didn't want to go home yet."

He reached out and grabbed her hand. "You know you could stay here, Ang. For as long as you'd like. It must be hard for you, living alone in that big house. Think about it, will you? No pressure, just an offer."

She nodded and sipped the last of the remaining soup, down to the last drop. Then she pushed the bowl aside and leaned back in her chair.

"Why did you turn to addiction psychiatry as your specialty?" she asked. "I don't think you ever told me."

"Because all these people, my patients, and addicts in general, they turn to drugs in search for pain relief. Their lives can't be just about the chemicals in their brains; it would be such a waste. Of spirit, of individuality, of sentiment and meaning. There has to be more, and there is. I like to believe that helping them find that 'more' in their lives is a worthy goal."

She laughed quietly and looked away from her father's perceptive eyes.

"It's strange," she said, "how you and I believe in the same core values, yet chose such different paths."

"Yes, you surprised me when you became a board-certified psychiatrist, only to throw away your prescription pad and favor psychotherapy all the way. I was proud, but surprised."

"I believed, and still do, that people shouldn't resort to chemicals to find happiness and meaning in life. That should come from deep within themselves, not from the Rx counter."

"Yet sometimes drugs help. Take your mystery patient, for example. Don't you think an SSRI could attenuate his suicidal tendencies? Don't you feel temped to write that script, if only to buy yourself more time to help him?"

"He wouldn't take anything, anyway. But no, the thought hasn't even crossed my mind."

"No?"

"His issues aren't chemical in nature. Unlike your patients, Dad, this man endured his pain without seeking relief. He's punished himself with it and continues to do so. For some elusive reason, he strongly believes he deserves to die. To reduce his case to the conclusion that his serotonin and dopamine levels are low, therefore he's depressed, would be superficial, to say the least."

A long moment of silence engulfed the room, making the tick-tock of the grandfather clock sound ominous. Time was running out, second by second.

"How is he, by the way?" Dr. Foster asked. His voice reflected the concern written in his eyes.

"He won't let me get close. The moment I believe I found a path, he withdraws."

"He's former military, you said?"

"He mentioned being deployed overseas only this last session. But that was it, a single word, 'deployed.' No idea where, when, for how long, or what happened to him over there. I don't even know his name, still."

"Your suspicion of posttraumatic stress is confirmed?"

"There are symptoms, but he won't discuss them. There has to be something; his reactions are altered and his coping mechanisms are... uncharacteristic. He has these pebbles he keeps playing with, whenever he's interiorizing or reliving past events. When he touches them, he seems transported to another world, probably in the realm of his trauma."

He listened without saying a word. She lowered her head into her hands for a moment, feeling her frustration rise to the surface.

"It's heartbreaking, you know, seeing this healthy, intelligent, strong man believe he doesn't deserve to live anymore. It's... unspeakable."

"He's not your first suicidal patient, is he? I remember you had others."

She raised her head from the comfort of her hands and searched his eyes.

She found support and understanding, empathy and warmth. "He's different. Out of all my suicidal patients, and there have been a few, this man is the first one I really fear I could lose, any moment now." She felt choked and cleared her throat quietly. "I can't let that happen, Dad. Just can't."

He squeezed her hand, and she relished the warm feeling of his strong grip. "You won't."

She shook her head a couple of times, keeping her head lowered and her face hidden by her long, curly hair. "There's no guarantee, none." She stared at their hands, her father's hand still gripping hers, and didn't say anything for a while. Then she recalled something, and stood up forcefully, almost yanking her hand out of his.

"Did you see the news yesterday? This goddamned city 'solved' the suicide problem at the Golden Gate Bridge," she almost shouted, making air quotes with her fingers and loading the word "solved" with all the sarcasm she could express. "They're installing a net, to catch those who want to jump to their deaths."

"No, I haven't heard," he replied. "I've been hearing rumblings about it in recent years, but I don't recall reading anything specific."

She paced the room angrily, then stopped in front of Dr. Foster with her hands propped on her hips.

"They call it a 'suicide deterrent system,' and it's supposed to be made of stainless steel mesh." She scoffed, filled with indignation. "First, it doesn't deter anything. People will kill themselves elsewhere, find another way. They've pledged some seventy-five million dollars to get it built. If they invested half of that in helping people, it would have meant something. It would've made a difference."

"And second?" he asked.

She frowned for a second, trying to remember what she'd wanted to say.

"Do you remember that article, a few years back, about the suicides at a Chinese manufacturing plant? It, too, installed netting to catch the poor people who couldn't handle their despair anymore. We were so critical of the Chinese for doing that; we called their factories 'sweatshops' and their practices 'inhuman,' from the heights of our hypocritical indignation. But now we're exactly like those Chinese, not an inch better. We do nothing to understand or ease the pain of these people, nothing but chain and enslave them, and make sure they have no way out. No one ever asks the right questions in these articles; no one ever asks why."

"Seems to me this is something you're passionate about," Dr. Foster replied. "You could become involved in raising people's awareness for mental health—"

"Ah, screw mental health for a minute, Dad, I'm talking about survival. What's a person supposed to do when he can't feed his family? We keep saying it's depression, but that empowers our society to blame it all on the individual, while failing to address the root cause. There are economic factors and societal and cultural issues that can't be ignored. That *shouldn't* be ignored."

"I agree," Dr. Foster replied. "And yet, as you well know, there's the individual's ability to cope and survive, to find new ways to adapt and thrive, and such abilities are hindered by a history of trauma and depression."

She lowered her head again and crossed her arms at her chest, still standing in front of Dr. Foster, only 3 feet away.

"Ang," he said, "don't—"

"What if there was a way I could save him?"

He raised his eyebrows, seemingly surprised.

"What do you mean? A new approach in his therapy?"

"No... action. I would have to get involved."

"Like an intervention?" he asked, deepening his frown. "Would you break any boundaries?"

"A few," she admitted.

"You could lose your license, Ang. Are you sure that—"

"He's not really my patient. Technically, I'm not his therapist. I never charged him a dime."

"Never?"

"Nope," she stated firmly. "He donates my fee to charity each week and brings me the receipt."

"Smart girl, I guess," he replied frowning, "although it makes me wonder why that happened in the first place. Did you see this coming?"

"Can't say that I did," she whispered. "Back then, I didn't feel comfortable charging someone who didn't want to be treated, that's all."

He scratched his beard, deep in thought. "If no money changed hands, and if no one ever sues you, you'll get to keep your career. But that's thin ice, Ang. Be careful, and only push that limit if you absolutely feel you must."

"I have to try. I'm running out of time."

# 27

# Referee

Dylan stood at the lane six starting block with a stopwatch in his hand, squinting in the morning sun and trying to focus on what he was doing. He'd given in to Taylor's persuasion and joined her for an inter-college swim event, and she'd coopted him as an impromptu referee, one who didn't really know what he was doing. His job was easy enough though; all he had to do was start the stopwatch the moment the swimmers were given the start, and stop it the moment the swimmer on lane six returned and hit the wall. He was backup, only in case the pool's electronic systems would fail.

A new group of swimmers approached the block starts and he took a couple of steps back, allowing them room to take their positions. His eyes wandered, searching for Taylor, but she was nowhere in sight. She was also competing that morning, and cheering for her was the real reason he was there, away from the semidarkness and relative silence of his home.

Outside the pool's wrought-iron fence, a man walked his dog at a brisk pace, and the animal rarely stopped to sniff anything. It was a large dog with pointy ears and proud gait; it reminded him of Lois. Had anyone taken her for walks after he'd deployed?

He heard the whistle and started the stopwatch, but his eyes remained focused on the man and his dog, about to disappear in the distance. The sound of the swimmers splashing in the pool and the cheering of the crowd melded and became a vivid memory. The incessant banter between Navajo and Texas, both picking at each other, making jokes, howling and whooping. Nickel's quiet conversation with Terrell, who knows about what. His own hands, ripping open the envelope of a letter from Taylor, under the barrage of wolf whistles and lewd comments from Griffin.

Then the call to "deploy in fifteen," and how they all scrambled to gear up and get ready for the unexpected mission, triggered by the sighting of a top ten, most-wanted terrorist in a nearby village. He saw himself putting on his flak jacket and checking all pockets for ammo mags and the first-aid kit. Tightening his knee and elbow pads. Putting on his helmet and adjusting the chin strap.

Checking his night vision gear, and putting on ballistic goggles. Grabbing his M40, then trotting to the Humvee, the engine already running.

He saw Terrell climb in the back, next to Navajo, and, on the other side, Texas hopped in. He took the front passenger seat and shouted, "Go, go," to catch up with the other Humvees, already stirring up clouds of dust in the early evening sun. The driver floored it, and the vehicle set in motion abruptly, throwing rocks and dust behind, bouncing badly on the uneven surface.

Then Navajo's voice, "Heard this one? Goes like this: Marines are better, just ask the sailor's wife," and then the ensuing roar of laughter. The driver's face, covered in dust and grime, his white teeth sparkling when he laughed at Navajo's old jokes. His gloved hands, gripping the wheel, and his eyes fixed on the road ahead. Who was it? Who was driving the Humvee? He had something important to do... he had to reach and grab that man's sleeve, make him turn around so he could remember. He had something important to say. *Shut up, Navajo, for once. Shut the fuck up.*

A splash of water landed on his feet as his swimmer approached the finish. Still confused for a split moment, he managed to kill the stopwatch in time, but the tension on his face still lingered.

"What, man? What's wrong?" the swimmer asked, panting from the intense effort.

Dylan didn't reply; he walked away from there, looking everywhere for Taylor. How long was this thing going to take?

Then he saw her, svelte and wet and breathtaking in a black swimsuit with a design of curvy lines that swirled around her waist, surrounded by men in Speedos standing way too close to her, smiling, chatting.

Why was she doing that to him?

He looked around and saw half the men there were ogling her, even some of the women. Did she like flaunting her stuff in public like that, half-naked? Was that what her passion for the gym was about? He clenched his fists and started to walk toward two bystanders with cameras, two jerkoffs who laughed and made obscene gestures toward the swimmers, toward Taylor.

A short whistle, then the announcer's voice, via the PA system, "Referees, take your stations."

He frowned, but didn't slow his stride. Then Taylor looked for him and, when she locked her eyes with his, she beckoned him over.

"Dylan, meet Gary and Maxwell. These guys won the fifty-yard competitions for freestyle and butterfly, respectively. Maxwell's time is within the national time standards."

He shook their hands, and the two young men held his gaze with honest, friendly looks.

"Two more races, and it's my turn," she said, grabbing his arm tightly and leaning into him.

"Uh-huh," he replied, still itching to go teach those assholes a lesson. He searched for them in the crowd but they'd vanished.

"Take your place at the starting block, they're waiting for you," Taylor whispered, then let go of his arm, but reached up to give him a quick kiss. He leaned over and kissed her, feeling numb from having to put a lid on his suffocating anger, then walked back to the starting block and took his position on lane six.

A whistle and a splash of water sent droplets on his feet again, and he clicked the button.

# 28

# Once A Marine

Angela looked out the window, waiting for DJ's car to pull up. For a change, she felt more confident about her planned course of action, although she was going to ignore most of the rules of psychotherapy, and those rules had their value. Unfortunately, they didn't apply to patients who weren't really patients and didn't want to be treated, at least consciously. For those, the rules hadn't been written yet.

She frowned when the digital clock chimed discreetly, marking the hour. He was running late. Was he even coming? She breathed deeply, refusing to get pulled into a vortex of renewed anxiety. For her half-conceived plan to work, she needed to hold it together.

DJ's black sedan pulled to the curb at precisely 6:02 p.m. She pulled away from the window, making sure she couldn't be seen from below, and waited for the intercom to buzz. Moments later, DJ opened the door and nodded once, his typical greeting.

She smiled, as she usually did, and invited him in.

"Would you like some tea?"

"No, I'm good, thanks," he replied, then took his seat.

She made one for herself, and brought the cup to the coffee table in front of her chair.

"What's on your mind today?" she asked, stirring the hot liquid.

"Aren't you going to start the recording?"

"Oh, I almost forgot," she replied, then found the remote and clicked it. The red LED turned on, and DJ seemed relieved.

She looked at him, noticing differences from the previous week. He seemed calmer still, his hands steady and relaxed alongside his body. He leaned against the sofa a bit more, although not completely letting his spine relax. His eyes were focused, present, and there was less tension in his jaw. She decided to test a theory, a chilling assumption that it could have been the thought of his death that calmed him, that made him feel more relaxed than the thought of living ever did.

"So, tell me," she asked, looking at him intently, prepared to capture microexpressions, body posture changes, clues into his inmost thoughts. "How are you planning to take your life?"

Nothing. No tension, no recoil; he was just a bit surprised, that was all the reaction her blunt question had triggered. She had less time than she'd estimated.

"You know I can't share that with you, Doc. Was that a trick question?"

"Why do you feel you can't share that with me? This is a safe place; we can talk about anything in here."

A crooked grin appeared on his lips. "Yeah, right. I still remember what you said during our first conversation. You said, and I quote, 'If you pose a danger to yourself or others I'm obligated to engage the authorities.' Why would I tell you where to find me, if such a situation should occur?"

"Ah, I see," she said, making an effort to refrain from showing her frustration. "But you have given it some thought, haven't you?"

"Yes. It will be in a place where witnesses, maybe even video surveillance will attest that my wife wasn't anywhere close. It will be at a time when she will be surrounded by people who'll testify she was acting normally, like nothing was supposed to happen. Yes, I thought of it."

"You think that's all there is to it, making sure she was acting normally the day of? She'll never be the same again; you do realize that?"

A cloud darkened his eyes, and his eyelids dropped, heavy under the pressure of a furrowed brow.

"I meant I don't want any cops to give her grief. I want her to be happy, to have a chance at a happy life."

"Happy?" she scoffed, against all principles of therapy that demanded she showed a supportive, nonjudgmental attitude, no matter what words were spoken. "Let me tell you a few things about the suicide survivor's recovery."

He pressed his lips together, but nodded and looked her straight in the eye. "Go ahead."

"First, there's shock and denial. It can't happen, it couldn't have happened, they must be wrong. The cops must have him confused with someone else; someone must have stolen his wallet. Then there's the unanswered question of why. She won't understand why you chose to abandon her, why you chose to end your life instead of living with her."

"You'll be there for her; you'll explain."

She shook her head, but decided to ignore his comment.

"Then there's guilt," she continued. "She'll blame herself, for years. She'll relive every argument you two had, and think maybe it was because of something she said, or something she did. Maybe it was because of her, um, gym going, or the stuff she's collecting. Even if I explain your decision to her, she'll blame herself for not making more money, for not taking better care of you. For not being with you every minute of her life. Do you realize that?"

He nodded again, his eyes darker, but his calm unperturbed.

"Think carefully what she'll be doing while you take your own life, because that thing she'll be doing, she'll never be able to do again. Guilt and sorrow will keep her from enjoying the same things after you've gone. She'll feel inadequate, so inadequate she'll believe you preferred to kill yourself rather than share another day with her, which is what you're going to be doing. She'll hate herself, because of what you're going to do, and she'll be fierce hating herself, that self-loathing will poison all her thoughts and all her days."

"She'll have you, Doc. You're good," he stated calmly, as if commenting on a fact that was completely removed from his emotional being. "You're actually way better than I thought. She'll be in capable hands."

"Do you care if she'll forgive you?"

He turned his head away, and his shoulders hunched forward. He clasped his hands together, with fingers intertwined.

"I hope she'll be able to, eventually," he whispered, his voice choked and weak, as if all strength had left his body and all breath had deserted his lungs.

She held her breath, hoping he'd continue. Instead, he forced himself back into composure, into the appearance of serenity that fueled her concern. Minutes passed, and no other words came out of his mouth. Two deep tension lines formed at the root of his nose, and his jaws clenched, willing words to stay locked inside, unspoken.

"Tell me about your deployment," she changed direction abruptly, and thought she heard his breath catch.

"What about it?" he asked morosely.

"When did you enlist? How old were you?"

"Almost twenty-two."

"Why did you enlist?"

"We had no future, no money for college, just like the rest of the grunts."

"We?"

"Yeah... I dragged my best friend in it with me."

She gazed quickly at her notes. "Was that Nickel?"

"Yeah."

She noticed the darkness that came upon him abruptly. Until that moment, she'd seen a hint of it, the threat of a storm on a relatively calm day. Now, under her scrutiny, he descended into a blackness that touched his entire body. His pupils dilated and his eyes lost focus, staring into empty space. He lowered his head, letting it drop all the way down in a despondent bearing. He unclasped his hands, and while his left hand clutched into a white-knuckled fist, his right reached inside his pocket and retrieved two white river pebbles. The rhythmic sound of pebble against pebble returned.

"What branch of the military did you join?"

"The Marine Corps," he replied quietly, while his fingers caressed the two stones.

"Ah, so you're an ex-Marine," she said admiringly.

He scoffed quietly. "I'm a Marine, not an ex anything. First off, it's *former* Marine, if you feel the need to underline that I'm not in active service anymore. Second, once a Marine, always a Marine," he added, looking at her with steeled eyes.

"Oh, I apologize, I didn't know."

"Uh-huh," he replied, staring back into nothingness again. "Most people don't."

"How was boot camp?" she asked, quick to move on from the tension-filled issue.

"Okay, I guess."

"Were you and Nickel able to remain together? Were you deployed to the same, um, place?"

He sighed and slowly shook his head.

"I don't know what you want to hear, Doc. We were in boot camp, then we were deployed. Period. Nothing to tell."

"I can't believe nothing worth mentioning happened during all that time."

"Well, you better believe it," he snapped, and glared at her, but then quickly controlled himself and resumed his earlier posture.

She frowned and decided to insist, in a situation when she would've normally backed out, respecting her patient's reluctance to discuss the subject.

"Look, if you tell me a single story about your deployment, I won't ask again, not today."

"What, you think I'm some stupid kid you need to play games with? Dangle some candy in front of my eyes, so I climb quietly in the back of your van? Jeez!"

She lowered her head, embarrassed with herself. "I apologize, you're right, that wasn't appropriate. I only wish you'd share with me some of your experiences over there, what it was like, what Nickel and you did, your life after coming back home."

"That's all you want, huh?" His voice was heavy with sarcasm.

"I believe it would be beneficial. It would complete the picture of who you really are," she added, gesturing vaguely toward the camera.

"It wouldn't be that beneficial, but it would satisfy your morbid curiosity. It would give you the excuse to say, 'oh, he's just another troubled veteran.' It would provide you with a nice label to slap across my forehead and feel good about yourself."

"That's not it, DJ, you misunderstood. In psychology, we don't slap labels, as you called it. We work with people to help them understand more about themselves, on *their* terms."

"Then these are my terms: no war talk."

She didn't flinch under his dominating glare.

"I believe there are strong emotions buried inside you, and you'd—"

"Shut up already, Doc; you're driving me crazy!" he shouted, then stood and carefully put the pebbles back inside his pocket. "What do you want to hear, huh? That I got really good at killing people? Is that what you want to hear? Well, I did. I got really good at it, from a distance, and from up close, as close as it gets." He stared at his hands as if they were covered in blood, spreading his fingers, studying them on both sides with a fierce look in his eyes. "Anything else you want to know today?"

She didn't reply immediately, stunned by his violent outburst. "Um... I'm sorry if I—"

"Ah, save it, Doc," he said, then walked out of her office, leaving her speechless.

It might have been the wrong outcome of a session conducted with the wrong methods, but she'd uncovered a path inside the labyrinth that could help him find his way back from the abyss. Yet there was no way of knowing if she'd ever see him again.

# 29

# Enemy Unseen

Dylan was stuck in the notorious traffic jam that's a synonym to Highway 101, one of the major San Francisco Bay Area routes. Cars crawled hopelessly, going less than five miles an hour, reflecting the oblique afternoon sun still visible above the incoming fog bank. But fog wasn't there yet, and the rays of the sun, the deep blue color of the sky reminded him of another time, another place.

He recalled how his Marine Corps unit had crossed into the Zabul province of Afghanistan fifteen years ago, after a long, bone-rattling ride though most of Kandahar. They'd set camp at the edges of new Taliban territory, ready to engage in a series of combat missions to stop the expansion of the neo-Taliban insurgency, as history was about to name the spewing poison that came from the Pakistani border, hiding in caves and coming out to kill anyone in its path: Afghan or foreign, civilian, combat, or relief personnel. Men, women, and children equally, savagely killed in the dead of the night by cowards living under rocks during the day.

The unit had gathered in the compound in the early morning chill, fully equipped and pumped, eager to head out and weed out some Taliban. Waiting for their captain to give the orders, Dylan's eyes veered to the left. If he were only looking at that segment of landscape, at a few degrees out of the 360 that covered the entire horizon, the view would be almost idyllic. Flowering almond trees at the foot of a green hill. In the distance, the snow-covered peaks of the Spīn Ghar mountains, peaceful and majestic in the brisk morning light. How deceptive it was, as if someone had packaged a chunk of hell in a candy wrapper. A few miles in that same direction it was Taliban-ruled territory.

"Good morning, Marines," the captain shouted. He'd seen a lot of action; it was his second tour in the Afghan desert, and his confident demeanor showed it, gaining him instant respect.

"Oorah!" the men replied in unison.

"Today we make history," the captain said. "You better believe that. We're going to board the helos and drop behind Taliban lines, in the Torgan Valley. Our mission is to locate and destroy the enemy. We're going to disrupt the opium operations in the region and cut off the lifeline. We're going to clean the area thoroughly, just like your momma taught you to sweep the floors. Not a speck of dirt will be left when we evac out of there. We'll take the Taliban head-on and wipe them off the face of this earth."

"Oorah!" the Marines shouted, and the energy of their voices electrified the air.

"We're two hundred Marines strong, going after a few hundred Taliban. I say they ain't got a chance in hell to see the light of tomorrow."

"Oorah!"

The captain looked a few of them in the eye, then stopped in front of Dylan. "I'm looking forward to this fight. We're going to smoke them out of their caves, like the fucking rats they are. What do you say, Sergeant Ballard?"

"Oorah!" Dylan shouted, from the bottom of his lungs.

"Sergeant Ballard will be your sniper support lead for today. You're in luck, because this man can wipe the snot off your faces with a bullet from 1,000 yards and not leave a mark, while scratching his balls at the same time."

"Oorah!" they all shouted again, and Dylan felt a strong emotion swell his chest. His fellow Marines and his captain counted on him; he wasn't going to let anyone down.

"One last thing," the captain said, "I haven't lost any of my men in combat. I'm proud of my record; few officers can claim the same. Don't you fucking ruin that today. Wheels up in fifteen."

"Oorah," they chanted one more time.

They scattered to get their gear inspected one last time and board the helos. Dylan saw Master Gunnery Sergeant Corbin head toward one of the helos and ran to catch up.

"Master Guns, permission to assign two more sniper support units. One won't be enough," he shouted, trying to cover the sound of the accelerating helicopter rotors.

"Load the M40s and lots of ammo. Who do you want?"

"Nickel and Texas."

Corbin nodded and hopped on the helo, and Dylan gave the orders.

A few hours later, they took positions near the Dehe Dawlat village, at the base of a mountain, near a course of water. The proximity of the water source made farming possible for a stretch of a mile or so along that river. The first lines were fruit crops, but a few yards inland, poppies replaced the orchards, and opium replaced the pomegranates, apricots, and melons. Along that river, the lucrative opium trade flourished, providing the Taliban with financial resources to fund the spread of terror in the region. Weapons, explosives, people, their food, and medical supplies, all coming from opium, cultivated by farmers who couldn't oppose the Taliban if they wanted to live.

Dylan lay on the ground, his M40 sniper rifle set on its bipod, loaded and ready to fire. He adjusted the scope and searched for any sign of movement on the northeast versant of the mountain range, while his fellow Marines were approaching the cave entrance slowly, taking cover behind boulders.

About a hundred feet up on the versant there was a crease in the rocks, a shaded crevice, and Dylan thought he'd seen a wisp of smoke coming from there. He looked at that spot for a minute, and nothing moved. He checked the surroundings again, and everything was still, death-like, as only rocks could be.

His platoon approached the cave entrance quietly, one careful step after another. Terrell led the men, holding his M16 firmly in his hands, ready to open fire at the sight of the enemy.

There was no movement anywhere; the caves of the Afghan mountains were Taliban strongholds for a reason. Complex cave systems could run for miles in depth, with multiple entrances, veritable rat mazes that could be easily turned into death traps for anyone uninvited who accessed them.

Terrell was only a few yards away from the cave entrance when Dylan saw it again; the faintest puff of smoke or vapor, coming out of a crack in the rocks, about a hundred feet above the cave entrance.

"Alpha Team, this is Sierra One, over," he spoke into his radio, breaking the radio silence order. "Do you read?"

"Go for Alpha," he recognized Terrell's voice.

"I have smoke, thirty-two yards overhead. Fall back."

"Negative, Sierra One, we're proceeding," Terrell replied.

"Alpha, do not enter the cave. Acknowledge the order."

A second of silence, then Terrell's frustrated voice acknowledged.

"Stay put, Alpha. I might have a round for that sentry's ass."

Dylan focused his scope on the spot and waited, barely breathing, his finger on the trigger ready to fire. He didn't even blink, for what seemed to be endless minutes, afraid he'd miss the exact moment that wisp of smoke appeared again.

It was barely visible, so thin Dylan doubted it was there, but he fired the shot nevertheless. The bullet ripped through the air and hit the center of that crack in the rock where he'd seen the smoke come from. A second later, the lifeless body of a Taliban fell to the ground with a dull thump.

"Tango Mike, Sierra One, we're proceeding," he heard Terrell's voice on the radio thanking him.

"Negative, Alpha leader, stay put."

"Copy."

"Send someone with a thumper," Dylan said, referring to the M79 grenade launcher. "I'm willing to bet my dick this cave's a trap."

"Sierra One, this is Sierra Two. I got the thumper," the radio crackled.

Dylan recognized Nickel's voice and call sign. "Fire when ready, Sierra Two."

The grenade whooshed and entered the cave, then an explosion soon followed, spitting dust and rocks out through the cave entrance. A split second later, a second explosion, much bigger, shook the ground and collapsed the cave entrance. Big boulders detached from the mountain's versant, and Alpha Team took cover at the base of the mountain, then withdrew in a hurry the moment the ground stopped shaking.

Through his scope, Dylan only saw smoke and debris at the base of the mountain.

"Alpha Team, report," he called. "Alpha Team, do you read?"

"Alpha Team all accounted for," Terrell's panting voice came to life over the radio static. "Sierra One, we owe you a big, fat one. Orders?"

"Hold positions. Damn if I go home with only one small-time kill to show for it. They're here, somewhere, and they might think we're dead. Go quiet."

"Copy that, going quiet."

He waited with the endless patience only a good sniper develops, listening, watching, searching. The wind howled over the steep, rocky mountaintops, scattering the dust quickly, helping him see again all the details of the terrain at the base of the mountain. The cave entrance had collapsed, taking with it a portion of the versant, but most of the mountain had stayed in place. The apparent crease in the rock, the crevice where the Taliban lookout had been, was still there, but no sign of smoke or movement anywhere.

The chirping of the few birds slowly resumed; their voices and the sound of the wind were the only sounds he could hear for a while. He swept the base of the mountain looking through his tactical binoculars, regretting the brief separation from his rifle's scope, but favoring the higher magnification and the depth perception of the combat optics.

Nothing.

Not a move, not a sound out of place. Not a whiff of smoke, or a cloud of dust, no matter how small. He was about to give the order to move out, when a boulder seemed to shift, several yards behind Alpha Team's location, maybe dislocated in the explosion. Yet the boulder didn't move naturally; it slid sideways, and a wrapped head popped right behind it.

He grabbed the radio.

"Alpha Team, on your six! On your six!"

Then he found that precise location and the enemy's head in his rifle's scope, and soon blood stained the rocks.

"Copy, Sierra," Terrell replied. "We're going in."

"Godspeed, Alpha Team. Make me proud."

They had decorated him for that day; he was given a Bronze Star for what they called "meritorious service in combat." His unit came back with fifteen Taliban names scratched off the list, including a couple of most-wanted names. Most of all, they hadn't lost anyone on that mission; they all made it back.

He smiled sadly to the bittersweet memory, one of the last decent ones from that war. He remembered how it felt to be young and feel invincible, beyond death's grip. How he believed he made a difference. He'd entered the Torgan Valley as a twenty-seven-year-old Marine sergeant who'd welcomed the recall into service for another four-year stint, who believed everything was possible, who knew he belonged.

Nothing lasts forever.

# 30

# Service Call

When Dylan finally got home that night it was after seven, and he opened the door with a sigh of relief, anticipating the moment he'd get into the shower. The smell of cardboard that he'd grown to hate was everywhere, impregnated in his clothes, on his hands, and, unfortunately, it was the first scent he picked up when he opened the door to his house. Although ridiculously expensive to own or rent, most Northern California houses lacked air conditioning, and summer brought stuffy air that didn't move, no matter how many windows they kept open day and night.

Taylor didn't greet him as usual; instead, he heard her talking to someone in the living room. He heard a man's voice, youthful and a bit adenoidal. He rushed in there and saw a young man curled underneath the desk, working on the Internet wiring. Taylor stood a few feet away, holding the old modem in her hand.

"Hey," she said, then reached up for a quick kiss. He responded, without taking his eyes off the stranger who sat on the floor.

"What's going on?" he asked in a whisper.

"You forgot we're changing Internet providers today," she replied. "I told you last night, didn't I?"

"Oh, yeah, sorry... I forgot," he admitted reluctantly, but his frown didn't dissipate.

He looked at the technician; he was a skinny kid, not a day older than twenty-three, with a spotty, undecided stubble on his face. He was incredibly filthy. His hair, unkempt and greasy, had stained the collar of his company-issued blue shirt. His fingernails were contoured by grime, and the back of his hands couldn't have seen soap anytime recently. His pants were also company issued, shiny in places where the grime had been beaten into the fabric by wear and friction. He wore beat-up running shoes, with the logo unrecognizable under dried, layered dirt. A faint smell of sweaty socks came from his direction, and Dylan thought for a second how grateful he was the young technician hadn't removed his shoes.

"I'll be done in five minutes," the young man said, "and I'll get out of the way. We're almost ready. We'll authorize the modem, then we'll measure the speed and make sure your devices work."

"Sure," he replied, a little appeased. Maybe the young man was that grimy after crawling on who knows what floors, in countless houses. But he hated having strangers in his home, in his space, his own personal bubble.

"All right, we're good here," the technician said, coming out from underneath the desk. He stood, unraveling a long, bony body that couldn't have weighed more than 125 pounds for his 5-foot 7 height. Maybe the cable company preferred scrawny techs, considering all the crawl spaces and narrow attic doors they had to fit through.

"Okay, we have signal, strong and steady," he said, checking the screen of a handheld device. "Check your laptop now, ma'am, and let me know if it connects."

Taylor leaned over the laptop and opened a browser window. It loaded instantly.

"Excellent," she chirped. "Thank you so much."

"If you have any issues with it, give me a call," he said, putting a stained business card on the desk. "I'll leave a cable extension and this splitter with you, in case you decide to move the modem to another room."

"There's no need for that," Dylan replied quickly.

"There's no trouble," the kid replied smiling, his teeth incredibly white against his grungy face.

He stifled a groan, then turned to Taylor. "Get him a Coke or something. He might be thirsty."

Taylor nodded and left; and the moment she disappeared from view, Dylan grabbed the kid by his shirt collar and slammed him against the wall.

"If you leave a single bit of your shit behind when you leave, I'll tear your throat out and shove it up your ass. Take a look around you," he gestured toward the pile of boxes in the corner. "Do I look like I need more goddamned stuff in this house?"

Blood drained from the technician's face, and he didn't move immediately after Dylan let go of his shirt. Instead, he remained affixed to the wall, shaking. Then he pulled himself together and gathered everything in a hurry, including the cable extension and the splitter he'd offered, dumping them in his tool bag.

Taylor stood in the doorway, holding the Coke she'd brought, pale, with an unspeakable sadness in her eyes. The technician bolted past her and out the main door, and, within a second, Dylan heard his truck's engine revving.

Without a word, Dylan locked the door behind him, then turned toward Taylor, whose tears ran down her cheeks without a sound.

"Honey, I didn't—"

"Why don't you throw me out too, with the trash? Why not get rid of me and my stuff, in one big cleanup, huh?" Her voice trembled with anger and sorrow; he couldn't remember ever seeing her so deeply upset.

He took a step toward her, but she put up her hands and took a step back.

He froze in place.

"I bet you wished I was gone, so the house would be all yours, clean of all my shit. Just be ballsy enough and admit it. I've seen your hate, right now, the way you spoke to that boy." She didn't shout, and that made it worse. The corners of her mouth had dropped in a deep pout, and her eyes were squinted shut. "Just say it and I'll go."

Dylan's heart raced against his chest, thumping hard. He reached out to take her hand.

"No, baby, please—"

"Don't touch me!" she snapped and swerved sideways, away from him. "Don't you fucking touch me. I'm nothing but a ball and chain to you, so quit lying. Now I know exactly how you feel."

"That's not true," Dylan said, trying to curb his anger and refraining from the urge to touch her, to sweep her up in his arms. "I love you... I've always loved you. Don't leave me, please don't. Forgive me... I didn't mean—"

"Yes, you meant it, all of it," she cut him off calmly. "You didn't mean for me to hear it, that I can believe, but I know you meant what you said to that guy. You don't need any of this stuff in here. All it took was one minute alone with a stranger for you to be honest, didn't it?"

"Taylor, please be reasonable," he pleaded, feeling anger starting to suffocate him.

"Reasonable? How am I not reasonable right now, care to explain?"

He sighed and sat down on the edge of the couch, palms clasped together in his lap, wondering if he could afford to answer her question, or he should just keep apologizing. He opted for another attempt to level with Taylor.

"Do you have another splitter, the one we kept after leaving Cleveland?"

She frowned, but didn't reply.

"Your turn to be honest, Taylor," he said softly, afraid she'd blow up again, but determined to give it one more try. "Somewhere in these boxes, do you have another cable splitter stashed away?"

She lowered her head. "Probably," she eventually admitted.

"How about cable extensions? I remember we had a couple of those, coiled up in there somewhere."

"Yes," she whispered.

"See my point? We don't need more. We already have spares, and spares for spares. Every time we moved, you packed these things and took them with you. If this guy would've left another set, you wouldn't have thrown it out."

She stood there, clasping her right wrist with her left hand, staring at the carpet. He tried to reach for her hand again, but she pulled back.

"Come on, Taylor, you have to admit it's hard," he pleaded gently. "Think of what happened last time we moved. In Indiana."

She looked him straight in the eye with a stern, yet tearful look.

"That wasn't my fault."

"No, it wasn't," he admitted reluctantly, "but you have to admit it would be easier for us if you... Just let me help you through it, okay? Keep what you need, what's valuable. Let's get rid of all the ballast, one box per day. Only what we don't really need."

She stood silently for a while, staring at him without speaking a word. Her sadness steeled and turned to anger, dilating her pupils, digging trenches across her brow, crinkling her nose.

"No!" she eventually shouted. "No need to help me with anything. Just throw it away. Have the balls to do it, already."

He stood, holding his hands up in a pacifying gesture. "There's no need for that... We can—"

"Get rid of it all, not just some. Every bit of what I have is trash to you, so take it out with the rest of the trash. Why bother to pick and choose?"

Disarmed, he let his arms fall alongside his body. That wasn't the result he'd hoped for. He knew better than to take her up on her offer, because it wasn't a true offer, it was a dare, fueled by the pain that ripped through her heart right that moment.

"Taylor..." he whispered, but couldn't continue, at a loss for meaningful words that could bring healing to her sorrow. Why did he even go there, when in a couple of months, it would stop being relevant? Stupid, reckless, fool.

She started sobbing loudly, long wails that made him want to do anything to make her pain go away. How the hell could he be such an idiot, saying those things to that tech? Why did he risk it? What big difference would another cable splitter have made?

"Please, don't cry," he whispered, "I'm just an idiot, that's all. I didn't realize."

Once again, he tried to take her hand in his, but she pulled away.

"Leave me alone," she said, then rushed to the bedroom and closed the door behind her.

He dropped to the floor, as if his knees weren't strong enough to support his weight, and leaned against the wall with his eyes closed, letting the nightmares back in.

No, what had happened in Indiana wasn't her fault... Like everything else, it was his.

# 31

# Leaving Indiana

There was always an effervescence, a flush of adrenaline that spiced up their lives when they were about to move. After all, a move to another state, to a new house, was nothing if not a new beginning, a fresh start where hope was renewed and the ugliness of defeat hadn't smeared anything yet. Where they could still believe they'd be successful, winning for a change at the rigged game called life.

Making things even more exciting, they were moving back to their home state of California, although San Francisco was their destination, hours away from Coalinga. Dylan had accepted a senior manager position with an office supplies corporation to manage their logistics and warehouse operations. It was a nice bump in pay, although not nearly enough to compensate for the huge increase in cost of living they were about to feel. Yet they didn't hesitate; Dylan didn't have another job offer, after desperately looking for more than five months from sea to shining sea, as he bitterly called his nationwide job search.

It was as if the nation had stopped having any need for men like him, men who were willing to work countless hours, who had skills and determination and willpower and strength. Somewhere along the way, the American, middle-aged man had become the most unemployed demographic of the nation, driven into poverty and despair by the senseless recruiting practices of the modern, greed-based economy.

That's why Dylan and Taylor were excited about the move, feeling they'd beaten the odds one more time, heading toward a new home, where maybe life would prove more favorable, where no one would tear down, yet again, the spider web they were about to weave anew.

They'd carefully packed everything in cardboard boxes and storage bins, and Taylor took pride in finding free resources to do all that. She'd raided the local supermarkets and came home carrying heaps of discarded boxes the stores no longer needed, heavy duty, colorful packaging for detergents and groceries, easy stackable and sealable, and, most of all, free.

The moving truck was going to cost them enough, even if Dylan was going to drive it himself. They needed a big one, the biggest one available, and even so there was no guarantee that all their things would fit. They still had things stashed away in storage, mostly things that they'd picked up along the way, adapting from one temporary home's needs to the next. In Cleveland, they had to buy a fridge, because the rental came without one. Now that fridge was in storage, along with a small washing machine they didn't end up needing in Indiana, but they were going to use in California.

Other things were kept in storage, things they hadn't bothered to unpack anymore, knowing Indiana wasn't their forever home either. From housewares to heavy clothing, which Indiana's warm climate didn't require, to books and music, and some of Taylor's collection of art supplies. These items filled two separate storage units, one of which was climate controlled.

Time had run away from them, packing and sorting, and they had less than two days before they needed to vacate that house, but they weren't even close to being done. An out-of-state move is complicated when there aren't enough resources in both time and money, and they'd eventually decided to get help loading, a decision they'd been avoiding for a while.

The man who rented them the truck and trailer had given Dylan the phone number for a guy named George, a mover who was always looking for work. They'd called him, and George had quoted $25 per hour for a two-person team. Still having some daylight left, they decided to meet the movers at the storage place and start loading those items.

Dylan had expected to see two men, but George had brought a woman with him, a sturdy, heavy-built woman who wore a wide, maxi, colorful skirt that reminded him of the ones worn in the Middle East by gypsy pickpockets. Once the thief would grab a wallet or a phone, she'd hide the object inside the skirt's many folds, which had pockets sewn into them, then have their bare hands in plain sight, above any suspicion. Dylan whispered a quick warning in Taylor's ear.

"Watch out for these people," he said. "You stay by the truck, I'll be inside with them. They might try to lift smaller objects."

They loaded in silence for a while, George and his partner moving quickly and efficiently in the mid-summer heat, almost putting Dylan's concerns to sleep. Then George approached Dylan, apparently taking a break to drink some water.

"Huh… you're rich," George said, panting a little.

"No, we're not," Dylan reacted with a scoff. "This is just stuff, nothing else. Books, clothing, that kind of stuff."

"You got stuff, that makes you rich," George replied.

Dylan didn't push back, realizing the man's simple and straightforward logic actually had a point. Maybe, by comparison with others, they were rich. They had a few things, even more than a few.

"I hope you'll make good on our seventy-five dollars per hour," George added. "You won't stiff me, will you?"

"What? You said twenty-five dollars! That's what you said," Dylan pushed back.

"No, man, I didn't. It's two of us, working hard in this heat. Who do you think I am, some two-bit loser?"

Dylan measured up the man's 6-foot-4 frame and muscular arms. He was younger and stronger than Dylan was, not a stranger to the prison system, judging by some of his tattoos, and definitely someone who wouldn't hesitate to beat both of them to a pulp and steal all their stuff. If Taylor weren't there, he would've handled things differently, but her presence changed everything.

"All right, seventy-five dollars an hour it is," Dylan replied, swallowing his sweltering anger.

George cracked a smile and wiped his brow, then patted Dylan on his arm. "Excellent, my man, we're in business."

"Actually, we're not. You see, at seventy-five dollars, I can't afford you anymore. We stop now, and I'll pay you what I owe you so far, and that's that."

"Don't do this," George growled. "I know you have the money."

"You know wrong," Dylan replied, "I don't. You two worked an hour and thirty-five minutes, I'll pay for two hours, not a penny more. We're leaving now."

He locked the storage unit, thankful for the video surveillance present everywhere in that facility, and gestured Taylor to get in the truck.

"Follow me to the bank, I need to pull some cash. Like I said, I was expecting today to cost me under a hundred bucks," he added, thinking that the bank's parking lot must have also been under video surveillance. He wanted every bit of interaction he had with this man to be recorded somewhere, in case things turned ugly.

At the bank, he pulled some more cash from the ATM, while George waited in his beat-up Pontiac, then beckoned him over, where the light was better, right under the ATM's camera. He paid the man $150, then turned to leave.

"You're making a mistake," George said quietly. His eyes glinted weirdly in the dusk, and his partner had a malicious grimace on her face. "Moves like that, if you're loading your stuff without professional help, you're going to run into a lot of trouble."

Dylan understood the threat, and, for a split second, he wondered what it would come down to. Set the truck on fire? Slash its tires? Everything was insured; he didn't care much about anything in there, anyway. He remembered giving George their home address, but his condo also came with video surveillance, and Dylan had a gun. He'd probably not sleep much the next two nights, but then they'd be free of this jerk, on their way to California.

"I'm going to take my chances," Dylan replied coldly. "I paid you what you asked for, now we're done."

He turned to leave, but heard George call after him and stopped. "I'd hate to see you not get where you want to go, man, just for a few hours of labor, a few pennies."

He shrugged and climbed behind the wheel of the truck, without bothering to reply.

"What was that about?" Taylor asked.

"Trouble," he replied, checking his mirrors to see where George's Pontiac was headed.

LESLIE WOLFE

"What kind?" she whispered, clasping his hand.

"Not sure yet."

He spent the night dozing on the couch, gun in hand, while Taylor slept in their bed. Nothing happened, and, at the first light of day, he went outside and found the truck to be intact, tires and all, precisely the way he'd left it. Relieved, he started loading boxes himself in the cool morning breeze, putting the few hours to some good use, until he could call another mover.

He'd loaded about a third of the truck on his own, his strength fueled by anger for the rip-off he'd been subjected to the night before, for not being able to teach those thieving assholes a lesson. He was downing another bottle of water in the kitchen, taking five minutes to catch his breath, when the doorbell rang.

With one hand ready to draw his gun, he opened the door and found two men in suits, holding out badges.

"Special Agents Jenkins and Munroe," the taller one said, "Homeland Security." By the way he'd gestured while identifying themselves, he must have been Jenkins.

He nodded and frowned. What the hell did they want with him?

"We have questions regarding your storage unit," Munroe said.

"Which one?" Dylan asked, still frowning.

The two agents looked at each other for a split second. "May we come in?"

Dylan remembered the gun he had under his belt, probably not the best way to welcome federal agents inside.

"Just give me a second, to make sure my wife's decent."

He went inside and stashed the gun in a kitchen drawer, and told Taylor what was going on. Then he opened the door and let them in.

"Pardon the mess, we're moving. What's this about?"

The two men didn't say anything; they looked around, as if searching for something.

"We have reasons to believe you might have, or had, explosive devices stored in your cold storage unit," Jenkins eventually said.

"What? Heck, no. You think I'm a terrorist? I'm an Afghanistan war veteran, for Chrissakes!"

"So, you have no explosive materials or devices?"

"None," he replied, looking them in the eye.

"Chemical compounds that could be used in the making of a bomb?"

"None. Household bleach is all we have, a couple of inches on the bottom of the bottle."

The two agents walked through the house, looking at everything carefully, but not touching anything.

"Do you want to see the storage unit?" he offered.

"How come you're so helpful?" Jenkins asked, looking at him with suspicion in his eyes.

"I believe in what you're trying to do," Dylan replied, "keep this country safe. We're on the same side, remember?"

Jenkins didn't respond; he moved on to the next room, under Taylor's petrified glance.

"Are you an American citizen?" Munroe asked.

"Of course, I am, born and raised."

"Can we see some proof of that?"

Dylan sighed. They were being ridiculous. "Um, our passports are buried in here, somewhere. We're moving to California, not overseas, so we packed them."

"Any other form of identification?"

"Driver's license," he said, then pulled out his wallet and gave it to him.

"How about you, ma'am?"

Pale, Taylor swallowed and nodded, then pulled hers out of her purse and handed it over.

"I'll be right back," Munroe said, then disappeared with their IDs.

"Where's your truck?" Jenkins asked. "You have a moving truck, don't you?"

Dylan stared at him, then he started to put things together. That asshole, that motherfucking crook George! He'd called Homeland on them, to get even. That was the trouble he'd promised.

"Yes, I do have a truck, want to see it?"

He led the way to the living room, while Jenkins headed for the front door.

"Trust me, it's quicker this way," he pointed at the living room French door. "We've been loading through here."

The truck was backed up almost to the deck limit, and the cargo door was open. Jenkins looked inside for a long minute.

"All this stuff, what's in these boxes? Are you running a business from your home?"

"No, it's my wife's stuff. She collects things."

"What things? Can we see?"

He frowned. Taylor hated when anyone looked at her stuff. Didn't these guys need a warrant? But probably it was quicker to humor them for a few more minutes.

"You can't expect us to unload the truck and open all the boxes, right? Pick one or two at random, and I'll open them for you."

Munroe came back into the house without bothering to knock and gave them back their licenses. Then he stopped right in front of the pile of empty cardboard boxes, all commercial packaging discarded by the local Costco.

"You sell detergents?"

"No," Dylan replied, rushing inside, "we used these boxes to pack up our stuff. These are leftovers," he said, then grabbed a few and lifted them in the air and let them drop, to demonstrate they were empty.

"Can I see that one?" Jenkins said, pointing at a stackable plastic bin with a yellow lid.

"Sure," he replied, after a split-second hesitation. He had three such bins, and two of them were trouble. One held his ammo, and the other one an unregistered handgun. The third held Taylor's favorite dish set. "Let me tell you what I think happened here," he said, dragging the bin out of the truck. "We contacted this guy to help us load, and he tried to rip us off. I think he called you guys as retaliation. He wanted seventy-five dollars an hour, can you believe it?"

"Yeah, yeah," Jenkins said dismissively, after exchanging another quick glance with Munroe.

Dylan popped open the lid, hoping for the dish set. Instead, several boxes of ammo came into view. The two agents took a step back, and Jenkins took out his weapon.

"Step away from that crate, sir."

"I have a concealed-carry permit. All this is legit."

"We'll need to see all the contents of that truck," Jenkins said, then to Munroe, "Get some help."

"No, I believe you'll need a warrant for that, and I'll need a lawyer," Dylan said, staring them fiercely in the eye. "I've got nothing to hide, but I have to move today. I'm busy. Please leave."

"Let's see that concealed-carry permit," Munroe said.

He produced it slowly, under the itchy trigger finger of Special Agent Jenkins. Munroe took it to their car, where he probably ran it. Then he came back, and whispered something in Jenkin's ear.

"You have a nine mil and a thirty-eight registered under your name, but that ammo is for a forty-five," Munroe stated. "We're taking you in, and we're getting warrants for all this stuff."

They took him out of there in cuffs, ignoring Taylor's sobs and cries, and put him in the back of their car. Minutes later, swarms of agents started ransacking every item they'd packed, going through every document, every box, and every drawer. Through some act of divine intervention, they completely missed the bin that held the unregistered weapon, the 45 he'd received from Nickel's dad when he'd returned from Afghanistan. At the end of a horrifying day, they released him and left.

Their house was an unrecognizable mess, with heaps of items scattered everywhere, damaged furniture, torn boxes, broken dishes, and spilled groceries. What made it worse, both Taylor and he were in bad shape, angry, shocked, exhausted. One way or another, they still had to leave in a little more than twenty-four hours. It was the end of the month; a new tenant was moving in the day after tomorrow.

Taylor lay on the slit couch cushions, scattered on the floor; she felt dizzy, and he could feel her heart pounding heavily against her chest. She didn't want to go to the hospital, although she was pale and weak and couldn't even stand on her feet anymore. She just lay there, trembling, curled in the fetal position, whispering she'd be all right every time he asked her what she needed.

Barely able to think anymore, Dylan managed to make a few phone calls and secure a moving crew that was willing to work overnight to pack whatever was left undamaged and load the truck. The new crew arrived within the hour, and they were expensive, charging a premium for the after-hours service. As he opened the door for the new crew, his phone rang, and he took the call without checking the phone's display.

A man laughed at the other end of the line, a raspy, hearty laugh. He recognized George's voice.

"I told you, didn't I?" George said, between cackles. "Lots of things could go wrong with a move, if you don't hire the right people." He laughed some more, then hung up, while Dylan gasped for air, choked with unspeakable rage.

"I'm going to kill him," he said matter-of-factly. "I'll find the bastard, and I'll end him. He won't do this to anyone else, ever again."

"Please, don't leave me," Taylor pleaded, pale and weak, leaning against the doorframe for support. "Let it go. Let's get the hell out of here."

He gave it up, for her sake, but for years he wondered what had happened to George. He hoped the son of a bitch would pay for what he'd done, at some point, even if at someone else's hand. He had no idea that, by the time of their move from Indiana, most federal agencies already had measures in place to ensure that false reports were not being used as retaliation or pranks. The practice was called swatting, and it had recently been categorized as terrorism. Dylan never learned that George had been arrested later that same night, together with his wife, who had, in fact, made the call to Homeland Security.

Regardless, the spider's delicate web had been crushed once more.

# 32

# A Complication

Dylan hesitated before entering Dr. Blackwell's building. He looked up from the sidewalk, dreading her office, the conversation, the mandatory process he'd subjected himself to for Taylor's sake. He thought of the weekly appointments as a necessary evil, and that's exactly what they were. He endured through them with his patience stretched to the max, hating how it made him feel, tense inside, about to break, about to scream.

He went inside and climbed the flight of stairs, instead of waiting for the elevator, then buzzed her intercom and was let in almost instantly. A few times before, he thought he'd seen her looking out the window, probably trying to see if he was coming. For a second, right before walking into her posh office, he stopped and wondered what she must really think about him, about his upcoming death. Was she going to get smart with him and pull off some twisted shrink deed in an attempt to foil his plans? He'd been coming there for three months, and so far, she'd respected his terms, but he still felt she couldn't be trusted. Who knows what damn tricks they taught them in shrink school?

She opened the door, and he walked past her, looking at her briefly, then sat on the sofa. The comfy cushions felt good, and he almost felt like stretching and yawning, tired after an endless day spent in the warehouse, putting up with Loreen's endless supply of self-serving crap. But he was restless and irritated, although he couldn't figure out why. He felt like pacing the floor, fast, like a caged animal yearning to break free, to get the hell out of there.

Instead, he took a deep breath and tried to smile. "Sorry about last week, Doc, I had a situation, something I had to deal with."

She sat in her chair like the whole world had come to a stop, relaxed, comfortable, seemingly self-assured, with a faint smile on her lips. She looked tired and drawn; she wasn't fooling him with her fresh lipstick and youthful hairstyle. She'd tied up her massive heap of long, curly hair in a loose ponytail that suited her, but she still looked drained; her eyes gave it away. It must have been hard for her to listen to people's whining all day long.

She smiled and nodded politely. "Is everything all right?"

He frowned. The hell it was; he had a big problem.

"Sure," he stated, trying to stay put, fighting the urge to fidget, to get off that bloody couch and pace the floor. Or better yet, to get the hell out of there.

He stared at his hands for a while, dreading her questions, wishing the hour was gone already. He had nothing to say, nothing that could be shared with a stranger. Nothing, really, that could be shared with anyone. There were two types of people in the world: Taylor and strangers. He couldn't share his thoughts with either.

"What does dying mean to you?" she asked, managing to take him by surprise.

"Is this a trick question?"

"Not at all," she replied calmly, while he wrung his hands together, as if to squeeze water out of a wet towel.

"Dying is dying," he said with a weird laugh, "you stop breathing. Then they put you in a hole in the ground, end of story."

"I agree, but what does dying mean to you? You told me you want to die; why?"

He shifted nervously in place, then angled forward, putting his elbows on his thighs and leaning into them. "It means the end of it," he replied reluctantly, after a few moments. "The end of it all. All the fight, all the endless pain I'm putting her through. All the worrying about tomorrow, about survival."

"So, you believe the only way to stop worrying about tomorrow, the only way to stop Taylor's pain is to take yourself out of the equation?"

He felt a wave of anger simmer in his chest. "What do *you* think, Doc?"

"I think it's a terrible waste of a good person, of a good life to end like this, that's what I think."

She sat there looking at him calmly, as if nothing was wrong in the entire world. His anger bubbled up, threatening to boil over. She had the gift to stir him up, to bring up the worst feelings inside him dangerously close to the surface. The calmer she was, the angrier he felt.

He slapped his thighs, then rubbed them a bit with wide, harsh up-and-down movements, as if warming his legs up before a run. He bit his lip, trying to abstain from shouting at her, but then decided to give her an example, so she could understand better and stop with the fucking questions already.

"If someone breaks into your home and jeopardizes your existence," he said, "the law is on your side if you shoot the bastard. If someone takes your money, all your savings, you're entitled to put a hole in his head. If someone kills your friend, you're in your right to take the motherfucker out, discharge a whole mag in him, if you so damn please. Now tell me, which one of these scenarios is a waste of a scumbag's life?"

She sat there holding his gaze, but her faint smile had vanished. Instead, he thought he saw in her eyes something different from what he'd expected, something... kind. Understanding. Bloody hell.

He stood and started pacing the floor, toward the window where the early evening light came filtering through the quiet thickness of the ocean fog, then he marched toward the back wall, where countless books were arranged on shelves and mixed with small décor items and memorabilia. A Phil Collins–signed vinyl. A baseball, signed by someone whose name he didn't recognize. A pretentious-looking award for remarkable contributions to the space program, given to someone named Michael Blackwell, probably the doc's late husband.

He studied the objects for a few seconds, then resumed his walk toward the window. He stopped and stared at the gray fog rolling in, covering the sun, bringing darkness soon. He slid his hand into his pocket and found the pebbles, and his fingers relished the familiar touch. He took them out and closed his fist around them, feeling their smooth surfaces, remembering the day he'd fished them out of the banks of Los Gatos Creek. The day Nickel's mother had died.

She hadn't deserved to die; she'd been nothing but kind. Him, on the other hand...

"What's on your mind?" Dr. Blackwell asked. "You seem preoccupied, angry even. Does talking about death upset you?"

"No, it makes me happy as a clam at high tide," he snapped. "What the hell, Doc, what kind of stupid question is this?"

"Oh, I touched a nerve, it seems," she said, with the tiniest of smiles. "If death is so upsetting, then—"

"Ahh, it's not that," he reacted, "I'm in a crappy mood today."

"Something to do with your absence last week?"

He sighed. "Yeah, you could say that."

"What happened?" she asked. "Would you like to share?"

He shook his head, then leaned his forehead against the cold glass. The sensation calmed his nerves somewhat. What the hell was he going to do? He'd tried everything...

"I found this... dog," he eventually said, "in the street, lost." He omitted saying that he'd chosen to spend time with a lost dog instead of coming to their scheduled session; he knew she wasn't going to react well to that.

"Interesting," she said calmly. "What did you do?"

"Fucked up my car, because she was filthy, covered in mud. It was raining last week when I found her."

Yeah, he thought, it was raining, and she was trembling in the cold rain, limping from a hind leg, looking miserable. He had to take her in. The hell with his car's upholstery; soon enough it wouldn't matter anyway.

"I took her home, gave her a bath, a meal, a place to stay for a while," he added, then he started rubbing the two pebbles together, absentmindedly.

"So, you have a dog now?" she asked.

"No," he replied quickly, with a sad, breathy smile. "Taylor's not happy having her around, and she's someone else's dog. All week long, I've been posting ads on trees and calling vet offices; maybe someone's missing her."

"And?" she asked, and, for some reason, she frowned.

"I haven't found her owner, not yet. She's not even microchipped. You'd expect people to microchip their animals in this day and age, but no."

"What kind of dog is she? Small?"

"Not really," he grinned, "she's a Belgian Malinois."

"I'm not that familiar with dogs," she replied apologetically.

He turned toward her.

"She's about this tall," he said, taking the hand that held the pebbles to his knee level. "She's beautiful," he added, and the doctor smiled. "She's about four years old."

"You can tell her age? How? By her dentition?"

"Yeah, by the state of her teeth," he replied, "although if she's been a stray for a while, she might be younger than her teeth are showing. It's a guess."

"What's her name?"

He frowned. "I don't know her name, don't know if she has one."

"You could give her a name," she said, smiling. "You could ask Taylor to help you name her."

"There's no point, Doc. She's not my dog, and she's not staying. I got other plans, and Taylor's not into dogs. End of story."

She didn't say anything else, but her smile disappeared.

There was no other way; there was no room in his life for a dog, not now. It was too late. Her appearance was nothing more than a complication, an annoyance, a problem he needed to solve.

He didn't share how he loved scratching behind her ears, seeing her eyes relax, her tail wag, how he enjoyed watching her fall asleep on the couch, leaning against his thigh, despite Taylor's frustrated groans. There was no point in sharing any of that, because soon it was going to end anyway.

Nine more weeks until November twelfth. Not a day more.

# 33

# Calm Again

Angela stared at the wall clock, watching the digits change, shift shape, morph into new digits with new meanings, but only one conclusion. Another week had passed, and time was running out. She'd just scratched the surface, barely getting an emotional response from DJ, and even that response she'd gained by brute force almost, not by consolidating and capitalizing on healthy, therapeutic principles. She felt as if she almost held her unwilling patient hostage, not unlike putting him on suicide watch, where patients are monitored intensively to prevent them from taking their own lives.

She knew she was getting close; she could sense how agitated he'd become lately, she could feel the storm brewing inside him, getting ready to break. She knew that without uncovering what lay hidden at the core of his despair, she couldn't hope to stop him from executing the death sentence he'd pronounced on himself.

The digits on the clock morphed again, as the intercom buzzed, right on the hour. She let him in, and he walked through the door slowly, calmly, irritatingly even-tempered. Where was that brewing storm she'd been counting on? What the hell was happening in this man's life?

They took their seats and sat quietly for a while. She studied his face, almost serene, all tension in his jaw gone, forgotten. He didn't lean against the back rest, but that was almost like his signature posture, as if he were afraid of getting too comfortable, of trusting her too much. He was cleanly shaven with an afternoon shadow, and wore the same business casual attire. Nothing really had changed since their last session, yet everything about him was dangerously different.

He was calm, too damn calm to be any good news. She waited for him to speak, but he didn't engage, leaving her no choice but to push forward, searching, hoping for a reaction to guide her through the maze.

"Tell me about your deployment," she asked, pretending she didn't remember his refusal to discuss anything from that time.

"There's nothing to tell," he replied, his voice even, steady, almost indifferent. He sounded as if he were talking about yesterday's boring ballgame, where no one had hit a single home run.

"I'm not buying it, DJ," she said bluntly. "How long were you deployed?"

"What difference does it make?" he snapped? "Could have been a year or a hundred, it's still the same."

"Humor me," she insisted. "Unless you have something else you'd like to discuss today."

He bit his lip nervously, and the knotted muscles in his jaws returned. He wrung his hands and fidgeted in his seat, shifting to the side, turning his face away from her.

"Seven years," he eventually said, in a low tone. "Four years at first, then they recalled me when the war on terror began."

"Okay, seven years, lots of things must have happened during that time. Any specific events come to mind?"

He lowered his gaze to the floor and didn't reply.

"Where did you first deploy?" she asked in a softer voice.

"I caught the tail end of Iraq, but not much action," he said, still staring at his shoes. "Then Kosovo."

"And then?"

"Then I came back home, got discharged."

"How was it, coming home?"

She'd hit a nerve. He scoffed and shook his head before replying.

"I don't know what I was expecting," he said in a low, morose tone. "Everything was the same. No one needed us, no one wanted us. I thought we'd be breaking free from that place, but we still had nothing. And Taylor…"

His words trailed off, leaving way to silence.

"What about Taylor?"

He shook his head again, and took his forehead in his palm, rubbing it slowly, as if to wipe away painful memories.

"She'd lived there all that time, waiting for me, alone, struggling. She'd hoped that when I came back, everything would turn around, and we'd finally have the life we wanted, start a family. Instead, I couldn't get a job anywhere. The oil fields weren't hiring, and we had no money to move anywhere else."

He pressed his lips together, doing a poor job at hiding his disappointment. She gave him time to process his thoughts, uninterrupted.

"When they recalled me to active duty, I was almost grateful, although it broke Taylor's heart."

"Then what happened?"

His shoulders hunched forward another notch. "Nothing. Just deployment."

"Where?"

"Afghanistan," he spat the word.

"What happened in Afghanistan, DJ?" she asked softly.

He promptly stood and started pacing the room with long, angry strides, while deep ridges furrowed his brow. His hand dove inside his pocket and retrieved the two pebbles, and he closed his fist around them so tightly she could see his knuckles turn white. Then he stopped in front of the window and looked outside, while his hand slowly relaxed and started playing with the two pebbles, shifting them around, rubbing them together, making them click quietly.

"There's no fog tonight, Doc."

"What happened in Afghanistan, DJ?" she repeated, in the same tone of voice as before.

He didn't reply; tension froze his shoulders and hunched his back. He lowered his head as if to look down at the street below, but kept his eyes on the horizon line, where the sun made its nightly descent. The soft clicking of the pebbles continued, quiet and level, almost soothing.

She glanced at the wall clock whose impassible digits shifted continuously, and decided to allow him another minute. But he didn't speak.

"DJ, what happened in—"

"For God's sake, woman, shut the fuck up!" he snapped, turning to glare at her. His flushed face was contorted in anger, and his rapid, strong heartbeats throbbed in the veins visible on his neck.

She didn't flinch. She looked at him steadily, waiting for him to continue, but he didn't. He managed to bottle up his anger and resume his earlier posture.

"How about when you got discharged? What can you tell me about the return to civilian life?" she asked, going after her hunch in a different manner.

He shrugged. "Nothing. I came home, to the same nothing that was there before."

"But you went to college?" she probed.

"Yeah, I did," he replied, still staring out the window.

"How was that for you?"

"Long. I worked nights to be able do it, and Taylor worked days. We barely spoke or did anything together for three years. I hated it."

"Ah, you finished early," she said. "Good for you."

"No need to drag it on," he commented. "It was a pain in the ass."

"How old were you when you graduated?"

"Thirty-two."

"Ah, I see."

He turned and glared hat her again.

"Do you really, Doc?"

"What do you mean?"

"Yeah, I had a degree, but I was already thirty-two and we were broke, stuck in that hellhole of a town where there wasn't any work. Taylor wanted children, and I... couldn't. Can you imagine, having a child like that? I robbed her of her life, that's what I did. Her shrew of a mother was right, had been right all along. Taylor threw her life away by marrying a loser."

"You're quick to put yourself down, aren't you?"

"And you think it's undeserved? Look at me now, getting ready to be laid off again, to move again, to struggle to find another job, nightmare on rerun. My entire life, I've crawled."

"Let's focus on the positive here, for a second."

"Stop doing that, Doc."

"Doing what?"

"Your job. I'm not here to get help. I'm here to get evidence, a testimony, nothing more. Stop trying."

"Ah, I see," she replied. "But if you feel you're so right in your decision, why does it bother you to acknowledge the few good things you have in life?"

"Such as?"

"Taylor, for example. You have a loving relationship with a good woman. Can you stop for a second to acknowledge that?"

He closed his eyes, and for a second, an expression of deep anguish tainted his face.

"You mean, the wonderful woman whose life I destroyed? Yeah, I can stop for a second and acknowledge that. I've been acknowledging it for a while. Every time I see her sighing when she watches other women play with their children. Every time people ask us if we have kids and her eyes turn dark. Every time she wants something we can't afford, and she doesn't want much, but I still have to say no. Yeah, Doc, I'm acknowledging stuff all day long."

Her eyes were glued to his right hand, and the way his fingers played with the two pebbles. What was the meaning of those? They were like an anchor to him, something he felt the need to touch to regain his balance, his strength. She wanted to ask about them, but didn't feel he was ready for that intimate question. He'd shut her up, or get angry, or both.

"How about your career? For a poor kid from Coalinga, you have a few things to be proud of."

He shook his head widely, looking out the window again.

"My career, Doc? Do you even know what you're talking about? I'm like a stray dog scouring for a meal, getting kicked and beaten, but licking every hand that's willing to fill the bowl, hoping that if I'll be good, they'll keep me for a while longer. That's my career for you, Doc, in terms even you will understand."

He glanced at her quickly, over his shoulder, then resumed staring out the window. He seemed overwhelmed by emotions, unable to manage his strong affect, and struggling to tolerate the weight of his feelings. He was sinking under the burden, but rejected her hand every time she reached out.

She needed to help him bypass the extreme feelings of despair he was facing; sending him home under such a dark spell could be a terrible mistake. She decided to change the subject, and ask about something that had been on her mind for a while, like a ray of hope peeking from behind a storm cloud.

"Speaking of strays, how's your dog?"

She thought she saw him sigh quietly, restrained.

"She wasn't my dog, I told you that. Taylor didn't want her, so I took her to the shelter. It's better if she finds a new home with someone who can give her a good life and keep her indefinitely. Taylor's not that person, and I have other plans."

She clenched her teeth and almost lost it. She wanted to stomp her foot and cuss out loud. Why did this incredibly stubborn man refuse to see what was good for him, even if it was right there, before his eyes? The only times she'd seen him smile was when he talked about that dog. The only times he'd shared stories with her without holding back were when he talked about the stray dog he'd found, and about Lois, his childhood dog, the superhero's girl.

Frustrated, she checked the time and felt almost relieved when she saw it was already a few minutes past seven.

"I see we're out of time for today. Same time next week?" she asked and stood, ready to see him out.

"Yeah," he said, then nodded and disappeared, closing the door behind him quietly.

She stood by the door, fists clenched, stirred up, wanting to break something. Just a few weeks was all she had left, and this man...

She grabbed her phone and retrieved a number from memory. The call was picked up immediately, after one short ring.

"Dr. Blackwell," the man said, "hello again."

"Hello, Barney, how are you?"

"I'm good... I am, you know. Some days are better than others, and today was one of those days, a good one. Saved a few lives."

She could hear the distant sound of dogs barking.

"That's great to hear, I'm happy for you."

"What can I do for you?"

"Did someone drop a Belgian Malinois at the shelter recently?"

"Yes, yesterday. A big dude, buzz cut, ex-Army or something."

She chuckled quietly. Yeah, that sounded like DJ.

"Barney, I need a big favor."

# 34

# Tenderloin

The first time Dylan was invited to attend a business lunch with Loreen and a major client, he'd been flattered, thinking that his career was going somewhere for a change. A business lunch with his boss? That must've meant something.

After a while, he noticed a pattern in Loreen's choice of companionship for these key account business lunches. She'd pick one of the senior managers to come with her, rotating though the entire operations team, and always feeding everyone the same corporate bullshit about opportunity, exposure, networking, and learning negotiating skills. Maybe it wasn't entirely bullshit, there was an opportunity in all that, but her real motives were different.

She only needed a lackey.

She didn't want to drive her own Lexus through the San Francisco downtown congestion, and risk scratching it. She didn't want to struggle finding a parking spot, or trotting for any distance on her 3-inch heels; she preferred to be dropped off instead, and have him arrive late, sweaty and apologetic, when everyone else had already made the introductions and read their menus. She liked having her own chauffeur and showing off her status to the unsuspecting clients.

Now that Dylan had her figured out, it was increasingly annoying to accompany her to these outings. On the drive back, she mostly kept her eyes riveted to her phone's screen, and her thumbs moved quickly, typing email and text responses. She rarely spoke to him; people seldom engage in meaningful conversations with their drivers, and she was no different.

They'd just finished an endless business lunch with one of their biggest clients, a Fortune 500 company in the tech sector, and Dylan's car moved incredibly slow on the southbound 101, caught in the afternoon traffic congestion. The roads were packed, and leaving the Marina District after two in the afternoon was probably going to be a costly mistake. He'd been going less than ten miles per hour for a while, and ignored Loreen's irritated sighs while he tried to figure out an alternate route back to the office. He looked at her discreetly, unnoticed, then started to think of the situation as a potential opportunity for an off-the-record conversation.

"How do you think it went?" he asked directly, as if they'd normally talk about their meetings afterwards.

She lifted her eyes from the phone's screen and frowned. "Went okay."

"You seemed to know them well, these guys."

"Yeah," she replied, resuming her typing. "They've been a key account for ten years, and we do this type of informal lunch every quarter. You know that, right? You've met them before?"

"Can't say that I have, no. Not in person. I've been working their account, but haven't met the brass."

"Ah, well. Now you have," she added, throwing him a quick glance.

"Yeah. Have you met Terrell Murray?"

"Who?" Her eyes didn't leave the phone's screen.

"He's in Order Entry, he works for me. African American—"

"The black guy with a limp? Yeah, I know him."

Dylan's hands squeezed the steering wheel until he felt his fingers go numb. "That's what you call him, that's all he is to you? A black guy with a limp?"

"He's weird, scary," she replied, without looking up from the phone. "He's always grim, can't smile no matter what. I hate that about people, not behaving professionally."

"He's not unprofessional, Loreen," he managed to say calmly. "He's been injured, you know. He has a prosthetic leg. He deserves some slack."

"Yeah, but still. We can't be expected to have him like that among ourselves, in meetings and all that. Not when the vice president is attending, at least. He should smile more. We're all happy to be here, thankful for our jobs, right? What's the harm in showing it every now and then?" She threw him another one of her quick glances.

Dylan forced some air into his lungs, feeling suffocated. What an idiotic bitch. He cranked up the air conditioning a notch or two, but it didn't help.

"He's a veteran, Loreen. I believe he deserves some respect."

"And I have all the respect in the world, Dylan," she replied, sounding irritated. "But this is a business, not a support organization. He sits there in our meetings, gloomy, barely present, if even, so my boss gets to ask me if I have personnel issues, or employee satisfaction concerns. How do you think that's helping my career?"

Dylan slammed the brakes, almost hitting the car in front of him that had stopped unexpectedly. He swallowed a curse and glanced at Loreen. She seemed her normal self, unperturbed, albeit a bit annoyed, tapping her foot rhythmically.

Then she set the phone aside, and sighed, a long, noisy breath of air, conveying nothing but frustration. "If he's in Order Entry, he'll land on your layoff list. Trust me, we're better off without him."

They were at the traffic light at Geary, and he abruptly shifted lanes and turned left.

"Where are we going?"

"Bypassing this traffic," Dylan replied, heading into the heart of the Tenderloin, San Francisco's highest-crime neighborhood, where most of the city's homeless gathered. Streets flanked by dilapidated buildings and littered with trash, homeless people dressed in rags and pushing shopping carts filled with all their possessions, or lying on the asphalt in the shade; that was the San Francisco Tenderloin on any given day.

He slowed, although there was no traffic on Geary. He turned onto Leavenworth, then he took Turk, zig-zagging through the neighborhood.

Loreen shifted in her seat, uncomfortable and wary.

"What's with the hobo boulevard scenic drive, Dylan?"

"Do you know the price of putting someone in the street?" he asked in a low voice.

She pressed her lips together and frowned, a deep frown that brought up a hateful glint in her eyes. She squinted her eyes and jutted her chin, but didn't say another word.

Dylan took another turn, driving slowly, looking for someone. Every time he drove by a homeless person, he slowed and turned his head, trying to see the person's face. Then he came to a stop, only a few feet away from a homeless man in a filthy, green jacket and brown pants.

The man sat on a frayed blanket that must have been yellow at some point, set directly on the asphalt, and leaned against the wall of a two-story, boarded building. He'd pulled some of the blanket over his legs, and clasped a black trash bag in his hand. He sat there with his eyes closed, immobile. His face was stained, and his unkempt beard and hair were yellowish and greasy.

"That man's a Desert Storm veteran," Dylan said, pointing at the homeless man. His gesture startled Loreen and made her withdraw toward the car door, putting more distance between them. "Take a good look at him. That's the price of putting someone on the street, Loreen. Don't kid yourself; this is where you'll find Terrell in a couple of months, when he'll get evicted. I hope your bonus will be worth it, boss. Do something worthwhile with it. Buy yourself some more shoes, or spend a week in the Caribbean."

"Take me back to the office, Dylan," she said coldly, glaring at him. "Now, please."

Dylan grabbed the wheel with a sudden gesture, and Loreen flinched again and threw him a terrified glance.

"What? If I'm a veteran, if I'm a Marine, I'm going to beat you up?" he snapped, raising his voice. "I must be crazy, right? Crazy... who knows how many people I've killed over there, right?"

She stayed silent, but her round eyes showed the fear she felt, while the glint of anger in them didn't vanish.

"That we did it for our country, for you, it doesn't matter, does it?" he continued, still suffocated, still unable to breathe. "Is that what you people think about us? Huh?"

She bit her lip and averted her look, but then spoke quietly, "Please take us back to the office, Dylan. Right now."

He shifted into gear and drove the remainder of the way without speaking. Loreen also sat quietly, not touching her phone, not taking her eyes off the road ahead. Until they pulled up to the office parking lot, and he stopped the car at the main entrance to let her off, not another word was spoken.

Then she opened the door to get out, but stopped and turned to him, speaking in a cold, unyielding voice.

"By November fifteenth, I expect those layoffs to be executed, Dylan. Not a day later."

# 35

# No Show

Angela didn't worry at first, when it was only six o'clock and DJ hadn't showed. It had happened before, him running late, either stuck in traffic or struggling with the idea of seeing her again, of opening painful wounds of the past. She'd seen it before, when patients couldn't deal with the burden of revisiting past trauma, strange things happened to them that kept them from arriving on time, strange things dictated by their subconscious minds as a defense mechanism of avoidance. Small household incidents or crises, like spilling cooking oil on the floor, or the cat running out of the house. Cars that wouldn't start, or drivers who got lost on familiar roads they knew like the back of their hands.

She waited patiently, although something gripped her gut in an unpleasant way, as she watched the wall clock incessantly mark the passing of time. That grip turned into the unwelcome seed of anxiety and started to grow, when thirty minutes into their session he still wasn't there. By 6:45, she paced the floor back and forth, stopping in front of her window and looking outside every minute, hoping to see the hood of his black sedan stop alongside the curb, in his usual parking spot.

Where the hell was he?

She'd checked her phone a few times, hoping there'd be a message, a voicemail, anything. Where was he, and what was he doing? Last time, when he wanted to skip a session, he'd called in and told her, albeit at the last minute, but still.

Whenever she thought she had a chance of getting somewhere with him, he did something to jeopardize that, to stop her in her tracks and resume his implacable journey to his set final destination. It drove her mad, the futility of her efforts, his self-destructive determination, the paradox of the entangled realities, one where his logic made sense, and another where she knew his trauma colored his view of life, like a pair of dark-lens glasses that killed all the light he could otherwise see. The insanity of not knowing where he was, if he was still alive.

She sat behind her desk and opened a calendar, staring at the day's date for a long minute. October fourth, a Wednesday like any other, yet dangerously close to that blurry deadline he'd mentioned, November. He didn't say anything else other than November; no day, nothing more precise than the month itself. But was it real? She thought she still had a bit of time left, and now, in his absence, she realized that time might have run out.

It was getting dark outside, and the hues of a fogless sunset colored her office, in deep harmony with the colors of her décor. Other nights, she would've relished the visual integrity, the melody of the result, but that night she didn't even notice it. She stopped her pacing in front of the window and looked at the quiet street below; no traffic, no car headlights disrupting the peaceful dusk.

At 7:34, she wondered how much longer she was going to wait, and why. What was she hoping for? He'd never before called or arrived later than his assigned hour. Not to mention she could forward her office number to her mobile phone and leave for the night.

And go where? The thought of entering her home, shrouded in darkness and silence, chilled her to the bone. Even if she started a fire and played some music, gloom would still linger in the corners of the rooms, in the coldness of the floors, and the chill of her bedsheets, memories of a life that existed no more, milestones of her loss.

She shook her head slowly, then picked up the phone and dialed a number. A man picked up immediately.

"Ang," he said cheerfully.

"Hey, Dad," she greeted him, trying to hide the sadness in her voice and realizing she was failing.

"Ang, what's wrong?" he asked. She hadn't fooled him once, not since she could remember. Not since she was seven and had fallen from the neighbor's orange tree, and failed to lie herself out of trouble.

She breathed, feeling unwanted tears blurring her vision. "It's my patient, he... didn't show."

"Oh, Ang," he whispered, "I'm so sorry. This must be really hard for you."

"He didn't say anything, and I thought I still had time." She stopped talking, afraid he'd hear the tears in her voice.

"Any one of us could lose a patient, and there's only so much we can do. You know that, don't you? We can try our best, but there aren't any absolutes in this line of work, sweetie."

"I know," she sighed, "but there are almost thirty days left to that deadline he gave me. I thought I had time." She argued with him against all logic, as if she'd convinced him, DJ would somehow still be alive.

"How sure are you of that deadline?" Her father spoke in a clinical voice, the tone she remembered from her early career mentoring sessions.

She didn't answer, suddenly aware she had no reason to believe that DJ's deadline was real.

"Considering you could get him admitted for forty-eight hours around that date?" he continued. "You know you have to take everything a patient says with a grain of salt or two."

"Oh, crap," she whispered.

"Do you know for sure something happened?"

"No, he just didn't show, that's all."

"Maybe he skipped the session and didn't bother to call. Don't jump to conclusions, Ang."

"Uh-huh, you're right," she said, invigorated by the urge to call every hospital and morgue there was in the San Francisco Bay Area. She needed to know, desperately.

"Why don't you come over for a cup of soup?"

"You made soup again?"

"No, but by the time you get here, it will be almost ready. Just say the word, Ang."

She laughed quietly, feeling renewed tears flood her eyes. "Not tonight, Dad; there's something I need to do. Maybe tomorrow?"

The moment she hung up, she retrieved her emergency contact list from her phone and dialed the first number, San Francisco Police Department.

"SFPD, how may I help you?" a woman said in a tired, dull voice.

"Yeah, this is Dr. Angela Blackwell. I need to know if you have any suicides or attempted suicides that match a patient of mine. Male, Caucasian, six-four or six-five, former military. Go back a week, please."

"Let me check," the woman said, and the line went dead for a long minute. "No, we have a few attempts in the past week, none that match your guy, and a Jane Doe who OD'd on sleeping pills."

"All right, thanks," she replied and hung up, somewhat relieved.

That didn't mean anything, really. He could've been taken to an emergency room without calling 911, and police would have no record of it. He could be hospitalized somewhere. She started calling hospital emergency rooms, working her way through a long list, call after call. At the end of an hour, she hadn't located him anywhere, which relieved her worries somewhat, but not entirely. Maybe he was floating somewhere and hadn't been found yet. Maybe he'd shot himself in a remote corner of the city, and no one knew about it yet. Maybe he'd traveled across the country, to make sure he was as far from Taylor as possible when he killed himself.

Or maybe she was going completely insane, and it had to stop.

She had to find him, find out who he was, and end that paralyzing anguish once and for all.

She spent the next couple of hours digging through the videotaped sessions, looking for a good image angle she could use. For someone who'd demanded to have his sessions recorded, Dylan had done an excellent job at hiding his face. For the most part, he'd kept his head lowered, turned away from her, away from the viewfinder. Distant profile views, shot against the light coming from the window, or images of the empty couch when he'd paced the room or looked outside the window. She had nothing.

She turned off her computer and left her office, then closed the door and locked it from the lobby. As she pulled her car keys from her purse, her eyes fell on the security cameras hanging from the ceiling, by the main entrance. She stared at them for a second, then unlocked her office door and went back inside.

# 36

# Identity

It took Angela almost an hour to get the property management company who owned her office building to deliver a few grainy shots to her inbox, but at least they'd delivered. DJ's frontal and profile headshots in black and white, blurred from the enhancement and grainy from the low-resolution cameras they used. A full body shot, showing him entering the building, and another partial profile showing him leave the building.

It was a start.

She checked the time and groaned; it was almost midnight on the East Coast. She hesitated for a split second, then dialed her daughter's number.

"Mom," she picked up quickly and spoke cheerfully.

"Hello, sweetie," she said, feeling her heart swell and, for a minute, forgetting all about her mysterious patient's identity. "I didn't wake you, did I?"

"Nah, you're fine," she replied. "How's life in Cali? I miss it, Mom."

"Come visit anytime, sweetie," she said, a little choked, then cleared her throat quietly. "Why aren't you on a date with the premed student by the name of Jamie?"

"Who says I'm not?" she giggled. "He's sitting across from me at the table, in this late dining restaurant-slash-diner that fits our budgets," she laughed, and Angela heard a man's youthful laughter in unison with hers.

She listened intently and closed her eyes, visualizing her daughter eating, chatting, laughing happily with her young man in a cozy, unpretentious restaurant setting. She grabbed hold of that idyllic image, pulling it close to her heart.

"Good girl," she eventually said, after letting that image linger in her mind for a while, undisturbed, cherished. "I need your help with something, then I'll let you go."

"What's up?" Shelley said quickly, a little worried.

"Do you know someone who's really good with the Internet, who could find—"

"Like a hacker?"

Young people, so impatient.

"Um, maybe, I'm not sure," she hesitated, not knowing how much information she should share with her daughter.

"Tell me what you need," Shelley said.

She breathed quickly. "I have a photo of a man. I need him found. I have to know who he is."

"Ah… Should I even ask?" Shelley quipped.

"It's better you don't," Angela replied. "Do you know anyone? I mean someone you can trust, not just anyone."

"I'll text you his info. He's one hell of a geek. You can call him now; he never sleeps."

"Thanks, sweetie. Have a good time, all right? I miss you."

"I miss you too, Mom."

She stared at Shelley's picture on her phone for minutes after she'd hung up. What would her daughter's destiny be? Would she spend her life with a loving man by her side, eager to come home to him every day? Would she be one of the lucky ones?

Her phone chimed with a new text message from Shelley, only a name, Ethan, and a phone number. Angela initiated the call, and a young man's voice picked up immediately.

"Who are you and what do you want?" he said, making her chuckle.

"Yeah, hi, Ethan, I have your contact from Shelley Blackwell. She said you might be able to help me track down a man's identity. I have a photo."

"Yeah, she told me. Send it over."

She quickly texted him the best of the photos she had, holding her breath, feeling her heart pounding in her chest. She was overstepping an important boundary, and knowing that made her uncomfortable, nauseous even. The thought of betraying a patient's privacy was unprecedented and unconceivable in her mind, and yet she had no other choice.

"Got it," the young man said. "Location?"

"San Francisco Bay Area," she replied.

"Give me a minute."

"I can call you tomorrow, if you—"

"No need. It won't take more than an actual minute, I promise."

She heard the keyboard clacking on the other end of the line as Ethan typed quickly, then he muttered, "Uh-huh, um, yeah. Got it. Your guy's name is Dylan James Ballard. I'll text you a link to his info. I have a home address, work, cell phone number, place of birth, age, military records, even work phone. Anything else you need?"

"No, that's awesome. Thank you very much, Ethan."

"Hey, anything for a hot chick like Shelley."

She chuckled and hung up. Seconds later, a chime alerted her to a new text message, this time from Ethan, with a long link. She clicked it, and it opened a page with a customized search result that showed all the information about DJ, including a recent, full-color picture. Yeah, it was him. Dylan James Ballard, of Coalinga, California. He worked as a senior logistics manager at a local distributor of office supplies, and there was a mobile phone number listed under his name.

She mapped his address and looked at the screen in street view. It was a small house in South San Francisco, one of the many colorful little houses packed tightly together and tucked against the Paradise Valley foothills.

Then she pulled up Facebook and looked for him; she didn't find a listing, but found one for Taylor Ballard. She was stunning. She had a glow about her, a smile that reached her intelligent eyes, a light that engulfed her entire being. That woman had been touched by love; Angela recognized the signs in her deep, blue eyes, the slight tilt of her head, the hint of the smile she wore on her lips, the confidence in the way she let herself be photographed.

Angela remembered feeling that certainty, having that poise herself, when she knew she was loved by Michael. With him by her side, it felt as if she owned the world, and nothing bad could ever happen to them. But in Taylor's eyes, despite the smile that touched them, there was a tinge of sadness, an indication of sleepless nights and deeply buried agony. She stared at Taylor's photo for a while, thinking, wondering what secrets she was hiding behind that smile.

It was almost ten, when she finally picked up the phone and dialed the phone number that Ethan had provided. She held her breath, hoping DJ would pick up, worried about his reaction. After four long rings, he answered in a sullen tone.

"Hello," he said, barely audible against a background of a TV movie with lots of action.

"Good evening, DJ, this is Dr. Blackwell—Angela. I was worried when you didn't show up today."

"Why?" he asked coldly, and she heard him walk through the house and close a door that muted the sound of the TV. "I told you I can't be saved, so stop trying."

She swallowed hard. "Are you coming in next week?"

"Yes," he replied, sounding defeated. "How the hell did you get my number? And *why* the hell did you get my number?"

"I've had it for a while, DJ."

"How?"

"I'm good at what I do," she offered quickly, hoping he'd drop it. "But don't worry, nothing's changed. Our agreement still stands."

"Yeah… Anything else?"

"No, I just—"

The call disconnected, as soon as she said the word, "No." With a frustrated sigh, she put down the phone and returned to the computer screen.

She studied what Ethan had dug up from his military record. It wasn't much; the years he'd served, a total of seven, concluded with an honorable discharge. Numerous medals and commendations, most of them for bravery, but also a Purple Heart; he'd been wounded and hadn't said a word.

She nested her face in her cold hands and thought of things she could do, approaches she could try to get him to open up about what happened during his second deployment. Based on his reactions, it was clear that was where the traumatic incident had happened: Afghanistan. But he wouldn't talk about it, and she was running out of time.

She stood and walked over to the window, to the particular spot that had turned into the place of choice for her patient and her, and looked outside. The night was clear, without a wisp of fog, and the crescent moon accompanied a bright star toward the horizon line, reflecting in the calm waters. Farther in the distance, numerous lights mapped the rugged, coastal terrain with homes, brightly lit against the shiny surface of the ocean. Picture perfect. Hard to believe on a night like that, a man could be counting the days until he'd be able to kill himself. Hard to believe that in a few days, a beautiful, loving wife could become a hollow, broken memory of what she'd once been, haunted by ghosts and ridden with guilt.

She took her phone and flipped through her contacts, searching for one name in particular, a person she hadn't spoken with in a long time. A former colleague of hers had married Colonel McCormick of the United States Marine Corps, back then a handsome lieutenant, and they had spoken on two prior occasions. Once, at their wedding, when Angela met the young lieutenant. The second time, when they happened to land in the same hotel for their Vegas vacation, and he was a lieutenant colonel. Without hesitation, she typed an email, asking the colonel for help deciphering the events behind a veteran's posttraumatic stress. She kept the note short, and sent it, together with her phone number and an invitation to call anytime, day or night.

Moments later, she received an email. It read, "Dear Dr. Blackwell, it's a pleasure to hear from you again. Unfortunately, I cannot disclose any particulars whatsoever about a veteran's service record; only the information available under the Freedom of Information Act. That said, because many years have passed since we last talked, I'd appreciate the opportunity to have a cup of coffee with you, at my Pentagon office, at your earliest convenience."

Ten minutes later, her flight was booked, and a note to her assistant advised she needed to reschedule all her appointments for the next couple of days. Soon after midnight, she boarded a nonstop flight to Washington, DC. In a few hours, she'd know.

# 37

# Coffee with A Friend

Angela followed Colonel McCormick's instructions to the letter, including taking a cab instead of renting a car to visit the Pentagon; the massive Department of Defense building didn't have a visitor parking lot. She'd arrived at DC's Ronald Reagan Washington National Airport a little after ten in the morning and didn't stop for breakfast or coffee; she hailed a cab and rushed to meet the colonel.

He'd sent someone to pick her up from the visitor entrance, a young woman dressed in military garb, and Angela followed her instructions quietly. Within minutes, she was screened and wore a visitor badge affixed to her lapel, then she was escorted to the colonel's office, room 3C215. That meant he was located on the third floor, C-ring, room 215. She couldn't help but admire the logical and intuitive building layout.

The colonel was still in a meeting, and she waited patiently on a chair, in front of his office, for what seemed like ages. Finally, two men exited his office, and he stepped into the doorway to invite her in.

"Dr. Blackwell, welcome," he said warmly, then stepped aside and showed her in.

She remembered him a bit thinner and with a lot more hair on his head, but several years had passed since she'd seen him. Michael was still alive, it was during one of their last vacations together, a week of exploring the little-known, but amazing Mount Charleston Ski & Snowboard Resort near Las Vegas.

The colonel had a large office, lined with bookcases and filing cabinets along the walls, and a massive desk. He sat behind it and buzzed his assistant for coffee.

"How do you take yours, Dr. Blackwell?"

"Just cream, no sugar," she replied.

"You heard it," he said into the phone's speaker, then hung up, not waiting for any confirmation.

Then he leaned forward, smiling. "Delia sends her regards. If you're in town for longer, we'd love to have you over for dinner."

"Ah, thank you, but no, I'm flying back out today. Please give Delia my best. I hope she'll understand; I have an urgent situation with, um—"

"I understand all about patient confidentiality," he replied, "no need to share more."

She nodded, thinking how best to approach the situation. He seemed guarded, unwilling to discuss openly. She reached and grabbed a pen and a sticky note off his desk, and wrote on it, "Dylan James Ballard, USMC." She pushed the scribbled note toward him, and he frowned as he read it.

The assistant knocked twice, then entered with their coffee on a tray. She laid it on the desk, then promptly disappeared.

The colonel made an inviting gesture, and she took a sip. It wasn't bad at all, not after the redeye flight and the DC morning chill. She smiled and quietly thanked him with a slight nod.

"I understand you're here to discuss veteran posttraumatic stress issues, Dr. Blackwell, is that correct?"

"Um, yes," she replied, a little confused by his approach.

She watched him get up and walk over to a filing cabinet, with the scribbled note in his hand. He flipped through countless file folders, then extracted one and brought it back to the desk. He quickly read through it while standing, then he took his seat and leaned back, clasping his hands together over his generous abdomen.

"Based on our statistics, PTSD impacts on average 9 percent of the veteran population, with that number climbing up to 20 percent in the case of Iraq and Afghanistan war vets." He put both his hands on the file folder he'd reviewed.

Then she realized why he was acting a little strange; he was probably cautious, in case his office was bugged. Maybe office surveillance was a given in the highly secure DoD building. Most likely, he couldn't talk much in there. Then why bring her to the Pentagon in the first place?

"What other veteran statistics interest you, Dr. Blackwell?"

"Suicide," she said quickly, and saw a cloud of concern descend on Colonel McCormick's chubby face. "Risk of suicide is elevated in certain veterans with severe PTSD," she added, communicating her question in a manner that he could hear it, without causing him any problems.

He propped his chin in his hand and sat like that for a moment, pensive, restrained. "Thousands of veterans kill themselves every year, Dr. Blackwell, despite the Department of Veterans Affairs' best efforts to curb these staggering numbers and help our service men and women heal and integrate better after their return from deployment."

Their conversation wasn't going anywhere; she was looking for specifics, for the truth buried in DJ's past, not for politically correct brochure speak. Concerned, she shifted in her seat and looked at him inquisitively. For sure he didn't fly her all the way to the East Coast for drip coffee and generalities.

He grabbed the file and put it in his briefcase, then stood. "We have excellent grounds, and the weather is nice. I'd be happy to walk you out, Dr. Blackwell. I'm on my way to a briefing at the Capitol. I apologize for having to cut our meeting short."

She was stunned for a moment, but then she noticed his demeanor didn't match his words. He wasn't apologetic or reassuring, he didn't smile, he didn't behave the way people normally do when they politely want someone gone.

Intrigued, she followed him through the long corridors toward the exit, barely keeping up with his determined stride. Several minutes later they were outside, after briefly stopping to turn in her visitor badge and sign out. Once outside, he didn't stop; he continued the same brisk walk toward the parking lot. She followed him quietly, not daring to ask any questions.

"I'd be happy to give you a lift," he said, stopping near a mid-sized SUV and turning toward her. "I'm in a hurry, so I won't be able to take you all the way to the airport, though."

"Thanks, I appreciate it," she replied, and climbed into the passenger seat. They buckled up and drove away, and for a few minutes not a word was spoken. Then he pulled the note with DJ's name out of his pocket and gave it back to her.

"No one must ever know," he said, not taking his eyes off the road ahead.

"Absolutely," she replied, "you have my word."

"He's an excellent Marine," he said, speaking evenly, with undertones of sadness in his voice. "A talented sniper and a promising leader. Great fitness reports, one after another. Decorated, commended. He made sergeant, and he would've rose higher in rank."

He fell silent, focused on driving through the dense DC traffic.

"Then what happened?" Dr. Blackwell asked quietly.

"They think it was an IED," he replied. "Took out his entire team; only two survived."

"Two?"

"Yes, Sergeant Ballard and Lance Corporal Terrell Murray. The lance corporal lost his leg that day. I was a captain back then, on my third deployment, had my own company stationed in Kandahar. Ballard and Murray, they were in Captain Wallace's company; they were sent behind Taliban lines, deep inside Torgan Valley. That's where it happened."

"What exactly happened?" Dr. Blackwell asked.

He shook his head. "No one really has any details. We know some sort of explosive device blew up, and enemy snipers took out most of the survivors. Murray said all he remembered was being blown to pieces, and Ballard patching him up, staying with him until CASEVAC arrived, and killing the Taliban who fired at them. Ballard saved his life. They got their man too, a Taliban on the top ten, most-wanted list they were sent to find. They found his body twenty yards from Ballard, loaded RPG in hand."

"And DJ—um, Ballard?"

"He didn't speak. He was in shock, and he'd taken a bullet in his left leg. It's possible he's blocked that memory, who knows... We lost many good men that day, good Marines. He was their sniper support; he must have felt responsible. Guilt is a tremendous burden to bear."

LESLIE WOLFE

"He never said anything?" she insisted, wondering if DJ's friend, Nickel, could have been among the men who died that day.

"Not a word. He never again spoke of Afghanistan, of that day, of the men who were with him. He got discharged soon thereafter and commended for his bravery. He received a Purple Heart. Last I saw him, he endured through the award ceremony, then disappeared. I still recall his quiet stoicism during the commemoration. It was... unusual."

"I see," she replied.

It was starting to make sense. His reluctance to share anything from his military past. His behavior, his decision to end his life, all driven by trauma and guilt, and compounded by life's incessant difficulties. But she still wondered it if wasn't more, more than an IED and being wounded. Maybe something he couldn't remember, an event so traumatic that his brain had cut access to it, protecting him with the veil of posttraumatic, temporary memory loss.

McCormick drove to a gas station and stopped at a pump.

"Colonel, do you happen to know the names of the men who died that day?"

"Let me see," he said, and pulled the file from his briefcase. He opened it and flipped through some pages. "Master Gunnery Sergeant Joe Corbin, Private First-Class Ben Griffin, Private Jack Austin, Lance Corporal Kenny Navas, Corporal Peter Coyne—"

"Sorry, what was that? The last name you just said?"

"Peter Coyne?" he repeated, intrigued.

"Nickel," she whispered, realizing the nickname must have been inspired by the man's last name. "They were friends, DJ Ballard and Peter Coyne," she clarified, "I believe they grew up together."

His eyes turned to the page, then back to her a moment later. "You're right, doctor. Corporal Coyne was from the same town as Ballard. A place called Coalinga, somewhere in California."

"Thank you, Colonel," she said quietly, "I can call a cab from here. I appreciate your time."

He shook her hand. "A pleasure seeing you after all these years, Dr. Blackwell. I hope you'll succeed with Ballard, I really do."

# 38

# Shards

October days rushed one after another, in a desperate scramble to make the month be November, the month Angela feared the most. She couldn't remember another time when she sensed the passage of time so acutely, so inexorably unstoppable. Every few minutes, she checked the time, and time didn't disappoint; it flew by, bringing six o'clock closer, and with it, the question that didn't let her sleep nights. Was DJ still alive? Was he going to step through that door in a few minutes, or would she soon be bound to look for him again at hospitals and morgues?

She stood and watched the approaching sunset, coming earlier each day by a minute or two as the winter solstice approached. Fog was rolling in, a thick wall of white, milky vapor soon to engulf the sun and cut the twilight short. It wasn't there yet, and that meant she could still enjoy the deep blue color of the sky and the sparkling hues where the sun's dying rays reflected the restless water. Not for long, but for a few more minutes, the world remained an incredible palette of colors and light.

A black sedan pulled to the curb and Angela breathed a quick sigh of relief; DJ had arrived. He walked toward the building entrance with a determined stride, right after slamming his car door shut so forcefully, she heard the noise clearly from inside her office. Then he buzzed the intercom two or three times with long, impatient buzzes, and she let him in immediately.

She opened the door with a raised eyebrow, wondering what was wrong. He walked in and barely acknowledged her, then went straight to his seat and let himself drop on the couch, instantly hunching forward, tense and silent.

He had deep ridges on his brow, and the corners of his mouth were clamped shut and curled downward, while tense muscles swelled his upper lip and his jaws. He ran his hands through his buzz-cut hair a couple of times, then clasped them tightly together in his lap.

She sat down and waited for him to speak, but he didn't.

"What's going on?" she eventually asked.

"Nothing," he muttered, not lifting his gaze from the carpet.

"You seem tense, agitated. Something must be bothering you." She waited, but no reaction came from the taciturn man. "Maybe I can help."

He threw her a quick gaze. "The hell you can, Doc."

"Try me," she insisted gently.

He sprung to his feet and started his normal routine of angry pacing, from the wall to the window and back again, staring intently at the floor, probably without even seeing it. Then he stopped abruptly next to her chair and searched her gaze.

"It's that dog," he spat the words. "The shelter called and said no one claimed her within thirty days, and they're going to put her down."

She nodded a couple of times. "I see."

"I... had to take her back. Taylor's fuming."

"Why?" she asked quietly.

His frown deepened and a glint of irritation lit his dark pupils. "Why what?"

She forced some air into her lungs. "Why take her back? After all, death is such a salvation, isn't it?" she said calmly.

He inhaled abruptly, and the air entering his lungs made a distinctive, sharp noise. "Damn you, Doc!" he shouted, so loud it made her windows rattle. Then he grabbed a vase from one of her book shelves and threw it across the room, where it shattered against the fireplace mantle.

She let out a quick, sad laugh. "I'm already damned, DJ."

Disarmed, he let his shoulders drop and his arms fall alongside his body. Tension escaped his body, leaving it inert, depleted of resources. He stood there by her chair, towering over her, seemingly unable to move or unsure where to go.

"With dogs, it's different," he eventually said. "They deserve to live."

"And you deserve to die?"

"Yes," he whispered, then walked back to the couch and sat down. "Hell, yes."

"Why, DJ?" she asked gently. "Why do you feel you deserve to die?"

He resumed his usual posture, body hunched forward and hands clasped together.

"The guy at the shelter said he'd dug up her paperwork," he said after a while, changing the subject. "She had a microchip after all, but it was damaged or something. She injured her left hind leg, a piece of shrapnel, the guy said. She's a war dog, a veteran, can you believe it? What are the odds?" The pain in his voice was scorching.

"Yes, I can believe it."

"No one needs a wounded veteran," he muttered, more to himself.

She struggled to hear his words, and leaned forward to reduce the distance. "Why doesn't anyone need wounded veterans, DJ?"

He wrung his hands, over and over again.

Reading the message in his silence, she moved away from the direct approach and tried a different one.

"Why wouldn't people want a dog like that?"

He pressed his lips together for a while, but eventually he answered the question. "They want clean dogs, dogs with pedigrees, tail-wagging, young, healthy, well-behaved. Just like with people, dogs aren't wanted unless they're perfect. They don't care how loyal she is, how strong, how courageous." He sprung to his feet again and clenched his fists. "What the hell am I going to do, Doc? I can't—"

He stopped abruptly, as if he were afraid he might say the wrong things. Then he stood and walked around the room, looking for something. He grabbed the trash can from underneath Angela's desk, and started picking up the glass shards from the floor, one by one.

"I'm sorry about that," he said.

"Don't bother, I have a service. They come in at night."

"I'll clean up my own mess," he insisted, without stopping from picking up the many shards. Then he reached under the sofa, and toward the edges of the carpet.

"Really, there's no need—" Angela started, afraid he might cut himself.

"It's my bloody mess, and I'm going to clean it," he stated so fiercely that Angela shivered. "No one else should have to."

There was an intensity about him, something that ran deep, touching his inmost core. As if his self-loathing had an extreme urgency about it, requiring immediate action. That something she couldn't identify. Maybe it was the traumatic memory that burned him inside, relentlessly. Maybe it was survivor's guilt, equally merciless, forcing him to walk the earth feeling he didn't deserve to live. She'd hoped she'd have a better understanding of his trauma after visiting the Pentagon, but even the little she'd learned gave her enough to understand the dimensions of his agony.

Instead of insisting, she decided to change the subject and steer him back toward the main topic of discussion. "What about Taylor? Maybe she could take care of the dog," she said, holding her breath. Her approach could prove dangerous, lethal, if she helped him find solutions to the problem that, at least for a while, kept him alive.

"She wasn't happy," he said quietly, saddened, abandoning the trash can on the floor next to the fireplace. "When I brought her back home, she told me as much. That dog won't last a day after I'm gone."

"After … you're … gone," she echoed his words slowly, one at a time. "You care about what happens after you're gone. You care about Taylor, and you care about this dog."

He wrung his hands, then ran both of them through his hair again, as if to remove a weight, a thick web entangling his thoughts.

"I've always tried to do what's right, Doc. Always. But I've done terrible things…" His gaze veered to the left, away from her, while his fingers dove into his pocket to retrieve the two pebbles. Clasping them in his white-knuckled fist pressed against his chest, he continued, tense, dark. "She deserves to live, and it's my fucking problem to figure out how to make that happen."

The soothing sound of pebbles clicking filled the silence for a while.

"What's her name?" Angela asked gently.

"Skye," he whispered after a while. "Taylor named her Skye."

A tiny crack appeared at the heart of the dark cloud, large enough to let a hint of a smile appear on his lips, when he said both their names in the same sentence.

# 39

# Golden Gate

He woke with a tongue flick on his nose and the sound of a subdued whimper. He opened his eyes to find Skye sitting next to his bed, staring at him and slightly tilting her head. When she saw him wake, she started panting slightly, showing an inch of rosy tongue between her teeth and thumping her tail against the floor.

With a groan, he sat on the edge of the bed, and Skye started wagging her tail faster and pacing back and forth between the bedside and the bedroom door, still whimpering.

"You need to go out, don't you?" he said quietly, then stood and got dressed quickly. He pulled on a pair of jeans and a clean, white T-shirt, then went into the living room. He stopped in place, as soon as he saw Taylor. She was dressed in her gym attire, wearing the black, tight-fitting yoga pants and a bright pink top, but she was sitting on the floor, surrounded by opened boxes and scattered stuff. Before she could sense him looking at her, the expression on her face had been one of deep sorrow, of heart-wrenching loss. But then Skye trotted over to her, and she turned and saw him. Her look quickly changed, replaced by a smile.

"Good morning, sunshine," she quipped. "Glad you could sleep in for a change. That's what November Saturdays are for."

"What's going on?" he asked cautiously.

"This?" she gestured to the scattered boxes. "Just sorting old stuff. I decided it was time to go through some of these things, see what stays and what goes."

He nodded, too surprised to say a word. She'd never sorted anything nor thrown away any one of her packed items for years; she kept things, more and more of them. He recalled the expression of suffering she had on her face only moments earlier, and wondered if that was the cause of the cleanup, or the effect of it. Still, knowing how sensitive she was to talk about her collected things, he decided to avoid the subject altogether.

"I need to take Skye out. Want to join us?"

"Not now, I want to wrap this up first," she replied, and a bit of that earlier sadness returned and touched her eyes. "You guys go ahead. I might go to the gym later, after I'm done here."

She had already turned away from him, carefully going through the contents of a box that seemed to be filled with magazine clippings of various fashion items. He made for the kitchen and grabbed a few slices of cheese from the fridge to share with Skye, then put her leash on. The dog started pacing around him more enthusiastically, wagging her tail and batting it against the walls and doors. He grabbed his car keys and wallet.

"I'll take her to the coast," he said, turning and staring at Taylor's back. "It would be like in the old days, when we used to have our threesome dates with Lois. You sure you don't want to hang with us?" He smiled at the memory.

She tried to smile, but looked away instead. "Yeah, babe, I'm sure. You guys run ahead."

"Call me if you need me, or if you want to do stuff together," he said from the garage door, throwing her one more regretful look. He would've loved to walk on the beach with her, to see her smile in the morning sunlight, to see her eyes light up at the sight of the Pacific waves crashing against the shore.

He pulled out of the garage with Skye sitting on the passenger seat looking all serious, and closed the garage door, as soon as his car cleared the bay. Then he stopped again, staring at the pile of cardboard boxes stacked at the curb, next to a large recycle bin filled to the brim. She must have been at it, sorting and throwing away stuff, since the break of dawn. He frowned, worried, wondering what had brought the change in her, why now? The perspective of yet another move? Or was it something else, some irreparable damage he'd done when the cable guy was there?

He considered going back inside and taking her into his arms, to kiss her face and make that sadness in her eyes disappear. But he couldn't move; he sat there in the car, engine running, afraid he'd upset the fragile balance of their lives, afraid he'd only hurt her more.

After a while, he drove away, absentminded, thinking of Taylor and the change he'd seen in her, a change that had recently crept up on them without him noticing the exact moment in time it had started. He drove to Golden Gate and parked along the coast, at the bridge parking. It was still early; not that many cars crowded the area, and Skye could follow him off-leash on the path descending to the beach.

She was a good dog; calm and reserved, well-educated and responsive. Most of the time she didn't take her eyes off him, waiting for him to lead the way, to take her places she could explore and enjoy. Just like Lois.

They walked south for a while, along the coast, then he sat on a boulder by the old batteries above Marshall Beach, and let Skye go free. She wandered around, sniffing, splashing in the cold water for a few minutes, then she returned to his side and sat next to him, as immobile as he was, staring, just as he did, at the waves that crashed against Helmet Rock. He put his hand on her neck and scratched gently behind her ears, and she panted a little, turning her half-closed eyes to look straight into his.

"I hope you'll forgive me," he said, taking quietly to Skye. "Maybe, if you're lucky, she'll let you help her forgive me too."

Skye panted quietly, licking her nose from time to time and sniffing the salty air.

"I'll have to leave you, but it's not your fault, it's mine," he continued, still scratching behind her tall, pointed ears. "I've hurt enough people... I'm not going to hurt more."

Skye let herself drop to a down position, then threw her hind to the side a little, relaxed. Her tail wagged lazily whenever Dylan spoke; she seemed to love hearing his voice. She kept her eyes mobile, sweeping the surroundings, then looked at him every now and then.

"For you, there's hope," Dylan continued, "I promise you that. I'll make sure of that. For me, there's—"

A football landed inches next to them, startling Dylan and making Skye leap to her feet, her hackles raised for a second. Then, recognizing the ball as a toy rather than a threat, she whimpered quietly and searched his eyes for approval, while her tail went in circles.

"Nah, it's not yours. Let's ask for permission, shall we?"

He stood and looked around, trying to find the ball's owner. Two young boys, maybe twelve years old, were coming down the path, hollering and squealing from the bottom of their lungs.

"This yours?" Dylan shouted toward them, trying to make himself heard over the sound of the crashing waves.

The boys stopped squealing, but kept coming down the path a little slower, unsure.

"Yes," one of them said. "May we get it back, please?"

"Mind if the dog brings it to you?"

They laughed happily. "Sure, why not?"

He made a head gesture and Skye rushed and got the ball, then ran uphill with it to the boys, responding to their whistles. Moments later, the ball flew back onto the beach, and Skye chased after it, limping a bit but barking happily.

"Note to self," Dylan mumbled, "need a dog toy."

He sat back down on the boulder and leaned forward, watching the two boys playing with Skye, throwing her the football and squealing every time she rushed to fetch it. Behind them, crashing waves foamed white over Helmet Rock, majestic in the blinding sunlight. Farther to the right, the elegant silhouette of Golden Gate, still wrapped in wisps of fog, completed the postcard image. Gulls shrieked, plunging and soaring above their heads, careless and free.

The happy voices sounded eerily familiar, and his vision blurred, as he stared into the horizon. Memories of another time came uninvited, yet he welcomed them, long-forgotten feelings tugging at his heart.

"Look, DJ, I got one!" Nickel had hollered, pulling a fish from the lake's water. Lois barked playfully and rushed to him.

It was small, so small it could barely feed a cat for dinner, not the two of them and old Mr. Simmons, who'd loaned them his fishing gear in return for their first catch. They couldn't take that 4-inch crappie back to him and expect he'd loan them his gear ever again.

It was getting late, and they had a long stretch of mountain road to pedal on their bikes to get home, but they put new bait on the hook and threw the needle back into the water.

"Knock, knock," Nickel said, starting one of his typical jokes. They were almost fourteen, but the same things made them laugh as when they were much younger.

Dylan grinned widely. "Who's there?"

"Lettuce."

"Lettuce who?"

"Lettuce in, it's freezing out here!"

The two boys giggled.

"Freezing? Are you crazy or something?" Dylan asked, still laughing, looking at the scorching sun.

"Hey, we got one," Nickel said, and jumped to his feet. He quickly grabbed the fishing rod, but it was hard to hold on to.

Dylan rushed to help, and together they barely held the fishing rod from snapping loose from their hands. It was bent almost into a half-circle, its tip touching the water surface, being pulled in all directions by what seemed to be a reasonably large fish. Dylan gripped the rod with his right hand above Nickel's, as tightly as he could. Lois pranced in shallow water, caught in the boys' excitement and barking happily every time they hollered.

"Let's get it out of the water, Nickel, let's go! It will run away!"

"I'm trying," the boy replied, reeling the fish in, inch by inch.

"Faster! It could break the line. I think it's big," Dylan added excitedly.

"It's a monster," Nickel replied, striving to pull the rod up, then quickly reeling while dropping the rod tip back down.

They walked backwards while continuing to reel the fish in, and soon it started splashing near the surface, 2 feet away from the shore. Lois went deeper into the water, eager to sink her teeth in it.

"Whoa, that's big," Nickel said, a little worried. "Lois, get away!"

"All right, we got it," Dylan said, and pulled vigorously at the rod handle, helping Nickel ease the fish in. As soon it was thrashing around on the shore, he let go of the rod and grabbed the skimmer. Soon, the dying fish was throwing its last spasmodic moves in the grip of the net, and the two boys were catching their breaths, exhausted but exhilarated.

"Look at this monster," Nickel said. "Must be at least three feet long."

"More like two," Dylan replied. "But whatever you say," he quickly caved, seeing Nickel's disappointed look and slack jaw.

They grabbed their gear and rushed toward home. They had a good three hours of biking on mountain roads before they got there, and soon it would be completely dark. The entire time they pedaled hard, debating which fish to give Mr. Simmons: the 4-inch crappie, or the 3-foot catfish?

"Think of it as an investment," Nickel said. "If we give this monster to Mr.

Simmons, he'll loan us his gear again."

Then he screamed, as he fell after hitting a tree stump, barely visible in the deep dusk. They'd just left Indian Valley Road, and still had a stretch to go.

Dylan jumped off his bike and rushed to Nickel. He'd broken his leg, and he couldn't get up. He was trying to play tough, but he still whimpered a little and his eyes had welled up.

"What are we going to do?" he'd asked.

"I'll put you on the bike, and I'll walk you home," Dylan said.

"No, you go ahead and bring Dad with the car."

"I'm not leaving you," Dylan said. "Now get up. Grab my arm."

"This is stupid, DJ. You'll be home in an hour on your own. I'll wait here."

"Not leaving you, Nickel. Not ever. Now stop being a pussy and get on that bike already."

He helped him climb on the bike, then used both their belts to support his broken leg against the frame, so it wouldn't bounce around as they traveled. He tied both fishing rods and the skimmer holding the big fish to the back of the bike, then started walking alongside that bike, pushing it by the handles uphill, on the dark, narrow, mountain road. Lois walked alongside, growling at times, alert, ready to pounce at the tiniest threat. They chatted all the time, sometimes louder than they should have, because it made them feel safe, but it was Lois who gave them the courage to face the night, to cross that mountain in the dark. It was Lois, and it was each other.

At almost four in the morning, they arrived home to a display of red and blue lights flashing from the sheriff's car. Dylan's parents were both at Nickel's place, debating what to do. The boys got away with a twenty-minute scolding, both dads too happy to see them return safely to stay mad for much longer. Even Mr. Simmons let them keep the catch, and settled for a slice of fried catfish with garlic and fresh-baked bread the next evening. Later on, he grudgingly signed Nickel's cast and promised them they could have his fishing gear anytime they wanted.

Now it was all but a faded memory, their first fishing trip across the mountain. The memory soon faded, leaving him to notice how familiar Skye's barking was... she had Lois's strong voice.

Without realizing, he took out the two pebbles from his pocket and started playing with them, running his fingertips against their smooth surface, holding them against the light to see their translucence, closing his fist around them to feel their warmth.

LESLIE WOLFE

# 40

# Stalker

It was almost ten at night when Angela stopped in front of her father's home, shivering in the cold mist. The fog had clung to her hair and clothes, slowly soaking them, and tiny droplets of salty water covered her face, mixing with her tears. She'd walked there, after aimlessly wandering the streets, trying to find a peace that eluded her, despite her best efforts. Then she'd stopped by the grocery store, hoping the bright lights and soft music would derail her thoughts and steer her into the practicality of choosing soup ingredients.

The light was still on in Dr. Foster's living room, so she climbed the three stone steps and rang the bell. Her dad opened the door in his pajamas and a loose bathrobe, his pipe hanging from the corner of his mouth. For a moment, he stared at her with bewildered eyes, then rushed to her.

"Ang, my goodness, what happened?" He grabbed her shoulders, as if to support her, and she felt his strength replenish hers.

She sniffled lightly, then followed him inside. "I thought we'd make some soup," she said, smiling between tears and holding out the grocery bag.

Dr. Foster frowned and looked at her attentively, the way a clinician examines a patient. She lowered her gaze to the ground, knowing he wasn't going to like what he saw, knowing there'd be questions.

Instead, he turned around and walked toward the bedroom.

"Let's get you out of those wet clothes, and then we'll make some soup together. It's a great idea."

She followed him and waited for him to pull out some sweatpants and a shirt, as if that hadn't been her home for many years. Then he added a towel and a pair of wool socks to the bundle, and closed the door behind him to let her dry off and change.

She stood there for a while, frozen in time, her mind empty of all thought. Then, slowly, she changed into the dry clothing that bore a faint trace of his aftershave, a scent she associated with comfort and safety and love.

When she came into the kitchen, he'd already uncorked a bottle of red wine and filled two glasses. The chicken was laid out on a cutting board, and he'd put

174

on an apron.

"Drink up, my dear, you look like you need it," he said, his frown still present, ruffling his thick, white eyebrows. "Water's boiling already, now we need to add these," he said, wielding the knife like a real chef and making quick work of cutting the chicken into bite-size pieces.

She sat by the kitchen counter on a three-legged stool and took a sip of wine. Slowly, she felt her blood revive and start flowing through her veins again, bringing back a little warmth into her heart. She watched him dice the scallions, then some fresh parsley she hadn't thought of buying, but he already had in the fridge.

"Thank you," she whispered, feeling choked, "for doing this."

"Anytime, my dear," he replied, keeping busy with mixing egg yolk into some sour cream. He threw her a quick, inquisitive look, but didn't say a word.

She held his gaze for a split second, then looked away. "He didn't show up today," she eventually said. "Didn't call, didn't say anything; just vanished again."

He put the sour cream bowl down, then took a seat himself, on another stool, right next to her. On the stove, the soup started to boil, throwing the occasional drop of liquid onto the heated stove where it sizzled and died.

"It's November, Dad," she said, undertones of urgency and despair coloring her voice. "The month he said he'd kill himself." She sniffled quietly again, and took another sip of wine. "You know what I've been doing lately?"

"No," he replied, slightly louder than a whisper. "Tell me."

"I've turned into a stalker. I call his work line at night, to see if the company has replaced his voicemail message."

"I thought you didn't know who this man was," he said, deepening his frown.

"I've, um, found out. I've broken all boundaries and had him tracked down. I know where he lives, where he works, his phone numbers, everything."

"Oh, Ang," he said quietly, his eyes filled with sadness and concern.

"I follow his wife's social media online, and breathe a little easier whenever she posts something that tells me he's not dead yet. I call hospitals and morgues whenever he doesn't show up. I called them today too." She shook her head and then nested it in her hands. She remained like that for a while, until she felt her father's hand touch her arm. "I've tried everything I could've done, and haven't made much progress. This man wants to die, and there's nothing I can do to stop him."

"I'm so sorry," he replied warmly. "This must be really hard for you. But you know you tried your best, and I can promise you that where you're not succeeding, no one else could, either."

"That's the father speaking," she replied, pushing back, but smiling a little.

"No, that's forty-some years of professional experience. We can't save them all. We, doctors, we're not God, we're not superhuman; we can't save everyone."

She frowned a little. "You keep saying the same thing every time. Don't console me, Dad. I don't need that. I need him to live. It's almost as if my own life depended on it, and I can't explain why."

He took a deep breath, then searched her eyes. "Let's talk about you, for now. What is it about this man's potential demise that upsets you so deeply? I know you care about all your patients, but I sense something's different about him. You're putting yourself and your career at risk. Are you sure you're not—"

"Falling for him?" she asked. "You asked me before, and I asked myself a few times. No, it's not that. He doesn't deserve to die, just like Michael didn't deserve to die. His wife doesn't deserve to become like me, empty, hollow inside, a haunted ghost overwhelmed with guilt. I guess I identify with her. In photos, she seems relatively happy, not knowing life is about to deliver a blow so devastating she'll never completely recover."

"I see," he replied, "and you want to stop that tragedy from happening. It's understandable." He seemed to think about it for a while, pinching his nose at the root, then rubbing his beard. "What makes him so determined to die?"

"He was severely traumatized during his deployment to Afghanistan. Something happened over there that he's most likely blaming himself for."

"So, he shared that? Ang, that's great progress," he said, smiling proudly.

She averted her eyes, ashamed. "No... I traveled to DC and had his record pulled. I have a friend who's—never mind, who helped me."

Dr. Foster's jaw dropped and his smile vanished.

"They don't even know what happened," she added, still not looking at him. "He never spoke about it, not with them, not with me, not with anyone that I could tell. Not even during the post-mission debriefing, or whatever that's called. All they have on file is he saved a man's life, but many others died, including his best friend. Can you imagine, living with that kind of unresolved trauma for all these years?"

He pressed his lips together, while an expression of deep concern spread across his face.

"And I'm supposed to let him die, then testify on his behalf?" she said, raising her voice. "I can't do that," she added, wringing her hands together, trying to shake the cold that still clung to her fingers. "I said I would, but that was when I thought I had six months to stop him. I never imagined I'd end up like this, completely and utterly defeated. I believed his subconscious cry for help was genuine, at least to the point where he'd actually let me help him."

"Do you believe you're close to reaching him?" he asked, his concern somewhat replaced with his mentoring tone she was so familiar with.

"I don't know, I really don't. I've been pushing him hard, and sometimes I believe I see a crack in his shell, but then it vanishes, and his all-consuming self-loathing, his survivor's guilt comes back with a vengeance, and I can tell he's counting the days until he'll die."

"But he's postponing it still."

"Huh?"

"He hasn't done it yet, has he?"

She shook her head. "As far as I know. But he said November. Something to do with life insurance policy clauses."

"Ah..." he reacted, "he still cares about something. Then you have an edge, my dear. Discuss your reluctance with him. Be careful and gentle about it, but use whatever means necessary to buy yourself some more time, and maybe you'll be able to reach him after all."

"That's almost unethical," she replied, looking in his eyes, "I gave him my word. That's a serious departure from my professional—"

"Oh, and stalking him isn't?" he asked, grabbing his pipe and putting it between his grinning teeth. "Breaching his confidence, invading his privacy?"

She bit her fingernail, then looked at him, ashamed. "It is, yes. You're right. You're always right."

She averted her eyes, wondering if she should share the things she hadn't dared to share with him yet, the other things she'd done to get DJ to reconsider his plans. She regretted not having the courage to tell him, but feared his reaction could erode her steeled determination to keep her unwilling patient alive, regardless of the methods she employed. She was lying to her own father and mentor, and she almost never did that. And worse, maybe she was lying to herself, thinking she could stop him from carrying out his plans.

He poured soup in their bowls, then added sour cream mixed with egg yolk and some feta cheese crumbles.

She took a spoonful and savored the amazing taste, while her mind grappled at her father's idea, playing with it, visualizing how it would work when DJ would come for his next session. If there was a next session.

"No matter what happens," he said, "please keep in mind we can't save them all, Ang."

She smiled sadly and looked away.

"No matter what happens, Dad, I can't let him die."

# 41

# The Dog Problem

Angela rarely started a fire in her office fireplace, but this time she went with her gut and broke the unwritten rule, for no conscious reason she could think of. She finished setting everything up, only a couple of minutes before six o'clock, and from the fireplace she went straight to the window, to look for DJ's car.

It was already there, in the same parking spot as always, but he was nowhere in sight, probably on his way upstairs. A second later, the intercom buzzed, and she rushed to push the button.

He entered with an angry stride, a deep frown marking his brow, and his eyes turned away, avoiding hers. She greeted him, and he mumbled something in response, then took his usual place, hunched forward, grim, tense. It was déjà vu.

She took her seat and was about to ask him what was going on, when he turned toward her, exposing a stubbly face painted in anger and restlessness.

"I have to put everything on hold until I can solve the dog problem," he blurted out, talking fast, in a raised tone of voice. "No one will take her, no one. Unbelievable. I've tried everything short of selling her, but she's not mine to sell. And why would selling her work any better than giving her away for free?"

She nodded slightly, listening.

"It's driving me crazy," he continued angrily. "It's messing up my plans, my timeline, everything."

"Why are you in such a hurry to die, DJ?" she asked gently.

He pressed his lips together and swallowed hard. "You don't understand. I have, um, I've chosen a date, and set things in motion based on that date. It's not like I can tell people to put things off for a while, because a lost dog I happened to find on some street can't be placed. And Taylor... Why are women so damn stubborn?"

"Why don't you show her how good a dog would be for her?" Angela asked quietly, looking at him intently, holding her breath.

"And what? You think she'll let herself be persuaded, when she didn't like

Lois too much before, and she doesn't like having a dog now? All she talks about is dog hair, and drool, and pawprints on the carpet. As if our house were anything more than a bloody warehouse filled with cardboard crap."

"You said she collects things, right?"

"Yeah," he said, clasping his hands together and staring at the floor. "She does."

"Maybe she does that because she doesn't have anything else. Maybe if she could have something of hers, something she'd value, she'd ease up on the collecting, don't you think?"

"I told you why she does that, and nothing changed. Well... She did throw out a few things recently, had me taken by surprise, because we're still living on the brink, and she's still afraid she won't have what she needs. So, what are you talking about? Something like what?"

"Something like a dog," she offered gently.

He was talkative, not his usual taciturn self. His emotions bubbled close to the surface, and anger had replaced his infuriating calm. She had a better chance to reach him, if his defenses were weakened from within, consumed by his own turmoil.

"Pfft," he scoffed, dismissing the idea without any other comment.

"Maybe if you showed her how much fun a dog could be, she'd change her mind."

"You don't know Taylor," he said angrily, standing up and shoving his hands inside his pockets. Then he paced the floor slowly, with his head lowered, lost in his thoughts. "She's strong, and stubborn, as stubborn as only a woman can be. She doesn't know it, but she's been my strength all these years, and her determination saved us. If it weren't for her, I'd be..."

He lost trail of his words when he stopped at the window, looking outside.

"What would you be, Dylan?" she asked gently, using his given name for the first time. He didn't react.

"Lost. Without her, I'd be lost," he said.

"Spend some time with her and the dog," Angela insisted. "Give it a try, and give that dog some credit. You loved Skye the moment you saw her, right? Maybe Taylor will fall in love too. Just give her time."

"She won't let me. She doesn't want to spend any time with me, with us. When I come home late from work, she's already had to take Skye out, to feed her. To her, Skye is nothing but a chore."

"Then you need to take some time off, to be with Taylor and Skye. Go to a sunny beach somewhere, have some fun."

He turned to her, livid. "Fun? What the hell are you talking about? I'll be gone by the end of next week, and that's the way it has to be. I'm tired of waiting, tired of counting the days until the nightmare will be over. I can't... not anymore. It has to happen."

He ran his hand through his hair a couple of times, then plunged his fingers inside his pocket and found the two pebbles.

Speechless, she watched his entire body transform as he touched them. It was different this time; they didn't seem to calm his anguish, they seemed to bring it out more. His shoulders hunched forward, and his head bowed. His right hand closed around the pebbles, tightly, until his knuckles turned white and cracked, then he cradled that tense fist at his chest, as his breathing accelerated almost to a pant, a series of gasps for air that threatened to turn into something else she couldn't yet define.

She was close.

"How about this?" she stated calmly. "Get some money from your 401(k) account and move with your wife and your dog someplace nice, remote, on a Florida coast, where it's always warm and sunny."

He shook his head, but his breathing pattern and his posture didn't change. "You're not hearing me, Doc. I'll be gone next week."

"Give it a couple of months. You can always be gone in February."

"I can't. You don't understand; I got a job, obligations."

"The hell you do," Angela pushed back, "you were going to not show up for that job one of these days anyway. Stop lying to yourself. Give your wife some time with you, before you leave her for good."

His fist stayed tucked against his chest, and he still breathed heavily. "Where would I go?" he asked, sounding almost defeated.

"There are semi-rural communities on the Florida Gulf Coast that she might like. I can tell you a few."

"And if I don't?" he asked, with a sudden wave of renewed, angry resolve.

"These are my terms," Angela stated firmly, standing up so she could be closer to his eye level. "You will move there, and you will spend at least three months with Taylor before you can come back and finish what you started. You owe her that much."

His pupils dilated and his jaws clenched so hard she could hear his teeth grinding.

"Unless you do as I ask," she continued boldly, feeling her heart thumping in her chest, "I will not stand in testimony for your wife after you're gone. Feel free to start this charade over with someone else," she added, speaking calmly, a calm she wasn't feeling, afraid she'd pushed him too far. What if he stormed out of there in a blind rage and jumped in front of a truck?

His blood drained from his face. He turned to her, his hand still clasping the two pebbles tightly at his chest.

"Why are you doing this to me?" he asked, in a low, coarse voice. "Why?"

"I've looked into it," she continued, trying to appear strong and unperturbed, when in fact her hands were shaking and she felt she couldn't breathe. "Even if you kill yourself in public with tens of witnesses, the insurance companies could argue that such a long, detailed plan to commit suicide for financial benefit is in violation of the spirit of the policy. There is such a thing as spirit versus letter in our law system. Your wife would have to prove that the suicide was a shock to her, most likely introduced by recent events or factors, and entirely out of character. If she conveniently produced these videos that stated you acted alone, they'd be more than suspicious, and most likely the insurers would win in court. She'd end up broke and alone."

His face had turned from pale to flushed in a matter of seconds, and his veins throbbed visibly in his neck. He closed his other fist and brought them both in front of him, ready to pounce. Yet she wasn't afraid of him; she didn't believe he could physically harm her.

"Unless, of course, you give me the three months I'm asking for," she continued, "in which case, I'll help your wife whenever she needs it. I know people; I have influence, I can make things happen… or not happen. Your call."

He lunged and got close to her in a split-second, in her face, glaring at her. She looked up at him and held his gaze firmly, even if it took all her strength.

"You fucking bitch! Why are you doing this to me?" he bellowed so loudly, so close to her face, she felt the air vibrate.

She continued to look at him, but softened the intensity in her eyes.

"Because what happened in Afghanistan wasn't your fault, Dylan, none of it was."

He gasped a couple of times and nearly choked, but then found the strength to fight back.

"How could you possibly know? You're wrong," he shouted, and as he spoke, his shouting started to sound more like a tormented wail.

"It wasn't your fault, Dylan," she repeated gently.

His shoulders hunched forward some more, while his right fist pressed against his chest again. His face was scrunched in anger and agony, but his eyes lost focus, staring into emptiness.

"You don't know that," he said in a heart-wrenching voice, weak, as if he'd lost all his anger-fueled strength. "I made him come with me… I killed him… I killed all of them."

His knees gave and he buckled to the ground, then fell on his side, still keeping his fist at his chest, but curled around it, wailing, letting out low-pitched, agonizing sobs.

"I killed him…" he repeated obstinately, between wailing breaths of pain. "I killed him…"

She crouched next to him and touched his shoulder gently.

"No, Dylan, the enemy did."

But he didn't seem to hear her anymore. His eyes stared into empty space, somewhere beyond the flames blazing in the fireplace, and long wails came out of his chest carried on pained, gasping breaths of air.

# 42

# Just A Kid

They'd been ordered to travel deep behind Taliban lines, at the heart of the Torgan Valley, toward a village named Sorkh Deh, a tiny spit on the map. Maybe three-, four-hundred people, not more, called that village home, but aerial surveillance had spotted hidden among them one of top ten, most-wanted Taliban.

Their platoon, code name Alpha Team, was going to approach the village from the southwest, and take positions as soon as they crossed the river. Another weapons platoon, approaching from the south, code name Bravo Team, was about to initiate the search for Abdul Rashid Omar, the son-of-a-Taliban-bitch who was the reason they were raising moon dust as fast as they could.

The road was terrible, barely deserving to be called such, an uneven path through the desert littered with loose boulders that made their Humvees bounce around, tin cans on wheels. They all donned their full battle gear, and with every hop and bounce, they rattled like sacks of loose hardware. And they cursed at the man behind the wheel, all the time, as if the driver were to blame for the bumpy road.

Dylan rode shotgun, holding on to the dashboard, half-turned toward the driver. His M40 sniper rifle was propped between his knees, handy, and his flak vest held as much ammo as he could fit in it. In the back, Navajo's endless supply of jokes, old and new, sprinkled laughter among the salvos of profanities, aimed at the Taliban in general, at that specific road, at Omar himself, and any others like him. Or spewed out there without targeting anyone in particular, a verbal form of stress relief, the only one they had available.

Master Gunnery Sergeant Joe Corbin, their leader, was in the Humvee ahead of theirs, and he was speeding ahead, while they were falling behind in a cloud of thick dust.

"Go, go," Dylan shouted, and the driver floored it, making the vehicle accelerate abruptly, throwing rocks and dust behind, bouncing badly on the uneven surface.

Then Navajo's voice, "Heard this one? Goes like this: Marines are better, just ask the sailor's wife," and then the ensuing roar of laughter. The driver's face, covered in dust and grime, his white teeth sparkling when he laughed at Navajo's old jokes. His gloved hands, gripping the wheel, and his eyes fixed on the road ahead. Then the driver turned and looked at him, and Dylan recognized Nickel's eyes through his ballistic goggles. He smiled tensely, and DJ jokingly punched him in the shoulder.

"We're going to nail Omar's ass today, guys," DJ said. "We're gonna be the names everyone sees on that most-wanted list, right under the line that crosses his name into oblivion, bearing today's date. We will make our mark on Taliban history, one so deep and painful they'll never forget, for generations to come. Oorah, Marines?"

"Oorah!" the four replied vigorously.

They'd arrived at their designated target location, and they pulled a few yards behind the leader's Humvee, then gathered around Corbin. They had a couple of hundred yards more to the village, but they decided to approach on foot, coordinated with Bravo Team's approach.

DJ took position behind a partially collapsed wall, probably what was left from a dwelling that had been destroyed in an explosion. The piles of rubble gave him and his team good cover, away from the eyes of the enemy, while offering a good vantage point with view of the entire village. He set the M40 rifle on its bipod, checked the magazine, and started to scan the neighborhood through the scope.

One hundred and fifty yards or so ahead, two rows of houses lined up a dirt road, all surrounded with masonry fences, all the same off-beige color, matching the dirty, yellowish-brown tint of the Afghan desert. All houses looked the same in that village, as they looked everywhere else in the Valley: flat and square, with tiny windows and dilapidated doors, sometimes just a rag hanging on a thread instead of a real door. He'd seen it on a recon map: The dwellings lined the riverbank on both sides, and beyond the edges of the village, poppy fields extended as far as the eye could see. Wherever the opium poppy grew, the Taliban wasn't far behind, like sand fleas on a desert dog.

"I see Bravo Team, two o'clock," he said, and Master Guns Corbin acknowledged with a grunt.

"Any unfriendlies?" Corbin asked.

He scanned the area again, left to right, then back, through the scope of his M40, then through powerful, tactical binoculars.

"Negative."

He kept scrutinizing the area, while Corbin radioed the Bravo Team lead to coordinate the search. Bravo conducted a door-to-door search of the village, while Alpha provided cover, hunting for snipers, sudden movement, anyone running.

Bravo Team had started banging on doors and conducting their search starting from the southeast end of the village, well within Dylan's range. He watched them move through his scope or through his tactical binoculars, go inside each dwelling with weapons in their hands while two Bravo Team Marines kept guard at the door, then saw them come out of there within a minute or two, and move on to the next house. No Taliban captured as of yet.

Corbin got off the radio and crouched next to him.

"Bravo said there's a suspicious man approaching. He's about to turn the corner, right behind that wall."

DJ focused on the edge of the indicated wall, nothing but a masonry fence surrounding one of the southernmost houses in the village, waiting for the man to appear. A silhouette, thin and not tall, dressed in a dirty, off-gray gown and loose pants, turned the corner and started coming toward them.

"I see him," he confirmed. "Orders?"

"Bravo's spotter saw him hide something under his gown, maybe an IED or a grenade. Don't let him approach our positions. Take him out."

DJ adjusted his scope to get a clearer view of the man's face. It was a kid, maybe thirteen, fourteen tops. He didn't have any facial hair yet, only some peach fuzz shadowing his lip and slightly extending his sideburns. He didn't wear a turban; his hair was cut like any young boy's hair would be cut in America.

"He seems Hazara, not Taliban," Dylan replied, without taking his eye off the scope's viewfinder, "and he's really young."

"Take the shot, Sergeant Ballard," Corbin repeated.

His finger squeezed the trigger a tiny bit, then released it. He frowned and pressed his lips together, then felt the burn of sweat dripping in his eyes. He wiped his brow quickly with his right sleeve, then put his finger on the trigger again.

"Master Guns, can we at least confirm he's rigged to blow?" he asked, keeping his eye glued to the rifle's scope and watching the kid approach unperturbed. He looked serene, unafraid. He had less than 40 yards left until he reached their position.

"Sergeant Ballard, I'm not giving this order lightly," Corbin replied. "Take the shot. Now."

"Permission to approach the target and confirm the threat?" he heard Nickel's voice behind him.

Corbin groaned and cussed under his breath. "Take Terrell with you and make it quick. Ballard, keep your damn finger on that trigger and be ready to take him out."

He remembered feeling the chill, that warning sign the survival instinct sometimes gives those who are about to make a terrible mistake. He remembered thinking he could still pull the trigger and take that kid out, before Nickel and Terrell got in harm's way. He remembered hesitating again, one second too long.

The kid froze in the middle of the dirt road, his wide eyes staring at the two approaching Marines. He saw Nickel gesture toward the kid, but couldn't hear what he was saying. Then, as in a slow-motion nightmare, he saw the kid put his hand inside his long shirt, and Dylan started to squeeze the trigger. The next moment, he released it again, breathing heavily, when Nickel's back blocked his view of the target.

"No shot, Master Guns, I got no shot," he said, surprised at the tone of urgency, almost panic tinting his own voice.

"Fuck," Corbin muttered, and ran to the left with his M16 aimed at the kid. "Too far, I could—"

That's when all hell broke loose. The explosion shook the ground and, after the sound of it subsided, he heard an agonizing scream. He looked through the scope but saw nothing but swirls of dust. He sprang to his feet and grabbed an M16 on his way to where Nickel and Terrell had fallen, and ran as fast as he could, screaming Nickel's given name.

"Peter! Oh, fuck, Peter!" Navajo and Texas were right behind him, while Corbin and Griffin were approaching alongside the wall, taking cover behind the occasional pile of boulders.

He heard shots, the whistling sound through the air that a distant sniper's bullet makes before hitting the target. He heard a thump, looked behind, and saw Texas lying on the ground, blood pooling around his head. He forged ahead, desperate to get to Nickel, not giving a damn about that enemy sniper's fire.

Then he felt something rip through his leg, the pain so brutal and instantaneous, it knocked the air out of his lungs and he collapsed to the ground. But he still didn't stop; he kept on crawling toward Nickel, who was only a few yards away. Behind him, he could hear the familiar sound of M16 rifles spewing fire, but he couldn't see the enemy anywhere. He knew they were there, somewhere close, and he saw their bullets flying through the air, silencing the M16 rifles one by one.

Soon all weapons, friend or foe, fell silent, and all he could hear was Nickel's agonizing cries. He crawled the final yards and stopped when he could grab his extended hand, then pulled himself closer to him, to make out the garbled sound he made, while blood spilled out of his mouth.

"Dylan... please," Peter said, clasping his hand forcefully, then he choked and coughed out more blood.

Dylan raised himself high enough from the ground to look at his friend's body. His legs were gone, and blood was everywhere. He'd taken a piece of shrapnel in the abdomen, and more blood was oozing from that gaping wound.

"We need CASEVAC here," Dylan shouted into his radio, then, without hesitation, he pulled out his CLS, the standard issue combat lifesaver kit, and started wrapping a tourniquet around what remained of Peter's right leg.

"No," Peter pleaded, reaching out and grabbing his sleeve. "Please..."

Dylan looked him in the eye and understood his unspoken request.

"No," he shouted, "I won't leave you. I won't," he repeated, unwrapping the combat gauze and pressing it against the wound in Peter's abdomen. "I can't."

"I'm already gone," Peter managed to say, then his hand found Dylan's and tucked something in his palm, a small, white, blood-stained, river pebble. "I'm just a heap of pain waiting to be set free."

"No!" Dylan shouted, "No! Helo is coming, I can already hear it," he lied, tears running down his face. Then he clicked his radio and shouted, "CASEVAC, where the fuck are you? We need you now, goddamnit, now!"

"Remember?" Peter whispered, wrapping his palm around Dylan's, where the little pebble was nested. "Set me free... my brother..."

Dylan dropped the dressing he was holding and searched his friend's eyes. Through the blur of tears, he saw agony in there, undeserved, hopeless pain. He saw his friend begging him for help.

He let an inarticulate cry escape his scorched lips and pulled out his handgun. Peter saw his hand hold the weapon and nodded, his eyes riveted to Dylan's, pleading, agonizing.

Dylan pulled himself to his knees next to him and removed Peter's helmet. Then he cradled his face at his chest, holding tight, while he wailed, rocking gently back and forth as his gun's barrel found Peter's ear.

The shot resounded louder than the earlier explosion, or so it had seemed to Dylan. He didn't let go of Peter's head, holding it tightly at his chest still, his mourning sobs resounding strangely in the silent valley.

Then he heard his name being called from a few yards away.

"DJ, I need your help, buddy," he recognized Terrell's voice. He stared at him, at his body laying immobile in the desert dust, but he couldn't move, not while Peter was still in his arms. He couldn't put him down. Not yet.

"Sergeant Ballard, this Marine needs your assistance," Terrell's voice made itself heard again.

He laid Peter's head on the ground gently, on the remainders of his combat lifesaver kit, and closed his eyes with trembling fingers. Then he stared at the pebble in his hand for a long minute, reluctant to let it go.

"Sergeant Ballard!" Terrell's voice called again, and he made himself put the pebble in his chest pocket, where it joined the other one.

Then he crawled to where Terrell had fallen. His left leg was smashed below the knee, and he was bleeding from a shrapnel wound in his arm. He wrapped a tourniquet under Terrell's knee and patched up his arm the best he could, then radioed again for help. He'd just finished working on him, when a bullet ripped through the air and dug into the ground, only a foot away from Terrell's head.

"Whoa, motherfucker," Terrell reacted, and started to crawl toward a pile of boulders, not even big enough to provide full cover.

Dylan took his weapon and started searching for the shooter with tear-blurred eyes. He didn't see anyone, but he thought he saw a glint near a distant wall, maybe the sun reflecting off the shooter's optics. He fired a carefully aimed shot, not expecting much, given the distance. He saw a body fall to the ground, but immediately bullets started coming their way from two other locations. He crawled closer to some boulders, and from that partially covered vantage point, he peeked his M16's barrel and started looking for targets.

He'd just taken out the second man and heard Terrell's weak voice yelling, "Yeah, eat that, fuckers, that's my man," when the familiar sound of a rescue helo chopping the air reached him, and he finally let go. He dropped his rifle and let himself fall to the ground, curled up on his side, wailing, his sobs resonating over ages.

Darkness had fallen for some time, and the fireplace was the only source of light in Dr. Blackwell's office. She hadn't moved from Dylan's side, listening to his haunting voice, as he relived his nightmares, there to help him find his way back from his own personal hell.

She didn't speak, didn't ask him anything, but she knew she'd finally reached him. He would talk when he was ready.

We don't fear death; we're terrified of losing life's
sweet droplets of elation.

# 43

# Saving Lives

Her last appointment for the day had just left, but Angela felt restless, unaccomplished, as if something were missing, something she'd forgot to do. It was a Wednesday afternoon, a day that had been reserved, up until a few months ago, for DJ's appointments. Now her day ended earlier, at four in the afternoon, but not a single Wednesday since Dylan had last been in her office had she made it out of there before seven.

He wasn't going to come back; she knew that. Yet her hesitant footsteps carried her to the window, where she leaned against the cold glass and looked down at the street below, as if she expected to see his black sedan parked by the curb. The spot was empty and had been every Wednesday evening since November of last year.

The intercom buzzed, and she made an effort to move away from the window and press the button.

"I have Barney here for you, doctor," her assistant said. "He doesn't have an appointment."

"Send him in," she said, smiling. She was always happy to see an old patient.

"He... has a dog with him, doctor," she added, and Angela could tell she was frowning, by the disapproving inflexions in her voice.

"Oh, that's fine," she replied, "send them both in."

She opened the door and stepped aside, making room for Barney and his companion.

"Barney," she said, then gave the bulky man a warm hug in the doorway, while the dog waited patiently.

"Dr. Blackwell," he replied, "thanks for seeing me."

"Always good to see you, Barney, come on in."

He entered the office and his companion followed, making tiny sounds when toenails clacked against hardwood.

She stared at the dog's beautiful face and almost found the courage to touch the big, pointy ears. She didn't know how the dog would react, so she pulled back her hand.

"Here's a GSD, just like the one you wanted, Doc."

"A GSD? You mean, this?" she asked, confused.

"A German Shepherd Dog, or GSD for short. Remember you sent me a dog's old picture a few months ago and asked me if I had one available?"

"Uh-huh," she nodded, with a cryptic smile. "Yeah, I do."

"Well, here it is," Barney said, ready to hand her the leash.

She smiled and lowered her eyes, but as she did, she met the warm gaze of the animal.

"Thanks for all your help, Barney," she said, "but the Malinois worked perfectly fine."

He smiled widely, showing two rows of white teeth that sparkled against his dark skin. "Glad to hear it, so glad."

She gestured an invitation for him to take a seat, and he did. The dog lay at his feet, and, for some reason, that gesture tugged at her heart.

"Hey, look, I'm sitting in my old spot," Barney commented, with a small laugh.

She laughed too, but her mind went to Dylan again; that used to be his spot also.

"That was some strange way to place a dog," Barney continued his earlier thought, "leaving her alone in the street like that for the guy to find. I was hiding behind that dumpster there, you know, the one next to your office building, in case he didn't see her or didn't take her with him. But, hey, I'm not complaining; anything to save a life."

"Barney," she said, slightly louder than a whisper, feeling choked, "just know that time you saved two."

"Huh?" he said, confused.

"May I?" she asked, approaching the dog.

"Have at it, Dr. Blackwell. She's gentle, won't say a peep."

She crouched next to the dog and extended her hand. The dog sniffed it, and she noticed her wet nose move, then a rosy tongue flicked quickly and touched her fingers, spreading warmth inside her heart.

She touched the dog's head, amazed at how silky and soft her coat was. As she continued petting her, the dog started panting quietly, savoring the interaction. Her tail thumped against the floor in a subdued, constant rhythm. She listened to the sound of her breathing, and imagined that sound breaking the cold silence of her empty home. She envisioned her toenails clicking against the floors in her living room, scratching at the door, and her strong voice barking at late passersby on the street. She saw herself rushing home after her appointments, even on Wednesdays, to spend time with her.

"Maybe it's time to slow down and discover what's important in life," she whispered, looking into the dog's half-closed eyes, "don't you agree?"

Barney looked at her with a frown of amazement.

"I don't know much about dogs, Barney, but do you mind if I give it a try?" she asked, smiling shyly.

He handed her the leash with a big smile. "She'll steal your heart, doctor."

"What's her name?"

"It's Lexi," he replied, and the dog's ears perked when she recognized it. "But you can name her anything you'd like. She'll learn her new name quickly."

"No, I wouldn't do that," she replied, continuing to pet the dog's head, then continued, half-jokingly, "A changed name could lead to identity issues, behavioral changes, unnecessary psychological distress. No need for that. Lexi is fine. I like it." She felt good about her decision, although she'd never been one for sudden changes in her well-established life.

"She eats twice a day, about this much," Barney said, making a gesture with both his hands. "She'll need a vet to make sure she's okay. At the shelter, we don't have all the bells and whistles, but we try our best. Her shots are up to date."

"We'll figure it out, Barney, and if not, we'll call you for help."

"Anytime, Dr. Blackwell, anytime," he said, then he left, still wearing a big grin on his face.

Lexi stood and tried to follow Barney, but the door closed in her face and she whimpered quietly, confused.

"Come here, Lexi," Angela called, and the dog obeyed, a little reluctantly, walking slowly, with dignity, then sat on her tail in front of Angela and searched her eyes.

"Welcome into my life, Lexi," Angela said, scratching her neck, right behind her left ear. "Apparently, the likes of you are worth living for."

# 44

# A Letter

*Almost a year later*

Taylor looked outside the window through breezy, white sheers and saw two familiar silhouettes by the water line. Dylan stood tall, hands propped on his hips, staring into the horizon. By his side, Skye sat on her tail, wagging it slowly, her pointy ears moving with every sound. It was still early, and the sunlight bore hues of orange and gold, reflecting in the water's trembling surface and sending playful, inviting glimmers her way.

Her lower back hurt a little, and she rubbed it quickly with both her hands, then sat in front of her desk. There was something she needed to do, and she took a moment reflecting on the best way to do it. Then she pushed aside her laptop and took out a few sheets of paper instead, laying them in front of her. Pen in hand, she stared at the forbidding, white surface for a second, but didn't hesitate much longer and started writing in cursive, forward-slanting script.

*Dear Dr. Blackwell,*

*It's been almost a year since I received your sobering call. Sometimes, I close my eyes and still can't believe it happened, can't believe I came so close to losing him. I was running through dense fog, and didn't realize I was approaching the edge of a cliff, about to fall, when you stopped me. You saved me... you saved us. I'm still reeling from it.*

*I remember feeling as if I were living a nightmare, one from which there was no waking up, one that you helped me navigate. I remember not believing you at first, because I didn't want to believe he was planning to leave me, not like that. Then you held my hand and taught me what to do to help him hold on a little longer. Another day, then another week, another month.*

*You should know the hardest thing I had to do was to say no to that dog, knowing that it could push him over the edge and rush him into doing the unthinkable, seeing how she made him smile a little. You were adamant about it, and I had no choice but to take your advice. Talk about taking a leap of faith... I'm glad I was wrong and you were right about Skye. She helped him find his way back and yes, for a while I was jealous of that stray who came into our lives. What did she have that I didn't? Why did he hold on for her, while for me, he wasn't going to? But Skye grew on me, and I started feeling grateful for every smile she brought to his eyes, for every moment he chose to spend with us, here, in our reality, instead of letting himself be drawn back, prey to the nightmares of his past. Can you believe she sleeps on our bed now, and I'm okay with it? My goodness, people change...*

*Speaking of change, our lives couldn't be more different. We're in Florida these days, living at the far end of a small community on the Gulf Coast, a place called St. George Island. We live a simple life; it's peaceful, so peaceful that many times the only sound we hear is the ebbing and flowing whoosh of gentle waves crashing against the sandy shores. He's been slowly coming out of his abyss, much too slowly. I know you told me it will take him time, years even. I can wait, as long as I see him coming back to me, to a life together.*

*He was scary quiet for a couple of months after we moved, unpacking like we've always done it, but slightly different. This time he was putting thought into things, and I had done the same. Sadly, most of my things are gone; they never made it out of California. But that's in the past.*

*When we arrived, he bought a fixer upper on two acres of sandy land facing the sound, after only briefly consulting with me. I said yes, per your instructions, although this is not ideal for me, not to mention he threw away a promising career in business that we spent years building, and I was understandably disappointed. But he took the time to settle in, to get us comfortable, although during those months he was dark, quiet, absent, and I was scared. Then he started working with Skye, to help her with her limp. She'd been injured before she came into our lives, I don't know if you knew that, and her hind joints were a little stiff from that injury. He worked with her every day, taking her swimming in the warm, shallow waters of the sound, and she recovered.*

*People saw and talked, posted online, did what people do these days, and soon he opened our home and backyard to people who needed assistance with the recovery of their injured dogs. They came here, camped in our backyard or stayed in local hotels, for as long as they needed. Then they posted their experiences online, and now we even have people flying in from the West Coast to spend time with Dylan. I've witnessed some dramatic recovery stories here, but none as dramatic as his own.*

*After a while longer, he turned quiet and restless again for a couple of months, spending time locked inside the house, instead of being out there, with the visitors and their dogs. I was scared, seeing him like that again; I almost called you. But he wasn't planning to leave us anymore... he had applied for a grant with the University of California and later received funding. He built a shallow, saltwater pool with swim lanes, where dogs can swim alongside their owners, and a submerged treadmill. He bought the neighboring piece of property, where he's building a motel-like structure for travelers to lodge in. The Internet has dubbed it, St. George Marine Dog Haven.*

*He brought Terrell in to help us. You probably don't know who that is; they were buddies, back in Afghanistan, I think; they don't talk about it. He's a great guy and has a kid, a bright, nine-year-old whose laughter fills the room. The two of them drove in one day, and thus we weren't alone anymore; our small family had added two new members.*

*Sometimes, I see Dylan and Terrell sitting side by side on the beach, staring into the distance. By the way they sit there quietly, I know they're sometimes letting themselves be drawn into the past, but I'm happy they have each other to help find their way back.*

*Most important, Dr. Blackwell, he's alive. He's starting to look healthier, his eyes are smiling more and more. I'm fine too, although I'd lie if I said I don't regret the big city life. It took me a while to be fine; this isolated, uneventful existence isn't what I wanted, but I've made my choice of where I wanted to be a long time ago, when I said, "I do."*

*I've learned to make the most of it. I started to take remote work engagements as a virtual assistant, and I have my steady clients from whom I get enough work to pay the bills. Although Dylan never charges these families for their visits, they donate, and that adds up and helps a little. When the university sends one of their doctors for a few weeks, it can get quite busy. I help as much as I can, posting ads and success stories online, doing everything I can to extend the peace and quiet he needs to be healed.*

*You should know that I'm pregnant, almost five months now. I guess he stopped saying no to our child, when life stopped saying no to him. It's a boy, and we'll name him Peter. I'm excited and also a bit scared, thinking, worrying, hoping he'll be around long enough to see him grow. Hoping you'll be around to keep us safe, if he ever...*

*I don't even want to say it. No.*

*We're okay.*

*I know you told me I can never contact you about any of this, and I understand why. I'm eternally grateful for everything you've done for us; I hope you know that. But I had to write this letter to you, to let you know we're okay, and we're going to be okay. I'll keep uploading photos on Facebook, so you'll see how we're doing, and I hope you still look at them and think of us from time to time.*

She read the letter, wiped a rebel tear, and signed it. Then she powered up the crisscross paper shredder underneath her desk and ran the letter through it, page by page.

She then stood and looked outside, through the white sheers undulating in the gentle breeze. Dylan and Terrell were by the pool, and several people, some of them newly arrived, listened to their instructions. Dylan assigned lanes, showed them the water bowls and icebox he'd put in the shade, next to the big pine tree, then crouched down to pet a Border Collie who wouldn't put her front left leg down.

She hesitated for a minute, throwing long, guilty looks at her laptop, but then decided otherwise, put on a bathing suit, and decided to join Dylan and Terrell by the pool. They could use her help, and she could use the light exercise, not to mention it was a beautiful day, a shame to waste indoors, by herself in front of a computer screen.

~~ The End ~~

# From the Author:

# A Measure of Defeat

Every year, in the United States, more than 40,000 people end their lives. In 2015, that number rose to 44,193, out of which 33,994 were males (CDC Statistics, 2017). Suicide is the second leading cause of death for the 25–34 age group, taking more lives than cancer and heart disease, and the fourth for age groups 35–54.

An estimated 1.3 million adults, aged 18 or older (0.6 percent of the adult population), attempted suicide in the past year. Among these adults who attempted suicide, 1.1 million also reported making suicide plans (0.2 million did not make suicide plans).

Suicide rates are 53 percent higher for male veterans, and a staggering 5.51 times higher for female veterans (CDC Statistics, 2000–2010). Thousands of veterans decide to take the final step every year, in a distressing epidemic that plagues the nation.

Whenever lives are lost offshore, on the remote battlefields of the war on terror, our hearts bleed, our eyes well up, and our flags fly at half-mast. As of October 2016, there have been 2,386 military deaths in Afghanistan, since the battle started in 2001. We stand united in our grief for the fallen heroes of this nation.

At home, more than 7,000 veterans end their lives each year, and little is said or done about it. That shocking number is the measure of our defeat, as a nation and as a community. We lose more people on the home front, on a daily basis, than we ever imagined possible. Than the enemy has ever claimed.

In recent years, the problem has been acknowledged, and public awareness is beginning to rise; it's a start, and anyone can help, including people like you and me. There are many ways to get involved, to offer support, your time, if money is too tight. We can find a veteran organization nearby and start making a difference. We could invite that rather reclusive neighbor with a USMC bumper sticker on her beat-up Chevy for beers and burgers sometime; she might appreciate it more than you think. You know who I'm talking about; that neighbor who's never been quite the same since the return from deployment. We could look for service records on job applicants' résumés when hiring and choose wisely; steeled warrior hearts have a lot to offer in the workplace, maybe even more than Ivy League grads. We could be more tolerant and inclusive, and not be as quick to judge and dismiss when someone doesn't smile the right way.

We might save a life.

Read on for an excerpt from

## *Las Vegas Girl*

They're two fearless, driven, unrelenting cops. They trust each other with their lives… only not with their darkest secrets.

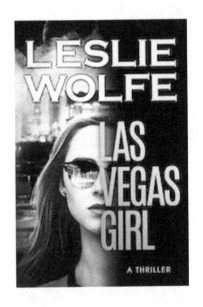

~~~~~~~~

# Thank You!

**A big, heartfelt thank you** for choosing to read my book. If you enjoyed it, please take a moment to leave me a four or five star review; I would be very grateful. It doesn't need to be more than a couple of words, and it makes a huge difference.

**Join my mailing list** for latest news, sale events, and new releases. Log on to www.WolfeNovels.com to sign up, or email me at LW@WolfeNovels.com.

**Did you enjoy reading about Dylan and Angela?** Your thoughts and feedback are very valuable to me. Please contact me directly through one of the channels listed below. Email works best: LW@WolfeNovels.com.

**If you haven't already, check out *Dawn Girl*,** a gripping, heart stopping crime thriller. If you enjoyed Criminal Minds, you'll love Dawn Girl. Or, if you're in a mood for something lighter, try *Las Vegas Girl;* you'll love it!

# Connect with Me

Email: LW@WolfeNovels.com
Twitter: @WolfeNovels
Facebook: https://www.facebook.com/wolfenovels
LinkedIn: https://www.linkedin.com/in/wolfenovels
Web: www.WolfeNovels.com

# Books by Leslie Wolfe

## BAXTER & HOLT SERIES

Las Vegas Girl
Casino Girl

## TESS WINNETT SERIES

Dawn Girl
The Watson Girl
Glimpse of Death
Taker of Lives

## SELF-STANDING NOVELS

Stories Untold

## ALEX HOFFMANN SERIES

Executive
Devil's Move
The Backup Asset
The Ghost Pattern
Operation Sunset

For the complete list of Leslie Wolfe's novels, visit:
Wolfenovels.com/order

# Preview: *Las Vegas Girl*

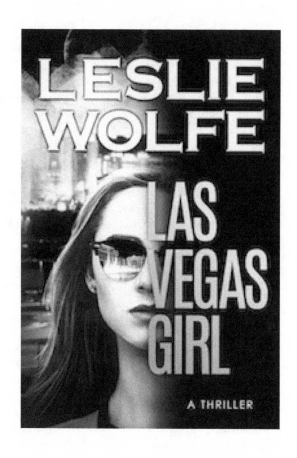

# 1
# Elevator Ride

Her smile waned when the elevator doors slid open and her gaze met the scrutiny of the stranger. She hesitated before stepping in, looked left and right uneasily, hoping there'd be other hotel guests to ride in the elevator, so she wouldn't have to share it alone with that man. No one came.

Her step faltered, and her hand grabbed the doorframe, afraid to let go, still unsure of what to do. The hotel lobby sizzled with life and excitement and sparkled in a million colors, as can only be seen in Vegas. Nearby, clusters of gaming tables and slot machines were surrounded by tourists, and cheers erupted every now and then, almost covering the ringing of bells and the digital sound of tokens overflowing in silver trays, while the actual winnings printed silently on thermal paper in coupons redeemable at the cashier's desk. That was Las Vegas: alive, filled with adrenaline, forever young at heart. Her town.

The elevator had a glass wall, overlooking the sumptuous lobby. As the cage climbed higher and higher, riders could feel the whole world at their feet. She was at home here, amid scores of rowdy tourists and intoxicated hollers, among beautiful young women dressed provocatively, even if only for a weekend.

She loved riding in those elevators. Nothing bad was going to happen, not with so many people watching.

She forced some air into her lungs and stepped in, still hesitant. The doors whooshed to a close, and the elevator set in motion. She willed herself to look through the glass at the effervescent lobby, as the ruckus grew more distant with each floor. She didn't want to look at the man, but she felt his gaze burn into her flesh. She shot a brief glance in his direction, as she casually let her eyes wander toward the elevator's floor display.

The man was tall and well-built, strong, even if a bit hunchbacked. He wore a dark gray hoodie, all zipped up, and faded jeans. He'd pulled his hood up on top of a baseball cap bearing the colors of the New York Mets. A pair of reflective sunglasses completed his attire, and, despite the dim lights in the elevator cabin, he didn't remove them. The rest of his face was covered by the raised collar of his hoodie, leaving just an inch of his face visible, not more.

She registered all the details, and as she did, she desperately tried to ignore the alarm bells going off in her mind. Who was this man, and why was he staring at her? He was as anonymous as someone could be, and even if she'd studied him for a full minute instead of just shooting him a passing glance, she wouldn't be able to describe him to anyone. Just a ghost in a hoodie and a baseball cap.

Then she noticed the command panel near the doors. Only her floor number was lit, eighteen. She remembered pressing the button herself, as soon as she'd climbed inside the cabin. Where was he going? Maybe she should get off that elevator already. Maybe she should've listened to her gut and waited for the next ride up.

A familiar chime, and the elevator stopped on the fifth floor, and a young couple entered the cabin giggling and holding hands, oblivious to anyone else but each other. She breathed and noticed the stranger withdrew a little more toward the side wall. The young girl pressed the number eleven, and the elevator slowly set in motion.

That was fate giving her another chance, she thought, as she decided to get off the elevator with those two, on the eleventh floor. Then she'd go back downstairs, wait for the stranger to get lost somewhere, and not go back upstairs until she found Dan. She'd call him to apologize, invent something that would explain why she'd stood him up. Anything, only not to go back to her room alone, when the creepy stranger knew what floor she was on.

A chime and the elevator came to a gentle stop on the eleventh floor. The young couple, entangled in a breathless kiss, almost missed it but eventually proceeded out of the cabin, and she took one step toward the door.

"This isn't your stop, Miss," the stranger said, and the sound of his voice sent shivers down her spine.

Instead of bursting through that door, she froze in place, petrified as if she'd seen a snake, and then turned to look at him. "Do I know you?"

The stranger shook his head and pointed toward the command panel that showed the number eighteen lit up. Just then, before she could will herself to make it through those doors, they closed, and the cabin started climbing again.

Her breath caught, and she withdrew toward the side wall, putting as much distance between herself and the stranger as she possibly could. She risked throwing the man another glance and thought she saw a hint of a grin, a flicker of tension tugging at the corner of his mouth.

With an abrupt move, she reached out and pressed the lobby button, then resumed leaning against the wall, staring at the floor display.

"I forgot something," she said, trying to sound as casual as possible, "I need to go back down."

On the eighteenth floor, the doors opened with the same light chime and quiet whoosh. The stranger walked past her, then stopped in the doorway and checked the hallway with quick glances.

She was just about to breathe with ease when he turned around and grabbed her arm with a steeled grip, yanking her out of the cabin.

"No, you don't," he mumbled, "you're not going anywhere."

She screamed, a split second of a blood-curdling shrill that echoed in the vast open-ceiling lobby that extended all the way to the top floor. No one paid attention; lost in the general noise coming from downstairs, her scream didn't draw any concern. It didn't last long either. As soon as the man pulled her out of the elevator, he covered her mouth with his other hand, and her cry for help died, stifled.

He shoved her forcefully against the wall next to the elevator call buttons and let go of her arm, pinning her in place under the weight of his body. Then his hands found her throat and started squeezing. She stared at him with wide-open eyes, trying to see anything beyond the reflective lenses of his sunglasses, while her lungs screamed for another gasp of air. She kicked and writhed, desperately clawing at his hands to free herself from his deathly grip.

With each passing second, her strength faded, and her world turned darker, unable to move, to fight anymore. The man finally let go. Her lifeless body fell into a heap at his feet, and he stood there for a brief moment, panting, not taking his eyes off her.

Then he picked her up with ease and carried her to the edge of the corridor that opened to an eighteen-floor drop, all the way to the crowded lobby below. Effortlessly, he threw her body over the rail and watched it fall without a sound.

The noises downstairs continued unabated for a few seconds more, then they stopped for a split moment, when her lifeless body crashed against the luxurious, pearl marble floor. Then the crowd parted, forming a circle around her body, while screams erupted everywhere, filling the vast lobby with waves of horror.

His cue to disappear.


~~~End Preview~~~

Like *Las Vegas Girl?*

Buy it now!

# About the Author

Leslie Wolfe is a bestselling author whose novels break the mold of traditional thrillers. She creates unforgettable, brilliant, strong women heroes who deliver fast-paced, satisfying suspense, backed up by extensive background research in technology and psychology.

Leslie released the first novel, *Executive*, in October 2011. It was very well received, including inquiries from Hollywood. Since then, Leslie published numerous novels and enjoyed growing success and recognition in the marketplace. Among Leslie's most notable works, *The Watson Girl* (2017) was recognized for offering a unique insight into the mind of a serial killer and a rarely seen first person account of his actions, in a dramatic and intense procedural thriller.

A complete list of Leslie's titles is available at https://wolfenovels.com/order.

Leslie enjoys engaging with readers every day and would love to hear from you.

Become an insider: gain early access to previews of Leslie's new novels.
- **Email: LW@WolfeNovels.com**
- Follow Leslie on Twitter: @WolfeNovels
- Like Leslie's Facebook page: https://www.facebook.com/wolfenovels
- Connect on LinkedIn: https://www.linkedin.com/in/wolfenovels
- Visit Leslie's website for the latest news: www.WolfeNovels.com

# Contents